FALSE PRIDE

FALSE PRIDE

A Bea Abbot Agency Mystery

Veronica Heley

severn
House

This first world edition published 2017
in Great Britain and the USA by
SEVERN HOUSE PUBLISHERS LTD of
Eardley House, 4 Uxbridge Street, London W8 7SY
Trade paperback edition first published
in Great Britain and the USA 2018 by
SEVERN HOUSE PUBLISHERS LTD

Copyright © 2017 by Veronica Heley.

British Library Cataloguing in Publication Data
A CIP catalogue record for this title is available from the British Library.

ISBN-13: 978-0-7278-8765-8 (cased)
ISBN-13: 978-1-84751-880-4 (trade paper)
ISBN-13: 978-1-78010-942-8 (e-book)

All Severn House titles are printed on acid-free paper.

Severn House Publishers support the Forest Stewardship Council™ [FSC™],
the leading international forest certification organisation.
All our titles that are printed on FSC certified paper carry the FSC logo.

MIX
Paper from
responsible sources
FSC
www.fsc.org   FSC® C013056

Typeset by Palimpsest Book Production Ltd.,
Falkirk, Stirlingshire, Scotland.
Printed and bound in Great Britain by
TJ International, Padstow, Cornwall.

ONE

'**M**rs Abbot . . .!'

'What is it?' Bea Abbot was terse. She hadn't slept well the previous night, the coffee machine had broken down and the prospective clients she'd interviewed that Saturday morning had all been rubbish.

So Bea Abbot snapped at the girl manning the phone . . . and then apologized. It wasn't the agency girl's fault that so many things had gone wrong. 'Sorry. There's a problem?'

'Someone's turned up without an appointment. I told her you were booked solid this morning, but she said she'd wait till you were free. I put her in the small office at the back that we don't use much.'

Bea Abbot's domestic agency was situated in the basement of her large, mid-terrace Georgian house. Being on a slope, there was a short flight of steps down to the agency's front door from the street at the front, while Bea's office – and the small one next to it – opened via French windows onto a garden at the back.

'Shall I tell her to get lost? It's nearly twelve o'clock.' The girl wore the harassed air of one who had hoped to leave work dead on noon and could see that hope disappearing.

Bea Abbot restrained herself with an effort. What she wanted to say was that she was dying for a cup of good coffee and was far too busy to see someone who'd called without an appointment.

She checked her watch. She was expecting her ward home from school for the weekend. The girl had a key to get in with, but Bea liked to be free to concentrate on her when she arrived.

'What did you say her name was?'

'A Miss Summerleys. She said she was on our books.'

Bea hesitated. 'Magda Summerleys? Yes, she is. One of the best.'

Magda could take over and run a household in an emergency, employees liked and respected her, and she could cook a decent meal on a budget. She even had some computer skills. Bea wished she had a dozen such on her books. Magda had never turned up without an appointment before.

She was working for one of their oldest and richest clients, wasn't she? They'd said Miss Summerleys had been tailor-made for the job. What had gone wrong? Somehow, Bea must fit her in.

Bea said, 'Tell Miss Summerleys I'll be with her directly.' And, in response to the girl's downcast look, 'I know you need to leave early today. It's nearly twelve so if you want to get away, that's all right with me. I'll see to locking up.'

'Oh, thank you. Yes, I will go, if you don't mind.'

Bea returned to her own office and threw open the French windows onto the pretty, paved garden at the back. She rubbed her forehead. Was she getting a headache? Pressure, pressure.

High walls enclosed the garden, giving it an illusion of privacy in the busy city. Birds sang in the trees, two large pots filled with hyacinths scented the air, the fountain splashed cheerfully in its little pond, and all was well with the world.

Well, almost all. Bea could have done with breaking off work at twelve herself.

The sun was on the back of the house. Bea breathed in, deeply, and closed her eyes for a moment. For two pins, she'd tell Magda to come back on Monday when she'd have more time to devote to her.

A tap on the door of her office and there was Magda Summerleys. 'Are you free now, Mrs Abbot?'

Magda was a study in the unremarkable. She wore dull brown clothes which did her no favours, and her pale pink blouse was finished with an old lady's pussy-cat bow. Her glasses were made of tortoiseshell-coloured plastic, she wore no makeup and smoothed her fair hair back behind her ears.

It was springtime, when birds do sing, tra-la, but Miss Summerleys wasn't singing.

No. Her tense body language was saying something else. If Bea were any judge of the matter, capable, thirty-something Magda Summerleys was on the point of screaming. Her voice was high with tension. 'Sorry to intrude. Piers said . . .'

Bea repeated the words. '"Piers said"? You mean, my ex-husband, Piers?'

Piers was charming but unreliable, a man whose tom-catting had ended their short-lived marriage many years ago. They were friends after a fashion nowadays, and he earned a good living as a portrait painter of the fashionable and newsworthy.

Bea stifled irritation. 'What on earth has Piers got to do with anything?'

'I know. It's crazy. He said I'd be safe with you while he tried to find Lucas. I do realize it was a bad idea. You're busy. I'd better go.'

Bea clutched at what she could understand of this. 'I haven't heard from Piers for some time. Why did he say you'd be safe here?'

Magda Summerleys wrung her hands. 'I don't know. Lucas went out for a haircut. We were to meet up at Piers's place. Lucas had an appointment with Piers to discuss arrangements to sit for his portrait. But he didn't return. Lucas didn't, I mean. Instead, his two nephews came looking for him. He – that is, Lucas – calls them Tweedledum and Tweedledee, though that's not their real names of course.'

She made a despairing gesture. 'I'm burbling. What does it matter what Lucas calls them? But they,' she gulped, 'they . . .' She pushed back the sleeves of her jacket to reveal as nasty a set of bruises as you might see in a month of Sundays. Someone had given her a Chinese burn. No, two of them. One on each arm. She took a deep breath, closed her eyes and swayed.

Bea thrust her into a chair. 'Sit. Put your head down.'

Magda sat, but kept her eyes tightly closed. 'I am *not* going to faint. Definitely not. I despise women who faint.'

Bea fetched a glass of cold water from the cloakroom and handed it to Magda, who managed to cup her hands around it, and drink. Finally she opened her eyes, and a little colour came back into her face. 'How ridiculous of me. What you must think!'

'Who gave you those bruises? And why?' Bea looked at her watch. How soon could she expect her ward to arrive for the weekend? Soon. 'Look, why don't we go upstairs and have a sandwich and a cup of coffee? Then you can tell me what's going on.'

'Sounds good. I'm so sorry to . . . but I didn't know what else to do.' She got to her feet, balancing herself by holding on to the back of the chair. 'If anyone comes, I'm not here and you haven't seen me. Right?'

Bea raised her eyebrows. 'That bad?'

'That bad. And you definitely haven't seen a brown leather briefcase. Right?'

'No. Well, I haven't, have I?'

'That's right. You haven't. Where shall I put it? A safe might be best, but they might look there.'

Bea told herself that she was not dreaming. She was standing in her office on a bright spring morning. She'd conducted a series of interviews that morning. She was expecting her ward Bernice to arrive for the weekend from school any minute now. They'd planned a family visit that afternoon, to be followed by a trip to the theatre. That was what she'd planned. That was normal.

This wasn't.

'You want a hiding place for a briefcase?'

Magda nodded. 'There's no initials on it or anything. It could belong to anyone. But its contents—'

'Paperwork?'

Magda shook her head. 'Jewellery. Diamonds.'

Bea smothered a desire to laugh hysterically. 'May I ask, have you stolen it?'

'What! No, of course not!'

'Who does it belong to?'

'Lord Rycroft. Lucas's elder brother. At least, I suppose so.'

'And who is looking for it?'

'Tweedledum and Tweedledee. But I'm sure they have no right to it.' Magda ran her fingers back through her hair, disarranging it. She was too far gone to care about how she looked.

She took a long, deep breath. 'Look, I agree there's no reason why you should take my word for it. I can see how it looks, my turning up like this, but Piers said you'd know what to do. Only, if you don't want to get involved and I really don't see why you should—'

'Shut up, and let me think!' Bea thought she knew enough about Magda to trust her.

And Piers? She wouldn't trust him with a woman under the age of sixty, but he did have a code of ethics. If he'd sent Magda here, there would have been good reason for doing so. Bea thought she'd probably regret helping the woman, but . . . well, how could she hide a briefcase full of family jewels?

Someone leant on the front doorbell upstairs, and they both jumped.

Magda shot to her feet. 'I'd better go. Will you let me out into the garden? Is there a back way out?'

'No, there isn't. Look, it's probably only my ward. She's twelve years of age, home for the weekend. She has her own key and can let herself in.'

The doorbell rang again.

Bea bit her lip. 'I suppose she might have forgotten her key, but just in case it isn't her ringing the bell—'

'They mustn't find the jewellery! Lucas would never forgive me. Look, I'll hide them in the garden somewhere, and then . . . shall I hide out there, too?'

The doorbell rang again.

Bea looked at her watch. 'No, I'll deal with it. Wait for me in my office.'

'Got it.' Magda was quick on the uptake.

The doorbell rang again. And someone started to use the knocker. Bea started for the stairs that led up to the ground-floor rooms. She opened the front door, saying with a smile, 'Did you forget your key?' And then, simulating surprise. 'Oh. You're not . . .? Sorry, I was expecting . . . Can I help you?'

Two men stood on the doorstep. Bea could see at once why they'd been called Tweedledum and Tweedledee. They were plump, thirtyish, hard men. They had fair hair brushed straight back, and full, pouting mouths. Like bad-tempered babies.

Identical twins? They wore black, both of them. Black tracksuit tops, and black tracksuit bottoms. And expensive trainers.

Bouncers at a nightclub? Did they work in a gym, perhaps?

The word 'enforcers' crept into Bea's mind and would not go away. It was not a warm day, but both men looked as if they might perspire a lot under pressure.

'Mrs Abbot, who runs—?'

'The agency?'

'Yes,' said Bea. 'I'm afraid we're closed for the weekend.'

They crowded in on her, forcing her to take a step back.

One of them said, 'This won't take a moment—'

'We just need an address for someone on your books. A Miss Summerleys, who works for our uncle.'

'Or perhaps she's going under a different name? Miss Harris?'

'Harris?' Bea was puzzled. 'Harris is a common name. We have several people on our books with that name, but my address list is confidential.'

They forced her to move back again. They stood close to her, hemming her in. She was tall for a woman, but they were taller and bigger and had much larger paunches. Their action was intended to intimidate, and it succeeded. She remembered the bruises on Magda's arms.

Bea also remembered that Magda had got away from them and brought the briefcase with her. How had she managed that? And how could Bea get rid of them?

They lifted their upper lips in amusement at having forced her back into the hall. One of them – the one who started each sentence – had a gold tooth, upper right jaw. Possibly he was the elder? Tweedledum? 'It's a matter of some urgency—'

'A family matter. Something important has gone astray—'

'We don't want to bring the police in on it unless—'

'No police. We will recover our property and no more need be said.'

Bea blinked. 'I regret I am unable to oblige you. Now, I must ask you to leave.' She was going to have to call the police to get them out. Only, where had she left her mobile phone? In the kitchen, or downstairs in her office?

'We'll leave as soon as you tell us where to find her—'

'Or them.'

Bea played her last card. 'If you don't leave now, I shall have to call the police.'

They both grinned at that. She was not holding a mobile phone, therefore she did not have one on her. Tweedledum lifted a bottle of mineral water to his lips and took a swallow. He passed it to his twin without either of them taking their eyes off Bea. The second twin took a swallow, too.

Taking their time. They knew they had her where they wanted her.

She was pinned against the chest in the hall, unable to move.

They knew and she knew that it had been an empty threat to call for the police. She tried for anger. 'This is intolerable. Who are you, anyway? You thrust your way into my house and—'

'Mrs Abbot, you are being unreasonable.'

'A Miss Harris – or maybe it was the Summerleys woman, we aren't sure – told us she got the job with the painter through your agency, so you must have her details on file, right?'

'What? A job with who?' Bea managed a light laugh. Had Magda actually told them she worked for Piers? Why? But that could be sorted out later. 'Look, I don't know who you are or what you want with Miss Summerleys or Miss Harris, but you can't just turn up out of the blue and demand access to the agency's books.'

'I told you; we need to retrieve something our uncle has stolen and given to the Summerleys woman—'

'Or maybe it's a Miss Harris, if that's her right name, for safekeeping. It's family property, Mrs Abbot, which we need to recover.'

'Urgently,' said his twin.

Bea allowed herself to frown. 'This is ridiculous. I don't know which Miss Harris you are referring to, but Miss Summerleys is not a thief.'

'No, no.' Perspiring. 'Not her. Our uncle has, well, misappropriated some family property. He is not precisely—'

'He's a trifle eccentric. That is why we don't want to bring in the police. We don't want him arrested. It was obviously a misunderstanding. He will have given it to the Summerleys woman on impulse, without telling her it was stolen goods. That is why—'

'If you can tell us where to find her—'

'We can retrieve the property and that will be the end of the matter.'

Bea opened her eyes wide. 'Surely you know where your uncle lives?'

A wriggle from Tweedledum Gold Tooth. 'We are confused. When we visited the painter, we found a woman with him. We thought she must be Miss Summerleys, and we know she works for our uncle. But the woman at the studio said she was a Miss Harris, working for the painter on a job arranged by you.'

Tweedledee said, 'You see why we're confused? Did that woman lie to us? Is she really a temp from your agency, or is she the woman who works for our uncle? We have to find out. So tell us where to find her, and we'll be gone.'

Gold Tooth said, 'We searched the studio, you see. It wasn't there. If that woman really was a temp called Harris, then we have to eliminate her from our enquiries and find Miss Summerleys.'

Tweedledee said, 'I've had a thought. The painter will know which one she was. Shall we go back there and ask him?'

A frown from Gold Tooth. 'We were rather rough with him.' He turned back to Bea. 'We are reasonable people. We don't wish to put you to any inconvenience but you must understand that, if you don't give us these addresses, we will be forced to take steps. Ask your friend the painter, if you want to know what we can do.'

Bea thought quickly. She was not going to give Magda away. What could she say to these two horrible men to get them to leave? 'You say you are related to Magda Summerleys's employer? Surely you know what his housekeeper looks like.'

'Well, no . . .'

'Uncle Lucas is not fond of visitors.'

'Then why don't you pay a visit to him?'

'She's his housekeeper, not his wife.'

'And housekeepers sometimes live in. Miss Summerleys does.'

'What?' They gobbled in unison. And turned to one another. In unison they said, 'She lives in!'

Tweedledee said, 'But the woman we found in the studio said she worked for the painter!'

Bea tried on a chilly smile. 'So you call on your uncle and find out what his housekeeper looks like, right? And the door is behind you.'

Tweedledee consulted with his twin. He was definitely the younger of the two. 'Is the bitch telling the truth, do you think? Should we check the agency's records while we're here?'

Gold Tooth grasped Bea's forearm. 'We make sure. We employ a little pain . . .?'

'No! How dare you!' said Bea.

He held her arm up high. His grip tightened. He might be carrying a lot of weight but he was solidly muscled with it.

Tweedledee said, 'Yes, it's best to make sure.'

Bea said, 'I shall scream, and—'

'Who will hear you? Do it, Bro.'

Bro – short for brother – did it. And Bea did scream. She knew that there was no one else in the house, but the pain was excruciating.

Only, there *was* someone else in the house, wasn't there?

Bea prayed that Magda would not interfere . . . and prayed that someone else would come to release her.

No cavalry came riding to her rescue. Nobody arrived to help her.

'Well?' said Tweedledum.

Bea gasped. 'I told you the truth. Miss Summerleys lives in.'

Tweedledum said, 'We had to make sure.' And, to his brother, 'Do you think the Summerleys woman is uncle's bit on the side?'

His twin snorted into a laugh. 'Unlikely. He doesn't even know which end is which, does he?'

They dropped Bea onto the carpet and stood over her.

'So, what do we do now?'

Bea pulled herself up against the wall. Her arm was on fire.

She prayed, *Lord, help me. Show me how to get rid of them. And, tell Magda not to interfere. Please.*

At least the twins had no idea Magda had come to Bea for

help. And what was that about their having been rough with
Piers?

Tweedledee was in two minds. 'He said she was with him
when he picked the stuff up.'

'He also said he was going to give it to her to hold for him
while he ran an errand. It's not at the studio, so she must have
hidden it somewhere.'

'He hardly knows which day of the week it is. Suppose he
intended to give it to her, but forgot? Suppose he did go off
with it?'

They didn't like that thought.

'Then where is he?'

They thought about it. Bea stayed where she was. What
weapon did she have against these two?

Tweedledum chewed his lip. 'He said he was going to have
his hair cut.'

'A likely story. He hasn't been to a barber in years.'

'He was supposed to be having his portrait painted. Suppose
he got delayed somewhere, and turned up at the studio after
we left?'

That wasn't a pleasant thought. 'We left the studio in a bit of
a mess. We damaged the painter. If we go back there now . . .'

'We'll find the police there.'

His twin nodded. 'Difficult to explain.'

Decision time. 'Maybe Herself knows?'

'She's not answering her phone. She said she'd be busy
today.'

'So, we go back to Uncle's place, to check on the Summerleys
woman?'

They looked down at Bea. 'Stay there, bitch!'

'If you've lied, we'll be back, understand?'

They waddled out, wheezing slightly.

Two bruisers, out of condition? But still capable of doing
a lot of damage.

Bea's arm was on fire. But at least they'd gone. And they
wouldn't be coming back. Would they?

TWO

Saturday noon

Bea pulled herself upright, checked that the front door was shut and leaned against it.

Magda's head hove into sight as she mounted the stairs from the basement. 'Are you all right?'

Bea nodded. 'Sort of. Why didn't you call the police?'

'It's complicated.' Magda was holding a mobile phone. 'I couldn't make up my mind whether to call them or not.' She gasped for breath, closing her eyes. 'I'm sorry. I don't usually give way like this.'

Bea pushed herself upright. 'I recommend strong, sweet tea and arnica for our bruises.'

Magda's smooth mop of fair hair fell over her face. She pushed it back with both hands and it settled into a more becoming frame around her face. 'Do you know what? I own a pepper spray. I used to carry it round with me all the time. At this very moment it's sitting in my bedside table drawer because I never thought I'd need it in this job. How wrong I was! Look at me; I'm trembling.'

Bea grimaced. 'Ditto. Come on. Tea and cake. And an explanation, if you please. I want to know why you didn't call the police when they threatened me.' She led the way to the kitchen at the back of the house.

Magda followed her. 'I didn't, because in the first place I don't believe Lucas is a thief, but also because the family is dead set on discretion and they never speak of their affairs to anyone. I'm sure there's a sensible reason for what's happening, though I haven't a clue what it is. I'm sorry. I shouldn't have involved you.'

She handed over the phone she'd been carrying. 'Actually, this is your phone. I picked it up off your desk when I heard the twins arrive. I was going to ring the police but then I thought

I'd wait till I heard what they planned to do next. By that time it was too late to stop them hurting you. I should have been quicker off the mark.'

Bea filled the kettle and switched it on. She told Magda to sit down. She found a tube of soothing gel and handed it over. Thinking hard, she made a big pot of tea and put the biscuit tin on the table.

'The job you're on now . . . I seem to remember the agency was asked to recommend someone discreet and efficient for a job as a housekeeper for an elderly bachelor. This is not the first time our services have been requested by that office. Every now and then they come to us for a housekeeper here or some office staff there. There's never been a hint of trouble before. Correct?'

Magda nodded. 'The Rycroft Foundation. The first Rycroft of any note made a fortune by what sounds like piracy under the Tudors. He managed to keep his head on his shoulders through some dodgy deals and acquired a title. The family made even more money in the Industrial Revolution. The title still exists, as do their splendid mansions in town and country. They own a nice slice of Mayfair. They've diversified into oil and shipping. They have investments here, there and everywhere. Some twenty years or more ago, a trust fund was set up to manage the nitty-gritty of everyday life for the family, as most of them seem to have lost the ability to work for a living and expect to be feather-bedded through life. The present Lord Rycroft is a case in point. He lives in luxury; he toils not and neither does he spin. He's something of a recluse. I've never even met him. And they're all pathological about privacy.'

'That's it.' Bea clicked her fingers. 'Two years ago, or was it three? Wasn't someone we supplied through the agency given the sack for tattling to the papers?'

'So I was told. When I got the job I had to sign a paper promising complete discretion. Any employee who talks to the press or posts something in the media is sacked that very day.'

Bea poured tea and took a biscuit. 'How many people have we supplied over the years? Off the top of my head, I can think of an office manager or administrator. And one, no . . .

two housekeepers. For different houses. And yes, someone to work in the office . . . collecting rents? Something like that. The Rycrofts have been good customers. Come to think of it, I don't think I've ever met the current Lord Rycroft, either.'

Magda took another biscuit. 'No, you wouldn't. I was interviewed by his son, flanked by a solicitor and Mrs Tarring, who acts as administrator and general dogsbody.'

Bea clicked her fingers. 'Mrs Tarring. Yes, I remember her. Well qualified. Efficient. We sent her over for an interview . . . when would it have been? Four years ago? Five?'

'She's brilliant. She keeps everything ticking over. She supervises the collection of rents, maintenance of the various properties, and so on.'

Bea said, 'But you didn't go to work for His Lordship. You went to another member of the family, didn't you?'

'I ought not to talk about it. I promised. But . . . what's happening . . . I can't keep it to myself. And if I can't trust you, who can I trust? No, they didn't want me to work for Lord Rycroft, but for another member of the family. There are – or were – three Rycroft brothers in the older generation. Lord Rycroft himself lives in the country and I don't even know what he looks like. Lucas Rycroft is the second in line. It was he who asked the trust to find him a replacement as his housekeeper was retiring.

'Mrs Tarring took me to see Lucas. We could smell the gin and the dirt in the place as we went in. Mrs Tarring apologized. She said Lucas didn't like visitors and that his old housekeeper seemed to have let things go. In spades! It's a big, rambling old flat on two floors, near Regent's Park. The rooms are large with high ceilings, but they hadn't been decorated or even cleaned properly for ever. Mrs Tarring was horrified, and so was I. The whole building belongs to the trust, which is supposed to look after it but, what with the housekeeper getting past it and Lucas not even seeing the dirt, nothing had been done about dripping taps, or rewiring, or anything. Mrs Tarring asked me if I felt up to tackling the mess and I said I was, because I do like a challenge.'

Bea patted Magda's hand. 'I don't know about you, but I need some painkillers. Those boys know how to hurt.' Bea found some aspirins in the cupboard over the freezer, and handed them over. 'So you took the job and had fun bringing the place up to date?'

Magda accepted the aspirins and overcame her reluctance to talk about the family. 'Thanks. And yes, I did. Lucas is no trouble. He's a gentleman of the old school and a scholar, who does actually bring in a pittance by writing articles for obscure publications on forgotten artists of previous centuries. He's adapted to some modern technology, though not all. He has a computer and a laptop and corresponds with art historians all over the world. Once or twice a month he travels to various conferences, or to exhibitions. He goes to his club for a meal several times a week and visits a gym to swim every other day. He is absent-minded, and sometimes forgets to tell me where he's going to be, but I can always work it out by looking in his desk diary.

'Yes, he is eccentric. He doesn't have a television set, though there is one in the housekeeper's sitting room upstairs, plus he bought me a small one for use in the kitchen, since I spend so much time there. On the other hand, he does keep up to date by reading *The Times* every morning and he listens to the radio, although . . .'

She paused, as if on the verge of adding something, then shook her head at herself.

'Go on,' said Bea.

A tinge of colour. 'Well, once or twice lately he's said he might get a television to keep up to date on the latest programmes in the art world. A couple of times he's even dropped into the kitchen to check on my set, and I think he might actually buy one for himself soon. But,' getting back to firmer ground – and had she really blushed at the thought of Lucas watching television with her? – 'he won't have visitors in the flat, disturbing his routine. He likes everything "just so". He can't stand the noise of the Hoover or the disturbance caused by decorators or workmen, so I see to all that when he's out or away. He grumbles about the smell of paint but I can usually get it out of the flat before he returns from wherever he's been. Last week he said how much brighter everything looked nowadays. He thought it was because the evenings were getting lighter.'

They both smiled. Bea said, 'I've often wondered whether the "forgetfulness" of these older professionals might have been Alzheimer's.'

'In this case, no. When he can turn his mind away from the fourteenth century, he's bright enough. Selective sight, you could call it. The trust allows him to live as he likes. He settled into the flat when he came down from Cambridge and walled himself in with books. He's learned basic computer skills, but his mobile phone is barely out of the ark. He's never bought or driven a car, hasn't had his hair cut in twenty years, wears the same four suits in rotation . . . ugh!'

'You took pity on him in his helplessness?'

'I needed another live-in job, what with my parents and all . . . you know?'

Bea did know. Magda's elderly mother and father needed full-time care in their own house in the country. Their pensions paid for some of the bills and if they had sold their house and moved into a home it would have solved their problems financially, but they were loath to move and Magda wouldn't make them. So Magda made ends meet by topping up their care bills from her salary, which was the reason she came to London to take jobs where she could live in.

Magda said, 'I enjoy creating order out of chaos. My salary and all the housekeeping bills are paid by the trust. If there's a problem – a leaking tap, a spot of damp – I ring Mrs Tarring at the trust and she sends someone along to deal with it. I'm gradually modernizing everything. Rewiring was the worst. I did that when Lucas went to America for three weeks. A spot of paint and some fresh wallpaper is working wonders in the main rooms. I brought in a microwave, replaced some shredded curtains, and all the bed linen. He never even noticed when I took his suits away to be dry-cleaned, and put him on a diet. It was a doddle. Mrs Tarring said how relieved she was that I cared. She said the trust hoped I'd stay for a long time and, to be frank, so did I.'

'Lucas has been married? Has children?'

'A bachelor, no children. He's not interested in women, or in men either, come to think of it.'

Magda gulped down the last of her tea and pushed her mug

forward for a refill. 'We'd settled into a routine that suited us
both, but a couple of months ago he began getting phone calls
from various members of his family. This surprised and
annoyed him. He said they weren't a close-knit family; they
didn't meet except for weddings and funerals. What had got
the family going was that Lord Rycroft – that's Lucas's elder
brother – appeared to be going gaga and they started fighting
about what should be done. Money was involved, in billions.
The question was: who was going to take charge of Sir, where
should he live, who should look after him and, above all, who
should manage the trust fund in future?'

'What age was the old man?'

'Not that old. Late fifties? There's quite a gap between him
and Lucas, who's in his early forties, although he looks older.
Lucas didn't want to get involved. He certainly didn't want the
aggro of running the trust. He said they should settle it amongst
themselves. But this, seemingly, was what they couldn't do. First
this one was on the phone to him, and then that. He's the next
most senior member of the family, you see, and some of them
seemed to think he should take over the running of the trust . . .
which I would have thought him the least likely of persons to
be able to do, but there you are. Often Lucas refused to answer
the phone, and I'd take messages for him. The twins were the
most insistent that he ring them back, but he never did.'

'Tweedledum and Tweedledee. Gold Tooth and brother.'

'Yes. They think and they act as one. As you've seen.'

'What do they do for a living?'

'They say they are part-owners of a gaming club in Mayfair,
but Lucas said it was more likely they were employed there
as bouncers. I don't know whether that's true or not. They do
get an income from the trust but are always in debt and agitating
for more. Their father, incidentally, was Lord Rycroft's and
Lucas's youngest brother. He was called Nicholas, I think.
Anyway, he passed away of a diseased liver some time ago.
Lucas went to the funeral, but didn't attend the wake. When
he died, the twins expected to move into their father's house
and to inherit the income which the trust had been giving him.
There was a terrible fuss when they found out they weren't
going to get either.'

For a moment Magda looked undecided. But then came clean. 'It's only gossip, but there was talk of the twins' business methods being unacceptable; apparently some debtor at the club had committed suicide and another had been beaten up.'

Bea was open-mouthed. 'I see what you mean about discretion being necessary. If the Rycrofts are so keen on privacy, how did you get to hear all this?'

'Lucas told me a little, and one of the workmen told me more. The Rycrofts always use the same firms of decorators and electricians and they talk to me because I'm one of them, if you see what I mean. Then if one of the family rings when Lucas is out or refusing to take the calls, they rant on at me as if I can do anything to help them.' She allowed herself a giggle. 'It was like disturbing an anthill. Tweedledum and Tweedledee screeched they'd been robbed. The others said it served them right, and they were not entitled to a penny more from the trust, and if anyone did get more, it would be them, and not the twins.

'I was told that when the twins did . . . whatever it was . . . the trust paid out considerable sums of money to stop the news getting into the papers. Lord Rycroft wouldn't let his nephews go to prison, but he tried to rein them in by threatening to terminate the lease of the gaming house at which they were employed, because that happens to be on Rycroft property. And you haven't heard any of this from me. Understand?'

'Understood. Another cuppa?' Bea poured again.

'Mm. Please. But this morning . . . I just don't understand it. Lucas has breakfast on the dot of eight thirty: orange juice, two boiled eggs with soldiers, two croissants with butter and black cherry jam. A pot of tea, strong Yorkshire, and *The Times*. The doorbell rang and I answered it. A courier was there with a package to be signed for. I signed and took the packet in to Lucas, who opened it straightaway. I noticed he'd spilled some tea in his saucer. He hates that, so I took away his cup and saucer and got a replacement from the kitchen. By the time I got back he was flapping sheets of paper around. He wanted to know if I'd seen a key which ought to have been in with the papers. I shook the envelope and a key dropped out onto the tablecloth. He put it in his waistcoat pocket.

'He abandoned his breakfast. That was unheard of. He'd only eaten one of his eggs and the other . . . I suppose it's still sitting on the table in the kitchen. He went off to make a phone call in his study. I don't know who to. When he came out, he put some paperwork in his old briefcase and told me to call a taxi. He said he had to run an errand at the bank, urgently. I reminded him that he had an appointment that morning to discuss sitting for his portrait—'

'With Piers? My ex-husband? So that's where he fits into this puzzle?'

'Exactly. Some society or other – something to do with his work on long-forgotten portrait painters in Italy – wanted to have a portrait of Lucas to hang on their walls. Lucas had grumbled when the project was first mooted. It would take time away from his work, he didn't know what to wear, and so on. He was really flattered, of course, but didn't like to admit it. I got his academic gown cleaned – he got a first at Cambridge and luckily still had the gown – and I arranged for him to have his hair cut before we met Piers to discuss arrangements.

'So there he was this morning, all set to go straight out to the bank until I reminded him about meeting Piers. He said he had plenty of time to attend to his other business first. Then he had second thoughts. He said I should go with him to the bank because he didn't want to tote his briefcase around all morning. He said that while he was having his hair cut, I could go on ahead of him to the studio and he'd join me in due course. He was pleased with himself for working that out. He also said it would be good for me to go, as I could take his gown to show Piers what he'd like to wear. It didn't occur to him that Piers might not be pleased if I arrived early. That was Lucas for you.

'So off we went to the bank. I sat in the entrance hall at the bank with his gown over my arm while he disappeared into the bowels of the building. He wasn't long. About half an hour, I suppose. When he came out, we took another taxi to Piers's place. In the taxi he took a phone call on his mobile.

I don't know who it was from. He said, "Yes, I've got it." He asked me for Piers's address, and I wrote it on a page torn out of my diary and handed it to him. He's hopeless about remembering things like that so I always have to write them down for him.

'He repeated the address to whoever was on the phone. He said he'd meet them there, and that if he were a few minutes late it wouldn't matter because I was with him and could look after the briefcase while he had his hair cut. When we got to Piers's place, he handed me the briefcase and said he wouldn't be long. He left me standing there on the pavement with the briefcase and his gown, while he took the taxi on to the barber's. And that was the last I saw of him.'

'What time was that, do you know?'

'About ten fifteen, something like that. Possibly a bit before. His appointment with Piers was for eleven, so he just had time to get to the barber's and back.'

Bea added it up: courier, key . . . safe deposit box. Jewellery?

Magda reached for a tissue in the box on the table, and blew her nose. 'The last thing he said to me was, "Guard it with your life!" Even at the time I thought it was odd.'

'You took the briefcase in to Piers's house?'

'I had to explain to him why I was a little early. I said about the haircut and Lucas promising not to be long. I didn't tell Piers why I was carrying a briefcase. Perhaps he thought it was a prop that Lucas wanted to use. He was so nice, Piers. Made me a cup of coffee, and we chatted about this and that.'

Piers was nice to all women, especially pretty women. He couldn't help himself. Mind you, thought Bea, Magda is not especially pretty. She had strong bones, though, and good skin. She'd probably age well. Piers would have liked that.

Magda said, 'The time passed quickly, but I couldn't help worrying about what Lucas had got himself involved in. Couriers and keys and taking stuff out of the bank. Stuff he didn't want to carry around to the barber's. I wanted to look inside the briefcase but it didn't seem right to do so because he'd trusted me to look after it for him. I was uneasy.' She stopped and looked at Bea. 'You know his studio?'

Bea shook her head. 'He likes to move around, takes

short-term leases. We keep in touch, but I haven't visited this particular place. It's in West London somewhere, isn't it?'

'Mm. A small, three-bedroom house, end of terrace. It has a loft conversion with huge skylights in the roof at the back, and that's the room he uses for his studio. He sleeps down below and works up above. At eleven o'clock the doorbell rang. He went downstairs to let Lucas in . . . only of course it wasn't Lucas.'

'It was the twins?'

'I knew about them. Lucas had said things in passing, and I'd had them on the phone many, many times, ordering me to put Lucas on, and him shaking his head and letting me make excuses for him. So when I heard them on the staircase, shouting for Lucas and telling Piers to get lost, I recognized their voices. I remembered Lucas telling me to guard his briefcase with my life. I had no time to find a good hiding place, so I put it on the stand in the middle of the room, the one with the chair on it for a sitter. I threw the gown over the briefcase and stepped away. They burst in and started yelling for Lucas.'

'What did Piers do when they broke in?'

'He got his mobile out. He tried to block their entry, saying, "Steady on," or words to that effect. They were rough. Pushed him back and back. He told them to leave. One of them punched him on the jaw, and he fell down. Knocked out! Just like that. I'd never seen it happen before. I couldn't believe it. They took his mobile phone and kicked him a couple of times. I thought they'd killed him. I didn't know what to do – they frightened me!'

'They'd frighten anyone.'

'I got my own mobile phone out to ring the police but they turned on me, plucked the phone from my hand and stamped on it. They kept demanding that I give them the briefcase. They'd never seen me before and all I could think of was to pretend that I was someone else, sent by the agency to do some work for Piers. I cried. It didn't take much to bring tears to my eyes. I wept and I sobbed, and acted like a complete drip, but I was so afraid . . . they had knocked Piers out so quickly. I was afraid they'd killed him and, if they'd killed

Piers, they could kill me, too. One of them punched me hard, on my breast.'

Magda put her hand to it. 'It hurt. They kept shouting, "Where's Lucas? What's he done with the stuff?" I kept shaking my head and saying I didn't know any Lucas. They pushed me down into a chair, the chair for the sitter. They held my arms up and . . .' She licked her lips. 'It hurt. But I wouldn't, I *couldn't* give them the briefcase. I made my mind blank so they couldn't see I knew about it. I kept saying my name was Harris, that I worked for an agency who'd sent me to Piers to do some work for him. I begged them to believe me, and eventually, I think they did.'

'You gave them the agency's name?'

'Yes. That was a mistake, but I was frantic to convince them I had nothing to do with Lucas. I'm sorry. I've dragged you into something which has nothing to do with you.'

'It can't be helped. What happened next?'

'They took the place apart. They opened every cupboard, every door. They overturned the table with Piers's paints on and pulled the blinds off the windows. I wept and cowered in a corner. I tried to creep away while their backs were turned, but they caught me at the door and brought me back. Dumped me back in the chair. I was so scared. My foot was touching the briefcase under the gown. I was sure they'd see it, but they didn't. I couldn't think how this would end. If Piers were dead . . .? He didn't move. When they'd finished searching the place, they asked me again where Lucas was, and again I said I didn't know any Lucas, but Piers had told me he had a sitting scheduled for that morning and was that supposed to be the Lucas they were talking about?'

'And that worked?'

'Yes.' She wept and rubbed tears away. 'The silly thing was that I really didn't know where Lucas was. Truly I didn't.'

Bea reached out to hold Magda's hand. 'You guarded his treasures for him.'

'Yes, but . . . at a cost.' She straightened her back. 'I don't regret it. Only . . . what will they do when they find out I fooled them again?'

THREE

Bea said, 'But they did leave, eventually.'

Magda nodded. 'Yes, but you should have seen the mess! And me in pieces. I looked for a landline phone to ring the police and an ambulance for Piers, but couldn't find one. Lots of people don't have them nowadays, do they? Then Piers began to move around. He sat up. He'd only been knocked out for a short time, had come round to find them searching the place and thought it best to play dead till they'd gone. I was so relieved. But worried sick. What was going on? What had happened to Lucas? Where was he?

'I told Piers what I knew about Tweedledum and Tweedledee and the family, and I know I shouldn't have told him anything, but I was so frightened that I did. I told him about Lucas giving me the briefcase to keep safe. We looked inside. Boxes of jewellery. Old boxes, leather. With a crest on. Inside, diamonds. Tiaras, necklaces, rings. I nearly fainted when I saw. Piers said there was a fortune there.

'I asked Piers what we should do. Go to the police, or . . .? The thing is, I didn't know why Lucas had taken the stuff out of the bank in the first place. He isn't a thief. I swear it. Surely, if he took things out of the bank, he must have had the right to do so? Only . . . he isn't the heir to his brother or his brother's estate, so what right had he to do that? I couldn't understand, Piers couldn't understand . . . Surely Lucas would never think of . . . but that's what he'd done. We decided we needed to find him.

'Piers had an old landline still connected, downstairs. He used that to ring Lucas's mobile. I was frantic to warn him. No service. Lucas is careless about charging up his phone and might well have forgotten to do so. He'd taken a call in the cab, but what if that finished the battery? He only uses his phone for emergencies, you see. My phone and Piers's smartphone were both in pieces on the floor. I thought, what if the twins had caught up with Lucas . . .? They had gone out looking for him, hadn't they? Piers said I should come here to you while he went to the barber's to find out what had happened to Lucas, and then he'd meet me here, too. Only, he hasn't come, and the twins have.'

Bea sighed. 'You'd already told them which agency you worked for, so they decided to check out your story.'

'Yes. I'm sorry. I didn't think quickly enough.'

'When Lucas took the phone call in the cab, was it from one of the twins?'

'No. No, I'm sure it wasn't.'

Then how had the twins known she was in the cab with Lucas? According to Magda, Lucas hadn't decided to take Magda with him to the bank until AFTER the phone call he'd made, interrupting his breakfast. Magda couldn't be telling the whole truth. Which meant . . . Bea wasn't sure what it meant. Also, the twins had referred to someone they called 'Herself', who was busy that morning. Who was this woman? Not Magda, presumably. Or was it?

Magda frowned. 'The twins . . .? It's difficult to explain, but . . . Lucas's manner with the twins is different. He didn't care for them. He said they were a waste of space, if not worse, and that the way they carried on, they were likely to end up in prison. He saw no reason why the trust should continue to support them. He said that if he'd been administering the trust, he would have made them pay rent for the very nice flat in which they lived, and reduced their allowances, and made them work for their living. They don't do anything much, you know. They hang around the gaming club and they go to the races and that's about it. When Lucas did have to speak to the twins, he was terse, monosyllabic. Would hardly give them the time of day. The man who phoned him—'

'It was a man, not a woman?'

Magda bit her lip. 'I can't be certain. No, I think it was a man. Lucas's tone to him was business-like, but he spoke to him as to an equal. I would say it was someone he respected.'

'His elder brother? Lord Rycroft would have had every

right to ask someone to get the jewellery from the bank,
wouldn't he?'

'Y-yes. But why would he do that?'

'Not married, no daughters wanting to show off their bling?'

A faint smile. 'No, not that I've heard about. Although I
suppose, if he did take up with a woman and want to marry
her, he'd have every right to show her the jewels. But, no.
Wouldn't he rather have taken her to the bank to see them?'

'What is your explanation, then?'

A hesitation. 'I'm being fanciful, but I have been wondering
if someone else in the family was in debt and wanted to lay
their hands on the jewellery. They themselves couldn't access
it because it was kept in the bank. They hoaxed Lucas into
taking the jewels out of the bank for them, and planned for
him to hand them over at Piers's place. Then they could sell
the jewels and blame Lucas when it was discovered they were
missing.'

'You think the twins arranged it?'

Magda leaked uncertainty. 'I don't know . . . I suppose they
could have forged a letter from Lord Rycroft, asking Lucas
to get the jewels out of the safe deposit box. Paid a courier
to deliver . . .' Her voice trailed away. She wasn't happy with
her theory.

Bea wasn't, either. 'For a start, how would the twins get
hold of the key to the safety deposit box, in order to send it
to Lucas? And presumably there was some kind of authorization in that paperwork which persuaded the bank to release
the stuff? How could they have forged that?'

Magda wailed, 'I know, I know! It doesn't add up, does it?'

'Is the paperwork still in the briefcase?'

'No. I looked. Lucas must have left it with the bank. I
suppose the officials there wouldn't have been keen to release
hundreds of thousands of pounds' worth of gems unless
they had proper releases. They would trust Lucas, though. I
mean, he's so clearly honest. I think he's been made the fall
guy for some kind of scam, though I can't see how it was done.'

'And, we've still got the jewels.'

'And the twins, and who knows who else, are going to come
after us for them.' Magda smoothed more cream on her bruises.

'Ouch. By the way, I hid the boxes in the hut at the bottom of your garden, and put a layer of plastic pots over them. Can you think of a better hiding place?'

'I can't think, full stop,' said Bea. 'I'm worried about Piers. He sent you here, but hasn't been in touch.'

'He hasn't got a mobile phone now, and neither have I.' She looked at her watch. 'It's well over an hour since he put me in a taxi and said he'd follow. Where is he? And if he's been held up somewhere, how is he going to contact me?'

Bea put on a brave face. 'Piers can borrow a phone, or get to a public phone box. He can always ring here.'

'But he hasn't.' She shivered. 'I'm not going to panic. I'm not! I am not hysterical, not in the least. But two of them went off to the barber's and . . . what happened? Did they drop into a black hole?'

'Is Sweeney Todd alive and living in . . . which barber's did you send him to?'

Magda pressed both hands to her head. 'I'm going mad. I do know, don't I? I wrote the address down on a card, and Lucas put it in his pocket so he wouldn't forget where he was going. It's on the tip of my tongue.'

'You'd have chosen a good one. Possibly not near Piers's studio?'

'No, of course not. It had to be good. Lucas hasn't had his hair cut in years. Wore it in a ponytail. Kept it clean, but . . . too, too sixties. Or is it seventies? Aging rock-star look. Ridiculous. I know; the place is called The Director's Cut. Men only. When I made the appointment I explained what was needed and they understood.'

'Might the long hair have been a good look for a portrait?'

'It might, but I think Lucas had got tired of it. As soon as the word "portrait" was mentioned, he said he didn't want to look a freak and it was time for a change.' She sighed. 'Actually, I quite liked the way he looked, but . . .'

It occurred to Bea that Magda had a soft spot for her employer.

Magda looked at her watch again. 'Where is he?'

Bea accessed a number on her landline. 'I'll try Piers's house. You said he's got a landline on the ground floor? Lucas

might have gone back there as he'd said he would. Or
Piers might well have returned by now.'

Burr, burr. Burr, burr. No service.

Bea cradled her receiver. She licked dry lips. 'No service.
Now what does that mean?'

She pushed the phone to Magda. 'Try the barber's?'

Magda retrieved her handbag from the agency rooms,
rummaged through pages in her diary, and dialled. 'Is that The
Director's Cut? I'm ringing because my boss, Lucas Rycroft,
had an appointment with you this morning, but hasn't returned.
Can you confirm that . . .?'

The voice at the other end was not amused. It quacked.
Indignantly.

'So sorry.' Magda put the phone down. 'I said it was a black
hole, didn't I? Lucas never turned up.' She took a deep breath
and closed her eyes. 'I am not going to panic. I am *not!*'

Bea tried to think clearly. Lucas and Piers had been missing,
or out of touch, rather – for well over an hour. It was no use
trying to report their disappearance to the police, who would
only act if someone were missing for twenty-four hours or more.

The two men were out there, somewhere. One had a mobile
phone, though the battery might have run down. The other
didn't.

Bea said, 'I think we must try to get hold of Lord Rycroft.
Find out if he knows about the jewellery being removed from
the bank.'

'I don't have his number. I was instructed never to approach
him. It's as much as my job is worth to do so.'

'Possibly. But . . .' Bea didn't add, but thought that if Lucas
had dropped off the planet then Magda would be out of a job
anyway.

Magda thought it over and probably came to the same
conclusion. 'It's the weekend and the trust's office will be
closed till Monday, but I could try Mrs Tarring because I do
have her mobile number for emergencies.'

Bea nodded. Magda located the number and dialled. No
reply. Eventually voicemail clicked in. Magda left a message
for Mrs Tarring to ring her on Bea's landline number, and put
the phone down. 'Any other ideas?'

Bea looked at her watch and half rose from her seat. She'd completely forgotten about her ward coming back home that weekend. Bernice ought to have been letting herself into the house with her key or ringing the doorbell half an hour ago. Or longer.

Now this *was* worrying.

There might have been a delay on the Tube? Yes, but Bernice had a phone and should have been able to ring and reassure Bea about what was happening.

The child might have been run over in the street and whipped off to hospital with fatal injuries. No. Stop right there.

There is absolutely no point in panicking just because someone is out of touch for an hour or so.

Bea tried to laugh at herself. She'd been playing down Magda's fears while getting ready to panic herself. Ridiculous!

On the other hand, perhaps a spot of prayer might be appropriate.

Dear Lord, keep the child safe, wherever she is. And as for Lucas and Piers . . . This is all too much! I can't think about them while Bernice is missing. Or not missing, as the case may be. Help, please!

The landline rang.

Magda started to her feet. 'Lucas! Or Piers?'

Bea grabbed the phone. It was Bernice. Oh, the relief! 'Bernice, where are you? I expected you over an hour ago.'

'Sorry, Bea; sorry. Should have rung you earlier, I know, I know. Things happened, and I forgot.'

Bea almost shrieked. 'You forgot! Here's me beginning to think about ringing the hospitals—'

'Keep your hair on. Honest, I'm fine. It's just that something came up. My friend Alicia was invited to go sailing this weekend. She didn't want to go by herself, so she asked me if I'd like to come, and I said – I really did – that I was due to stay with you this weekend, and she said her grandfather would ring you and fix it, and I've just checked and he hasn't.'

'No, he didn't ring me,' said Bea, telling herself to calm down, that all was well.

'Some men have no brains,' said twelve-year-old Bernice in world-weary tones. 'I just asked him, checking up, you know, and he said he'd meant to ring you, but things had happened. Like I said.'

'I see,' said Bea, who knew and liked Alicia's grandfather well enough, while not going into rhapsodies about his stock of common sense. 'But this really won't do, Bernice. If you've been invited out for the weekend, I need to clear it with your hostess. Do you have her name and contact number?'

'Dunno. Mrs Something double-barrelled. I'll ask her to ring you when we get there, right?'

'No, it's not all right. That's not how things are done. Had you forgotten that we've got theatre tickets for this evening, and were planning to see your mother and stepfather this afternoon?'

'Yes, I know. Sorry about that, but you know how it is with Alicia, and I've never been sailing. Alicia's grandfather has a friend who has a boat on the Isle of Wight somewhere, and we're going to—'

Bea almost shrieked. 'The Isle of Wight?' She identified background noise. A car, being driven at speed. 'Bernice, don't tell me he's driving you down there as we speak!'

'I told him you'd be cross. Here, I'll hold the phone up so you can speak to him.'

A male voice, rather too hearty. 'Hi, there, Bea! How you doing?' William Morton, aiming for insouciance while very much aware that he was at fault for not having spoken to Bea and asked her permission to take Bernice away for the weekend.

Bea was incensed, and not inclined to let him get away with it. 'William Morton! Do you realize I could have you arrested for kidnapping a minor?'

'Sorree. I thought Bernice had asked you, and she thought I'd asked you and—'

'You didn't think it was important to get my permission?'

'It was a spur-of-the-moment thing – wait while I just pass this lorry – I've only just met someone and she invited us to go sailing with her. Alicia said she wouldn't go without Bernice and Bernice said she'd love to go, so . . .'

Ah-ha. So he'd just met someone who'd invited him to go sailing with her? Bea hadn't encouraged William when he'd shown signs of wanting to make her his second wife, but she was undeniably narked that he had now found someone else. Yes, it was a dog-in-the-manger attitude and she ought to be ashamed of herself, but . . . and then she was struck by the thought that it was going to be easier to deal with Magda and Piers without having Bernice around. Bernice was a great girl, but yes, she was a demanding guest.

Bea said, 'Oh, very well. But get your hostess to ring me when you arrive. I can't let my ward go off into the blue for a weekend without knowing exactly what's happening. I'll see if I can return the theatre tickets, but Bernice had better ring her mother and make her excuses there. Will you bring her back here on Sunday evening, or take her straight back to school?'

'We have an invitation for Sunday lunch. I'll take them back to school on Sunday afternoon, right?'

Bea ground her teeth, and told herself not to do so. 'Very well. Drive carefully. And, have a good time.'

She put the phone down, torn between wanting to smash something and relief.

Magda was pacing up and down, putting her hands under her arms and taking them out again. Magda didn't know what to do with herself. 'The phone! He could be trying to get through to us!'

Bea said, 'Piers, or Lucas?'

'May I try Lucas again?'

Bea handed over her phone, and Magda dialled. And listened, and replaced the phone. 'Still no joy.'

Bea tried to be positive. 'Piers knows both my mobile and landline numbers, so he can get through to me on either. And it wouldn't be Lucas trying to ring because he doesn't have either of my numbers. Now, calm down. That phone call means I'm free for the weekend. So let's go and see what's happening at Piers's place, shall we? My car is parked in the mews at the end of the road. It'll only take me a few minutes to get it.'

Magda grabbed her handbag. 'Won't it be easier to take a cab? Parking is always so difficult. And it will be quicker, won't it?'

She was probably right. Bea phoned for a cab, grabbed a jacket and set the alarm on their way out.

Five minutes later they were in a cab and speeding towards
West London.

On the way, Bea said, 'Magda, let's talk about the twins.
They're loose cannons, aren't they? Almost feral. They think
the quickest way to achieve results is to inflict pain. I wonder
how they've got away with it for so long. You say there was
a problem with some people who owed them money, but that
it was all hushed up for the family's sake? What does that say
about them?'

Magda was hesitant. 'I've told you what I've heard. I really
am not supposed to pass the gossip on to anyone else.'

'Only now you have to because Lucas is missing.'

Magda winced. 'Well, one of the maintenance men said
they've been a problem since they were born. Their father got
through a fortune, gambling and drinking. He died a while
ago. Last summer some time? Their mother walked out on
them when the twins were little. It explains something about
them. They live together, drive each other around in an expensive sports car, have never married. The maintenance man
warned me never to let myself be alone with them. He said
they like tormenting people who can't hit back. He said they
used to confine their attentions to people they didn't think
would run to the police, but then it escalated and there was a
nasty case which the family had to hush up.'

Bea said, 'One thing: they're not overly bright, because first
you and then I fooled them. But I must admit I don't wish to
meet them again without backup.'

Magda sighed. 'Me, neither.'

Bea said, 'So, about the jewellery, we haven't a clue whether
it's stolen or not. Or who it actually belongs to. Presumably
the head of the Rycroft family? I expect you'd like to get it
back to the trust, but we can't do that till we neutralize whoever
it was who organized its removal from the safety deposit box
in the first place. Someone was supposed to collect it from
Piers's place, but . . . who?'

Magda nodded. 'It must be someone Lucas thinks has the
right to it.'

'These professor types. Did he forget what he was supposed
to be doing this morning, and head back home?'

Magda objected. 'Lucas is not that far gone. He wouldn't forget that he was supposed to be meeting Piers. He really was looking forward to having his portrait painted.'

Bea handed over her mobile. 'On the off-chance, see if he's gone back to the flat. Try his landline there.'

Magda tried. Burr, burr. Burr, burr. She handed the phone back to Bea. 'He doesn't have an answer phone, said they wasted his time. As I said, they've both dropped into a black hole.'

The taxi slowed to a crawl as they turned into the road where Piers had currently rented a house.

'Uh-oh.' The cab driver stiffened. 'Police. Is this where you want to go?'

There were two police cars parked in front of Piers's house, and a policewoman was standing at the door. Then came the wail of a siren, and an ambulance loomed at the taxi's back bumper, urging it to move on. The cabbie drove on, slowly.

'Piers is injured?' Bea felt faint. Piers had been in her life since she was eighteen, and though their marriage had not lasted, he'd always been there. They were on good terms nowadays; when they met, it was as if no time had elapsed since they last talked to one another.

'Is it Lucas?' Magda's voice went high with anxiety.

There wasn't enough space for the ambulance to park. It continued to loom over their taxi, wailing away to get their cab driver to move on. A small group of bystanders had gathered on the other side of the road.

A large policeman thumped on the taxi's window. 'Move on. If you please.'

The cab driver moved on, saying, 'Do you want me to stop?'

Bea said, 'I don't know. I can't think. Can you find somewhere to park?'

Piers has always been there in the background of my life. What will I do if he dies?

The traffic built up behind them. The taxi driver rounded the corner while the two women turned in their seats to watch as the ambulance double-parked outside Piers's house.

Magda's voice wobbled. 'The police are there. What do we tell them?'

'Make up your minds, ladies.' The driver was relaxed about it.

Bea was sharp. 'If only we knew who the ambulance was there for! Cab driver, could you let me out, please? I need to see who's been injured.'

'I can't stop here.' The cab driver was being reasonable. They were in a moving stream of traffic and there was absolutely nowhere to park. Bea said, 'I'm going to get out! Now! Circle the block and pick me up when you can.'

Pray God it wasn't Piers who was hurt!

Bea got out and ran back, dodging through groups of people speculating as to what all the fuss was about. A policeman was holding back the groups of gawpers.

Bea caught his arm. 'Please, who is it?'

He took no notice. 'Back,' he said. 'Let them through.'

A gurney was being taken across the pavement, with a man strapped to it. Pale face, floppy fair hair under some kind of bandage. Floppy fair hair? It wasn't dark-haired Piers!

The gurney was lifted into the ambulance. The policeman turned on the bystanders. 'Come on, now. Show's over. No one's dead.'

No one was dead. And it wasn't Piers!

Bea leaned against the nearest garden wall, trying to control her heartbeat. Another patrol car arrived. The taxi chuntered up again, with Magda's alarmed face at the window. Bea stumbled into the taxi.

The policeman loomed up. 'Move on, please!'

Magda craned to look out of the back window. 'Did you see who it was? Was it Lucas? The ambulance is leaving. They don't take dead bodies in ambulances, do they?'

Bea comforted herself with the reflexion that Magda was right, and that if someone had died, instead of an ambulance there would have been a forensic team on site. So, nobody had died. She said, 'A man, I think. I couldn't see much of him, but I think he had fair hair. Rather fine and floppy.'

Magda tried to smile. 'Not Lucas, then. He's fair haired but turning grey.'

Not Lucas, and not Piers. It must have been someone who'd collapsed on the pavement? But, glory be, it wasn't Piers or Lucas.

Magda fretted. 'But where could he be?'

Bea said, 'Let's try Lucas's place. Perhaps, if he did have an absent-minded turn, or if something happened to distract him, he might just have forgotten all about the meeting with Piers, and gone back there.'

'Yes, yes.' Magda's colour had risen. 'That will be it. I suppose. No need to get all excited.' She wasn't convinced, but she gave the cab driver the address.

Lucas lived at the end of a terrace of expensive houses set back from the road by a strip of communally planted gardens behind iron railings. Millionaires' territory. Stucco-faced in cream, there were pillared porticoes over the front doors and smoothly glistening old glass in the tall windows. So far, so eighteenth century.

The cab driver parked and, while Bea paid him, Magda shot up the steps to an imposing doorway and used her key to let them into a wide, black-and-white paved hall. She ignored the door directly ahead to take a curving staircase up to the first floor. Bea followed her into the hall at a slower pace and started up the stairs behind her. Magda put her key into a door on a first-floor landing. Entering a square hall she called out, 'Lucas?'

Bea followed her. Daylight streamed down from a lantern two floors above. A second, graceful staircase curled up the inner wall. The walls were dressed in fresh-looking wallpaper in a subdued green and cream and the woodwork was painted white.

Magda ignored an alarm panel to drop her handbag on a hall table and dash around, opening doors. Then she shot down a short corridor under the stairs to what, presumably, must be the kitchen quarters.

'Lucas?'

No reply. The very air seemed dense, unused. The tiny sounds they made as they walked about seemed muffled. They couldn't hear any noise from the street. There was a faint trace of paint in the air. Good-looking pictures on the walls. Victorian watercolours and some old engravings, which Bea guessed were antique Baxter prints. Low bookcases lined every available wall space. Everything looked clean and tidy – thanks to Magda, no doubt.

Bea made a note to herself. Magda hadn't turned an alarm off when she let them in, therefore one couldn't have been on.

Why not?

Magda appeared in the doorway at the end of the corridor. Her eyes were wild. 'He's not here. He hasn't been here. He always drops his keys in that brass bowl on the hall table when he comes in. But someone else has been here, in every room on this floor.' She wrung her hands. She was only just about under control. 'We've been burgled!'

FOUR

'You're sure?' said Bea, and knew it was a stupid thing to say. Of course Magda was sure.

'See for yourself.' Magda gave Bea a tour of the rooms. 'The library, where he works; every drawer has been pulled out from his desk and someone's toppled books out from their shelves. Why would they do that, for heaven's sake?'

The walls in the library were lined with built-in shelving; mahogany, no expense spared. Each shelf had been stuffed with leather-bound books, many with a crest on them in gold. There was a Victorian kneehole desk with a modern adjustable typing chair behind it and a Pembroke table laden with more books, some open and some shut. And, looking out of place, a modern business desk with computer and printer on it.

Yes, all the drawers in the desks had been pulled out. This room hadn't been painted yet. Where they could be seen for books, a greyish-cream wallpaper begged for renewal.

Bea said, 'They were looking for a safe?'

'There is no safe.' Magda ushered Bea into the next room along. 'Dining room. It gets the morning sun. He was having breakfast here when all this started. He left *The Times* neatly on the table when he went to do his phoning, and look at it now . . . tossed anyhow into the fireplace. His chair is always placed so that he can see out of the window over the gardens below, and now it's turned right round.'

There was no fire in the grate to set *The Times* alight, fortunately. Ah, but efficient central heating radiators had been installed, so there would be no need for real fires any more. This was a nice, bright room, almost square. Wallpapered – where the walls could be seen for yet more bookcases – with a blue and white Chinese-inspired pattern. The woodwork was all white. There were signs that the breakfast table had been hastily cleared away. A napkin had been thrown down; there were crumbs on the tablecloth and toast still in a toast rack. A small hand bell, no doubt used to summon the attention of servants, lolled on its side.

Magda righted the bell. 'There's an electric bell push beside the fireplace in all the rooms down here, but he prefers to use a hand bell.'

She led the way into the next room along. 'His bedroom. I didn't have time to make his bed before we left, but he never leaves his wardrobe open like that, and look, the drawers are all pulled out from the chest of drawers and the side table.'

Massive mahogany fitments, a bed with a high, carved back. Only two pillows on the bed, and a duvet thrown on the floor. The room had been repapered recently, in an elegant ochre and cream pattern. More white paintwork.

'His bathroom, next door. Nothing seems to have been touched here.'

Bea peered in, hoping to see a mahogany surround to the toilet and bath, but no; the fitments had been updated at some point, although she was pleased to see the old cast-iron bath did have claw feet and there was real lino on the floor. More fresh paint. Magda had definitely been earning her keep.

'The sitting room,' said Magda, leading the way. 'It's the next room on my list to be done. Please note that he refuses to have fresh flowers or plants anywhere, but he collects jade . . . it's all there in the cabinet between the windows. Or rather—' a catch in her voice – 'it was. It's gone! He'll go spare.'

The cabinet's doors hung open and the shelves were empty.

The furniture here was a three-piece suite by Chesterfield out of Harrods. Massive. Cretonne covered. Probably hadn't been re-covered in this generation. The walls were covered with a lilac wallpaper, which had been bleached almost to white where the sun had struck it. Bea thought it would be interesting to see what Magda intended to do with this room.

There was a newish radio with modern speakers, and yet more bookcases and more books. No television.

Magda said, 'That leaves just the kitchen and utility room. I can't see that anything's been touched there. Do you want to look?'

Bea did. She was fascinated to find a thoroughly modern kitchen and utility room with a dishwasher half filled, waiting for the breakfast dishes from that morning to be added to it. The used tableware was currently sitting on the central unit. And yes, a small television had been hung on the wall by a landline telephone. Beyond the kitchen, a small toilet had been carved out of a capacious utility room, which held the latest in washers, driers and freezers. Very nice, very Magda.

Bea said, 'What's upstairs?'

'Servants' quarters. Lucas doesn't go up there, or hardly ever.' She flew up the stairs, followed closely by Bea, and banged doors open. 'Junk room housing ancient pieces of luggage and some broken bits of furniture that I haven't got round to dealing with yet. Spare room, never used in my time. Bathroom, ditto. My sitting room . . . I can tell you, nothing's been touched here, thank the Lord. Then my bedroom and bathroom en suite. A small kitchen for my own use; the usual offices, a cupboard for cleaning materials.'

Everything was neat, bright and sparkling clean, with new paint and fresh wallpaper. The television in Magda's sitting room was one of the latest. In her bedroom, the bed had been made and there was no dust on the dressing table. Towels hung in orderly fashion in the bathroom.

Magda made a gesture of despair. 'What do we do now? If we ring the police and tell them we've been burgled, the papers will get hold of it and Lucas will go spare, not to mention Lord Rycroft. I'll get the sack, and I do like it here. But we must report the burglary, mustn't we?'

Bea put her arm round Magda and led her downstairs. 'Let me check on something before we decide what to do.' She went into the sitting room and pushed back the floor-length velvet curtains – sadly stained with age. 'The windows have been wired for alarms. There's a panel for the alarm in the hall. But Magda, you didn't even pause by the alarm pad to shut it off when you came in. Which argues—'

Magda ruffled her hair. 'No, it's broken. Again. He hates the alarm. Wants it taken out. I've told him and told him . . .' She was on the verge of tears. 'And now, look what's happened!' She sank into a chair and began to rock. 'What am I to do? Where is he? Oh, where is he?'

Bea was tracing wiring along the skirting board. 'How was it broken? Alarms don't usually break.'

'Lucas snipped the wires. In the hall. He'd set the alarm off by accident again. That's the second, no, the third time he's done it. He can never remember the code. I've written it down for him, and I make sure he's got the card in his pocket when he goes out, but one day last week he took a different jacket from the one I'd left out for him to wear, and he didn't have the code on him when he returned. I don't know what to do with him. When I told the alarm people what he'd done, they were so cross they wanted to cancel the contract, but I persuaded them to give him another try. They're coming on Monday. Oh, he's going to go spare!'

Bea said, 'Wait a minute. You said the alarm was going to be repaired on Monday. Who else knew it was broken?'

'Why . . . I don't know. Mrs Tarring knew, of course. I had to tell her what had happened, and she agreed that we'd probably have to pay extra to get reconnected. But she wouldn't have talked to anyone about it. Why should she?'

'Agreed,' said Bea. 'Unless—'

Magda shook her head. 'She wouldn't.'

'No, I don't suppose she would,' said Bea. 'She got the job as administrator to the Rycroft estate through me. I know her. She wouldn't talk to strangers.'

But she would have told someone in the office that the alarm had been put out of commission, wouldn't she? Especially since no alarm meant no insurance.

Unless, of course, there's a traitor in the camp?

'Magda, where's the main landline phone?'

'In the library, but there is a separate landline in the kitchen for me to order food, keep in touch with the office and so on.' Magda led the way back to the library, and groaned at the mess. 'What on earth were they looking for? We have no safe.' She picked up papers at random, and then didn't know what to do with them.

Bea located an old-fashioned Bakelite telephone on the kneehole desk. She picked it up, inspected it, and shook her head.

Bea had a wide circle of friends and one of them was a freelance bodyguard, whom she had employed on a couple of occasions. Recently he'd shown her a couple of 'bugs' he'd removed from a client's house, and had briefed her on their use. Now she might be completely wrong, but if someone had wanted to find out what was going on in this house, might they not have resorted to planting a bug or two near to the landline?

She squatted down to look under the desk . . . and stood up, attracting Magda's attention by putting a hand on her arm. 'Magda, do you think you could make me a cuppa? I'm dying of thirst.'

'Yes, yes, of course.' Magda dropped the papers onto the floor. 'Oh! What am I going to do?'

Bea urged her from the room. 'Everything will look better after a cuppa. Come on, let's leave this mess till later.'

Once in the kitchen, Bea went round opening and shutting all the cupboard doors, particularly near the landline on the wall.

'What are you doing?' said Magda, filling the kettle and switching it on.

'Bugs,' said Bea. 'I wondered whether someone was listening in to what has been going on here. I don't think there's anything in here, but there is a bug under the desk in the library, which is capable of relaying phone calls to an interested party.'

Magda nearly dropped the mug she'd been reaching for. 'What!'

Bea said, 'I did wonder how they knew where Lucas was supposed to be this morning and what time he'd get hold of the jewels. You say he went into the library to make a phone call at breakfast time. When he made that phone call, he must have said where he was going, that he planned to take you with him, Magda, and that he proposed to leave the jewellery with you while he had his hair cut. And someone was listening in.'

Magda sank into a chair. 'That's how they knew that Lucas was going on to visit Piers, which was where he was supposed to meet someone – someone different or the same someone? – and hand the jewellery over?'

'Two different people, or the same one?' Bea breathed out, slowly. And smiled at Magda. At least she now knew that Magda had not been responsible for leaking the news that they were all due to meet at Piers's place. That was a relief!

Magda ran her fingers back through her hair. 'I don't know what to think. Either way, what's happened to Lucas?'

And Piers. Please, Lord; keep him safe.

Bea said, 'Magda, I was serious about that cuppa. And maybe a sandwich, if you can manage it? I think it's safe for us to talk now. I can't be a hundred per cent sure, but I don't think there's any bugs in here. Now, I want you to think who had the opportunity to plant a bug in the library.'

Magda looked at her watch. Her lower lip trembled with the effort of restraining tears, but she managed to nod and produce a teapot, add tea bags and pour boiling water in. 'I can't think . . .'

Bea prompted her. 'You say you only had workmen in when Lucas was away. When was the last time that happened?'

'The decorators?' Magda crossed the room to look at a calendar on the wall. She stabbed at it with her forefinger. 'He hasn't been away this month. The decorators are due next Friday when he goes to New York for a conference. I'll have four days to get the furniture moved into the middle of the room and the walls done.'

'Will that be the sitting room?'

'His collection of jade figurines!' She swallowed. 'Oh dear. I realize it's no good panicking, but . . . yes, the sitting room. Willow green paintwork with William Morris wallpaper. Corny, but it works. It suits the furniture. One of Lucas's ancient uncles used to live here and that's why the furniture is mostly nineteenth century. Apparently he, Lucas's uncle, was an eccentric, too. But Lucas likes it, and that's why I try to go for the traditional look when I redecorate. I'm having new curtains made and the Chesterfield is going to be re-upholstered in the same willow pattern. It will look lovely and he probably won't even notice.' She poured tea into mugs and added milk.

'How do you arrange things with the decorators? Do they come here and discuss what you needed with them? And, can you manage to make us a sandwich? It's long past our lunch hour.'

'Of course. When I've tried Lucas just once more.' She used the landline in the kitchen. Pressed numbers. Listened, put the phone back. 'No signal. Dead. He's run out of juice. I usually recharge it for him overnight. He keeps the charger in the drawer of the old desk in the library.'

Moving like a sleepwalker, Magda found a sliced loaf and some ham and salad stuffs in the fridge. 'You asked who could have planted the bug in the study? I don't see how it could be someone from the decorators. The Rycrofts always use the same firm. I pass my suggestions to Mrs Tarring and she asks them to call and measure up, which they do . . .' She looked at the calendar again. 'Last month. Six weeks ago. That's the last time they were here.'

'Can you work out when the family started getting agitated about Lord Rycroft? That might give us a clue as to when the jewellery heist was planned?'

'And the jade . . .!' Magda struggled to contain her misery. She buttered sliced bread, and then broke off to start the dishwasher. 'I'm trying to think. I remember that the first phone call was on the first Saturday of the month. Lucas was getting ready to go out to an exhibition. I heard his phone ring in the library, but he's told me never to answer that one, so I don't. He came in, afterwards, to tell me he might have to go down to see his brother in the country after he'd been to the Royal Academy. This meant he probably wouldn't be back that night. He was annoyed. I asked if anything were the matter and he said it was likely to prove a storm in a teacup but he'd better check it out. When he returned, I asked how he'd found his brother, and he said his brother was no more ridiculous than usual, and that it was his nephew who needed his head seeing to.'

Bea took over making the sandwiches as Magda didn't seem capable of seeing any job through to its conclusion. 'Which nephew? One of the twins?'

'Oh, no. I don't think so.' Magda was doubtful. 'He could have meant Kent, Lord Rycroft's eldest son, but Kent's really sane, so I don't think Lucas meant him. There is another cousin, I think . . . but I really wasn't paying much attention. It didn't seem important at the time. After that there were a number of calls, all demanding that Lucas ring them back. They wanted him to call a meeting of the family to discuss some family problem or other, and he wouldn't. Sometimes he'd pick up the phone, hear who it was, and put the receiver down without speaking.

'That's when they started on me, ringing on my landline here, asking me to get him to phone them back, making me take down messages to give him . . . messages he tore up and dropped in the bin. One of them told me the old lord was going round the twist so it was imperative that Lucas took action, but he just laughed when I repeated that to him. They must have got my phone number from the office. That is, my own personal, housekeeper's phone number.' She pointed to the modern phone hanging on the wall. 'There is a phone upstairs in the housekeeper's room but I spend a lot of my time in here so Mrs Tarring arranged for that extension on the wall.'

'When was that done?'

Magda consulted her memory. 'Quite soon after I arrived. Two years ago in January? Yes. January.'

'So that's not it. We're looking for someone who came in this month, after the general hoo-ha began.'

Magda muttered to herself, tracking down notes she'd made on the calendar. Eventually, with some hesitation, she returned to the eighth. 'Would the eighth be about right? Lucas has a meeting of some Ancient Society of something or other on the second Wednesday of every month, so he was out when a man came with some papers for Lucas to sign. The man said he was from the Rycroft Foundation and Lucas had made an appointment for that day and time. I didn't know him, but he had the right paperwork. He was respectable, well spoken. No, it couldn't have been him, could it?'

'Tell me about him.'

'I said Lucas was out. He said he'd heard that Lucas was a bit absent-minded, which of course, is true. He asked if he could use the phone to ring the office, to check that he'd got the right day and time. So I let him into the library and showed him the phone. I stood there, all the time. I didn't leave him alone. He took a file out of his briefcase and rang the office, told them what had happened. He listened, put the phone down and apologized to me for wasting my time. Apparently he'd come to the wrong address. It wasn't Lucas who was supposed to be signing the papers but one of the other Rycrofts. He tried to put the file back but it came loose and papers went all over the floor. Oh!' She covered her mouth with her hand.

'You helped him pick them up, and that was when he put the bug under the desk?'

'I could kick myself.'

'I don't see how you could have known he wasn't genuine. Did you tell Lucas about his visit?'

'The man begged me not to. He said he might lose his job if they found out he'd gone to the wrong Rycroft's house. Knowing how strict they are, I believed him. So, no I didn't.'

Was this the traitor in the camp? Did this 'respectable' man work for the foundation in some capacity or other? It sounded rather like it.

Magda said, 'When do you think we should start ringing round the hospitals?'

Bea had wondered that, too. She looked at her watch. Barely two hours had passed since Piers had gone off in search of Lucas, who had been missing longer than that. It was time enough for an ambulance to have travelled to a hospital, and for the patient to have been received into an Accident & Emergency department.

'We could give it a go. I don't know what else to try.'

A phone rang.

Magda reached for the one on the wall, and Bea reached for her handbag.

It was Bea's mobile ringing. 'Yes?'

A man's voice. 'Bea, where the hell are you?'

'Piers!' *Was it really him?* 'Piers, more to the point, where are you? Are you all right? Not in hospital?'

'How come you know about that? And where's Magda what's-her-name? She'd fled by the time I got back to the house and—'

'*Where's Lucas?!*' Magda all but screamed.

Bea put out a hand to Magda, grasping her arm. 'Quiet, Magda. Piers, this is important. We saw someone get taken off in an ambulance from your place. Who was it?'

Magda moaned with pain and Bea released her arm, mouthing, 'Sorry.' She'd forgotten about Magda's bruises, which she ought not to have done, since her own were still painful.

Piers said, 'Lucas Rycroft, you mean?'

Magda heard and gave a little wail.

Bea said, 'Was it him? Are you sure?'

'How can I be sure? I wouldn't guarantee to pick him out of a line-up. How could I? I've never met him. All I know is, someone called Lucas was expected to arrive at my place, and there this man was. He wasn't awake enough to introduce himself. What does your Lucas look like?'

'Long fair hair, turning grey, tied back. In his forties.'

'I don't think it's the same man. My body – whoever he was – would be in his late thirties. Fair hair, shortish, but longer over his forehead, small beard.'

Bea mouthed to Magda, 'It's not Lucas!'

Piers continued, 'Look, where are you? I've been round to your place, and there's no one there. Your car's still in the mews.'

'Can you grab a taxi and meet us here?' Bea gave the address. 'It's Lucas's place. He seems to have vanished.'

Piers grunted, and switched off.

Magda said, 'I'm going to have hysterics!'

'No, you're not. That was Piers on the phone. He's coming round here. The man taken off in the ambulance is a man in his late thirties, blond, with a small beard but short hair. So it's not, repeat not, Lucas.'

Magda gulped. 'But he might have had his hair cut, which he meant to do that morning. No, it can't be him, can it? Lucas is older than that and going grey. And,' almost a smile, 'he hadn't got a beard.'

'Do you know of another man answering to that description?'

'Oh. Well, yes, I suppose . . . I met a man like that once, when I was interviewed for the job. He's the Rycroft who runs the trust. Kent Rycroft, the old lord's eldest son. Pale blue eyes, very clean fingernails, beautiful suit, handmade shirt, silk tie, polished brogues. The sort of man you'd imagine might be a diplomat, or a mandarin in some ministry or other. But it couldn't be Kent, could it?'

'Did this Kent of yours have brains?'

'He didn't show what he was thinking, but yes; brains. I don't think he needs to raise his voice to be obeyed.'

'Wedding ring?'

Magda closed her eyes, trying to remember. 'No. A signet ring on his left hand, little finger. Beautiful watch, thin. Gold pen on the table in front of him. Smartphone. He had my file open before him but didn't need to refer to it. He had my details already in his head. Date of birth, and so on. Another man, not quite so smooth, not quite so expensive, sat on his right. He introduced himself by saying he was a solicitor employed by the Rycroft Foundation, and it was he who arranged my contract. Mrs Tarring sat on his left. I speak to Mrs Tarring on the phone quite often but I've never seen or spoken to either of the other two since the day I went for the interview.'

Bea arranged some cold meat on the buttered bread, piled on some cheese and a selection of salad stuffs. 'Why should Kent Rycroft be at Piers's studio? I can only think of one reason. He must be the person who'd arranged to meet Lucas and to take the jewellery off him.'

Magda shook her head. 'Why would he do that? He runs the trust. He could take the jewellery out of the bank any time he chose.'

Bea cut the sandwiches in half, and passed one to Magda. 'The most surprising people can run short of money.'

Magda said, 'No. Kent Rycroft is not short of a penny, believe me. When various members of the family got hold of my phone number and started ringing me, I asked Mrs Tarring what to do about it. She said to take the messages and pass them on to Lucas if I wished, but not to get involved. She said the only caller to take seriously was Kent, and he's something in the banking world as well as running the trust. I don't know much about him, except that he's divorced and lives by himself with a housekeeper who comes in daily. I think he had a son, once.'

She frowned, trying to remember. 'The son died last year? Tragic. Anyway, Mrs Tarring did tell me that Kent was one of the few members of the family who actually earns his living and that was one of the reasons why he got landed with the Rycroft Trust. The others are far too greedy to be relied upon when it comes to dealing with large sums of money. Well, she didn't actually say that because she's the soul of discretion, but that was what she meant.'

A doorbell rang. 'That must be Lucas!' Magda rushed down the corridor to open the door before Bea could warn her to be careful.

A moment's pause and Magda returned, looking downcast, with a somewhat battered-looking Piers in tow.

Bea held out her hand to him. 'I'm glad you're safe. I was worried.'

Piers was not in a good temper. Six foot of darkly charming testosterone, dented nose, shock of dark hair turning grey at the temples. A nasty yellow bruise on his chin which bore its usual five o'clock shadow. Casual clothes, originally good but rumpled.

He said, 'Will someone kindly tell me what's going on?'

FIVE

Bea echoed, 'What's going on? I wish I knew!'

Magda touched Piers's arm. 'You haven't seen Lucas, have you?'

'Maybe I have, and maybe I haven't,' said Piers, who looked about to explode at any minute. 'My life today can only be described as a farce. A dark farce, but one whose meaning is impenetrable to one of my limited intellect.'

Bea said, 'Have you had anything to eat?' She pushed the plate of sandwiches towards him. Men always feel better when they've eaten. And not only men. She took a large bite of hers and almost groaned. It was so good!

Piers bit into his, too. Round a mouthful, he said, 'Look, I make arrangements to have a quiet chat with someone who wants his portrait painted. I'm intrigued because I've heard his name mentioned here and there. I'm fully booked on Saturday but I decide to make time for him somehow. I tell him that I have an appointment out of town for lunch, so please would he not be late. And what happens? Not only does he turn up late, but he doesn't turn up at all. Instead—' he glowered at Magda – 'he sends his mistress—'

'I am not his mistress!' said Magda, turning red.

'To tell me he's stopped on the way over, to have his hair cut. His hair cut! Would you believe? Did he have to have his hair cut today of all days? Why didn't he have it cut yesterday, or last week . . . or better still, tomorrow?'

'Oh, I do agree,' said Bea, pouring out and handing him a mug of tea. 'Would you like some aspirin as well?'

'Aspirin!' Piers barked. 'Morphine might help. A massage in a quiet, dark room might help! Aspirin won't even touch the sides!'

'We understand.' Bea gave him another sandwich. 'What we want to know is—'

'What *you* want to know is irrelevant. What I want to know is why Fate has to rear up and kick me in the teeth like this. You do realize I have been made homeless?'

Bea frowned. Was that possible?

Magda grimaced. 'Oh, come. It's not as bad as that.'

'Not as bad? *Not as bad!* Apart from the destruction caused by those two apes who came after you, and you'll notice how restrained I am in calling them apes, my hallway is spattered with blood! Yes, human gore! I'm only renting that house, and I'm going to be held responsible for returning it in the same condition as when I first walked into the place. Do you know how difficult it is to get blood out of wood? And will my insurance cover the replacement of the floorboards and repainting the hall? Will it? No way!'

Bea said, 'Calm down. Magda told us you were knocked cold by the twins, and that you very cleverly played dead while they tried to find the bag which Magda was keeping safe for her boss.'

Piers shook his finger at Magda. 'I must say, you have a good shriek on you! Well done you!'

To Bea's amusement, mixed with horror, Magda squirmed with pleasure.

Ah, the well-known Piers Effect. If he so much as crooked his little finger at a woman, she was his. Except, of course, for Bea, who knew all his little ways and could see through the charm to the man behind. Well, she had to admit that the man behind the charm – apart from his inability to leave other women alone – was, in many ways, admirable. Honest. Hardworking. Intelligent. Talented. And, she had to admit, sexy.

Piers softened his tone to concentrate on Magda. 'If I'd only known you were carrying a time bomb, I would have got you out of the house earlier. I know they knocked you about. No lasting damage, I trust?'

Magda shook her head, and smiled at him.

That's not a smile, that's a simper if ever I saw one! And I had imagined she was half in love with her boss!

'Ah well,' said Piers, magnanimous as ever, 'it wasn't your

fault, Magda, or whatever your name is. But I don't think my insurance company is going to be that amused when I tell them that some idiots rampaged through my property, destroying my smartphone, overturning my easel, ruining canvases and scattering my paints and brushes all over the floor. They tore the blind from the window but, above all, they vandalized two portraits that were on the verge of completion. And who, may I ask, is going to compensate me for that? Will my two sitters be prepared to give me another appointment or two, so that I can start the portraits all over again? I think not.'

Without turning to Bea, he thrust his mug at her. 'Is there another in the pot?'

'Yes, yes,' said Bea, refilling his mug. 'We do understand that you have been shockingly badly treated. But I know you; you'll survive and dine out on the story for weeks, which will probably bring you in even more commissions. What we want to know is—'

'Why! That's what I want to know. Why me? Why have I been targeted?'

Magda said, 'I do feel terrible about what's happened to you. I'm afraid you were just in the wrong place at the wrong time. Those two men were after the jewellery which Lucas had given me to keep safe. That's why I hid it and pretended to be someone else. I couldn't stop them wrecking your studio. But when they'd gone, you were kind enough to go and look for Lucas. So what happened? Did you find him?'

Piers sipped his mug of tea. He closed his eyes to savour the brew. He opened his eyes and said in a normal voice, 'Aargh. Good cuppa. What I think is, that I should never have been sidetracked into going after your Lucas. Why didn't I phone for the police as soon as the Marauding Twins had gone? That's what the police want to know, and they have a point, don't they?'

'You were confused,' said Bea, soothing his ruffled feelings. 'You'd been knocked out.'

'True. And yes, I do have a headache and if you *can* find me some aspirin, I'd be grateful.'

Bea got some aspirin from her handbag and pushed them towards him. Then refilled his cup.

'Yes, yes.' Magda fidgeted with anxiety. 'So did you find Lucas?'

'I couldn't find any trace of him. He never turned up at the barber's. They were pretty busy. Were annoyed he'd failed to appear. Can't blame them.'

Bea said, 'So after you drew a blank at the barber's, what did you do?'

'Stupidly, I went back to the studio to report to Magda who, surprise, surprise, had scarpered, leaving my studio uninhabitable. Oh, and that's when I found the body in the hallway.'

'A corpse?' Magda paled. 'Really? But it wasn't Lucas?'

'Well, not a corpse, exactly. Or not yet. He was still alive when I got back, but whether he'll make it or not, I don't know. He'd been bashed over the head. Blood was spattered everywhere. I tell you, I nearly passed out when I saw.'

'What did he look like?'

'All I could make out was short, fair hair, small beard.'

'Ah,' said Magda, relaxing. 'I do think it must be Kent.'

Piers took the last but one sandwich. 'That shook me, I can tell you. But, stiff upper lip and all that. I did what I ought to have done in the first place and dived for the landline phone in the sitting room to report my findings to the police, only to find someone had been there before me. Torn the wiring out of the wall. Dead. And me with no smartphone. So I called up the stairs, thinking that you, Magda, might still be on the premises. No such luck. Out I lurch into the street and flag down the first passer-by, who probably thought I was mad but did phone for the police, clearly thinking I needed restraining for my own sake. The police turned up, and then an ambulance . . .'

'We saw the ambulance arrive,' said Bea. 'We were trying to connect with you, but the police kept moving us on and we didn't know what to think.'

'You may well apologize. Do you realize how it looked? Mad artist says he went out to run an errand for a friend and returns home to find a man lying at death's door in his hall. Mad artist's studio has allegedly been wrecked by two men whom he mistakenly refers to as "Tweedledum and Tweedledee". No, he doesn't know their names, but that is what his visitor had called them. Which visitor? Ah, there's the rub. She's vanished, leaving not a trace behind. Or rather, a smashed mobile, but that's all. A whiff of brimstone would be more helpful.

'Rather naturally, the police can't make head nor tail of this story. They think the Mad Artist is hallucinating, and ready to be carted off to the Funny Farm. Worse, when he's asked who the man in the hall is, all he can say is that it might be someone called Lucas, whom he'd been expecting to meet that morning. "What's his surname?" they say. I say, "Can't think, but the details are on my smartphone." So we look at what's left of my smartphone on the floor, and they say, "Who did that?" and I say, "Tweedledum and Tweedledee," and they think I'm taking the Mickey, and I can't blame them for that.'

Bea smoothed out a smile. 'You'd been knocked out. You were concussed. No wonder you gave them confusing answers.'

'Confusing?' Piers yelped. 'What else could I tell them? I didn't know the man from Adam. Anyway, while they're waiting for the ambulance, they search the man's pockets and find no wallet, no cards, no diary. So they tag him as "Mr Lucas" and he's borne off to the hospital.'

'If he had a beard, it wasn't Lucas,' said Magda. 'I'm more and more sure that's Kent Rycroft.'

Piers clicked his fingers. 'Rycroft. Ah, that's the name. I knew I knew it.'

'Being knocked on the head can do that to you,' said Bea, perturbed that Piers had not been able to remember the name for so long.

'I'm fortunate the police didn't arrest me there and then, or get me sectioned and in need of locking up. As it is, they announced they'd take me down to the station to make a statement. They thought I was either cuckoo or being very cunning and hiding relevant information, such as the address of this Lucas what's-his-name. I told them I usually record information for work on my smartphone, and they were welcome to take the pieces away and see if they could make sense of them, but they shouldn't expect me to remember such details offhand. I closed my eyes for a nap and they went into a panic, said I'd got concussion and carted me off to hospital for a check-up, at the same time warning me not to leave town and saying they'd need me for more questions later. And me not even able to ring my client and say I couldn't make our lunch date.'

'What did the hospital say?' Bea told herself that Piers was perfectly all right really, but . . .

'I sat in A & E till a doctor was found to shine a torch into my eyes and tell me I should take it easy for twenty-four hours, and discharged me. Then I wandered off till I found a public phone and contacted you.' He managed to take the last sandwich just as Bea was going to swipe it. 'Aargh,' he said. 'That hits the right spot. Oh, and to add insult to injury, do you know what this Kent was knocked out with? My cast-iron doorstop in the shape of a cockerel. It was a birthday present and I am rather fond of it. Or rather, I was.'

Bea said, 'You mean, the doorstopper I found for you in the antique shop? The one I got for you because you were always complaining about a door which wouldn't stay open when you wanted it to.'

'That's right,' said Piers, eyeing the sandwich sitting, untouched, on Magda's plate. Magda might have lost her appetite, but Piers was still hungry. 'Cock-a-doodle-do. Victorian. Hefty. And now, merely an exhibit in a case of assault.'

Bea said, 'We must inform the Rycroft family of what has happened.'

'We can't,' said Magda. 'We have to wait till Mrs Tarring phones me back. I don't have a number for anyone else.'

'What about the messages you took from the family? Didn't they give you a number to take down so that Lucas could ring them back?'

'Yes, but I gave all those notes to Lucas, and he put them in the bin.'

'So, let's look in the bin. Also, *you* might not have the family's contact details, but I bet Lucas did. The last one to find his address book is a sissy . . . but let's search in silence. Yes, Piers. No talking, please. There's a bug in the library which is going to record or relay everything we say.'

'Why not remove it?' said Piers, being practical.

'And carry it around with us, so that someone can overhear everything we say?'

'Put it in the fridge or freezer. That should give it a headache. I'll deal with it for you, shall I?'

Saturday early afternoon

While Piers dealt with the bug, Magda found Lucas's address
book under some papers which had been turfed out of a drawer
in the kneehole desk. She seemed reluctant to hand it over,
but Bea insisted. Meanwhile, Bea herself had been investigating the contents of the waste-paper basket and had retrieved
a couple of screwed-up memos. Each one stated that so and
so had called and asked Lucas to ring back. Telephone numbers
included.

They retreated to the kitchen to make the necessary phone
calls.

'We'll try Mrs Tarring again first,' said Bea. 'There are two
numbers for her in Lucas's address book: one landline and
one mobile. Magda, she hasn't responded to the one you tried
before, which was her landline, wasn't it? Yes? So let's try
the other. And, Magda, would you put the call on speaker
phone so that we can all hear what she says?'

'She'll be furious at my ringing her at the weekend,' said
Magda, pressing digits.

Piers said, in a forlorn, die-away voice, 'Are there any
biscuits, do you think?' He was as thin as a rake. He often
went without food for hours when he was painting, but at
other times he binged on junk food, while never seeming to
put on weight.

Bea said, 'Mrs Tarring will be even more upset when we
tell her she's got a traitor in the camp.'

'I do hope she doesn't give me the sack,' said Magda,
ignoring that and clearly wishing herself elsewhere. And then,
to Piers, 'There's some biscuits in the tin in the cupboard
here.' She pointed, and Piers investigated. He found the biscuits
and promptly removed himself and the tin to another room.

At last, Magda's phone call elicited a reply. 'Mrs Tarring,
I'm sorry to disturb you, but—'

'Yes, Magda? What is it? You do realize this is the weekend.'
An older woman's voice. A pleasant voice. One accustomed

to command, but displeased at being contacted outside office hours.

'Something has happened. Lucas has disappeared. He's not where he should be, and he's not answering his phone. And, we think Kent is in hospital, though we don't know—'

'What! What nonsense is this?'

Magda gibbered.

Some people go to pieces far too easily.

Bea took the phone off Magda. 'Mrs Tarring, this is Bea Abbot here from the agency. Magda called me to help because various crimes appear to have been committed—'

'Mrs Abbot? Nice to hear from you. Did you say "crimes"?' A light laugh, amused.

'In order of importance: a man answering to Kent Rycroft's appearance has been assaulted and taken to hospital, labelled with Lucas Rycroft's name; the Rycroft twins assaulted Magda and wrecked a portrait painter's studio; the Rycroft jewels have been removed from the bank and are now in limbo and Lucas Rycroft has disappeared. Oh, and his flat has been burgled and his jade figurines have gone.'

A silence in which hard breathing could be heard. Mrs Tarring's voice came at last, faint with shock. 'Repeat that, please.'

Bea continued, 'Yes, it's hard to take it all in, isn't it? I'm at Lucas Rycroft's place, with Magda. I suggest you ring round the hospitals to see where Kent Rycroft is. We think he may have been admitted under the name of Mr Lucas. Meanwhile, I'll ring the police to inform them of the burglary here at Lucas's place. That is, unless you know where he might be?'

'What? No, I don't. But you mustn't ring the . . . Lucas often visits exhibitions at weekends and sometimes he . . . I'm sure there's a perfectly good explanation for . . . he'll have forgotten to tell Magda about this change of plan, that's all. I'm sure she's worrying unnecessarily. Mrs Abbot, I don't understand the rest of what you said. Is this some practical joke?'

'Far from it. Lucas had an appointment this morning to discuss having his portrait painted. He didn't turn up. Instead, the artist found a strange man lying in his hallway, who'd been attacked by person or persons unknown. The artist had been expecting a visit from Lucas, and told the police that. But, from his description of the victim, it sounds more like Kent Rycroft than Lucas. Whoever he is, he was taken off to hospital under the name of Lucas.'

'You think Kent has been attacked? But why? It doesn't make sense. Are you sure?'

'I'm sure. I suspect the Rycroft twins may have been involved.'

'What? Which . . .?'

'The two boys. Tweedledum and Tweedledee. They've been rampaging around, trying to find some jewellery which Lucas withdrew from the bank early this morning.'

'I don't understand. Why would Lucas withdraw—'

'You may well ask.' Grimly. 'The pair of them also paid me a visit at my home. Magda and I have both been recipients of their attentions, which I may say were forceful in the extreme. We're back at Lucas's place now, and that's how we discovered that his place has been burgled.'

'You are at Lucas's place?' Faint but pursuing. 'Why? I don't understand.'

'Neither do I. I suggest that if you see the Rycroft twins, you take evasive action. I'll stay here with Magda while we wait for the police. When you've found out what's happened to Kent, will you let me know?'

'No police! No, the Rycrofts wouldn't want that.'

'You can't cover up an assault and a burglary!'

'Mrs Abbot, the Rycrofts are pathological about privacy. Believe me, they will not want the police called in.'

'But we can't ignore—'

'We had a break-in at the office a couple of years ago and all our computers were stolen. I was ordered to replace the equipment and say nothing to the police. I pointed out that the insurance people were not likely to pay up if we didn't inform the police, but Lord Rycroft insisted.'

Bea said, 'He's the one going gaga, isn't he?'

'No! No, that's a lie. He's eccentric, that's all.'

'Mrs Tarring, the only reason Lord Rycroft wouldn't have

wanted the police involved, was that he knew who had organized the break-in at your office. Am I right?'

Silence. A cautious, 'It did occur to me, yes.'

'You think the same person or persons might be responsible for the theft of Lucas's jade pieces?'

'It is a possibility, yes.'

'Someone who has access to keys, not only to your office but also to Lucas's place?'

'I can't be sure, of course, but—'

'There were no signs of forced entry here. Magda let us in with her keys. But someone has definitely been through the place, searching for something. And the jade pieces are conspicuous by their absence.'

More silence.

Bea said, 'If we call the police to investigate this break-in, they will test for fingerprints and identify the intruder.'

'No, no. Please! No police. I do see that this is an emergency. I'll see if I can get Lord Rycroft to come to the phone, although it would be unheard of for . . . Well, if he says to let the police in, then I'll ring you back and you can contact them.'

'What about Kent Rycroft? Do you want me to start ringing round the hospitals to see if he's been admitted, or will you do it?'

A wail. 'What are we going to do? If it's Kent . . . Oh, dear! Kent is the only one who ever gets anything done. Mrs Abbot, I'll ring you back as soon as I've spoken to Lord Rycroft.' She ended the call.

Magda wrung her hands. 'She still says not to call the police?'

'There was a break-in at the office and all the computers were stolen. Who does she think did it?'

Lowered eyelids. 'It was before my time.'

Bea said, 'Magda, come clean.'

'All right, I did hear about it. It was Tweedledum and Tweedledee, of course. One of the Rycroft maintenance men told me about it. No one was *supposed* to talk about it, of course, but he told me so that I'd never leave them alone if they visited Lucas. He said the twins organized the break-in because they'd been refused an increase in their allowances. It was their way of reminding Kent that they were not to be trifled with. I think myself that he ought to have called in the police, but he didn't. I can only assume the old lord told Kent to let the twins have what they wanted.'

'You think it was they who broke in here as well?'

Magda said, 'I don't know. It's possible. The people who went through these rooms were definitely looking for something and I suppose it was the jewellery they were after. Well, they didn't get it. I think they took the jade out of spite.'

'You think that Lord Rycroft will continue to protect them, no matter what they get up to? Surely he knows that people who indulge in this thuggish behaviour don't turn into saints with age? They may have started by twisting a few arms, but unless stopped they will progress to beating people up . . .'

'Or hitting them with a doorstop?' Magda swallowed. 'Let's hope Kent's going to be all right. He's the one who keeps everything going. Without him . . . I mean, who's going to authorize payment of my salary at the end of the month? And that's supposing I keep my job after this.'

'And who is going to compensate Lucas for the loss of his treasures? What's more, the twins – if it was them – didn't just take the jade. Someone was searching through the drawers to find something. Does Lucas keep money at home?'

'No. He uses cards, like everyone else.'

'So they must have been after the jewellery.'

Magda said, 'I suppose so. Oh dear, oh dear.'

Bea got out her mobile phone. 'Mrs Tarring was too shaken to call the hospitals, so we'd better do it. You start with Hammersmith Hospital. I'll try Charing Cross first.'

Five minutes later Magda signalled to Bea that she'd got something. 'Yes,' she said. And again, 'Yes. I'll see that someone contacts his family. Yes, his name is not Lucas. It's Kent. Kent Rycroft. We think so, anyway. The next of kin would be his father, Lord Rycroft. I don't have the address, but I can tell you the telephone number of his office and someone there can give it to you.'

She read out Mrs Tarring's two numbers, and put the phone back on the wall. 'That was Hammersmith Hospital. They have admitted a man under the name of Mr Lucas, but they won't give me any more information than that because I'm not a relative.'

'I'll see if I can get through to Mrs Tarring.' Bea tried the woman again. One line was not answered. The other was busy. Was Mrs Tarring still on the phone to Lord Rycroft? If so, she'd ring back when she'd finished. Bea smoothed out the memos she'd taken from the waste-paper basket. Neither of these messages had been from Lord Rycroft. One was from Mrs Tarring. The other . . .? She said, 'Who is . . . what's this name? It looks like Shirley?'

'Shirley is a c-cousin, I think. Not c-close.' Magda's teeth were chattering.

She was in shock. Bea put the kettle on. She tried Mrs Tarring's number again. Still engaged. She made Magda a cup of sugared tea, and gave it to her.

Now what? Lucas's address book beckoned. There were two entries for Lord Rycroft; one for an Eaton Square address, and one for a place in Oxfordshire. She tried the Eaton Square number first. The agency had supplied another housekeeper to the Rycrofts in the past, hadn't they? Would this be the one Bea knew?

SIX

Saturday afternoon

The phone rang and rang. It didn't give the 'engaged' sound, and it didn't click through to voicemail. Finally, a woman answered.

'Yes?' Middle-aged? A little hoarse? A housekeeper?

Bea said, 'This is Mrs Abbot, from the Abbot Agency.'

'Who?'

Not one of Bea's clients, then. She said, 'May I speak to Lord Rycroft? It is rather urgent. It's concerning his son.'

'Lord Rycroft is not in residence.' The phone clicked off. A standard reply, delivered by someone who wasn't going to waste time talking to strangers.

Bea tried Mrs Tarring again. As before, one line was engaged and there was no answer to the other. 'Mrs Tarring must be ringing someone else. She's not on the phone to the Eaton Square address because that number wasn't engaged. Perhaps she's speaking to the hospital.'

'Or the Oxfordshire number? Lord Rycroft lives there most of the time, nowadays.'

Bea tried the Oxfordshire address. Another long wait, again no engaged signal, or voicemail. Again, a woman replied. 'Yes?' A livelier, younger voice.

'This is Bea Abbot speaking, of the Abbot Agency. May I speak to Lord Rycroft? It is an urgent matter, concerning his son.'

'I'm afraid Lord Rycroft is not in residence.' The standard reply. And no recognition of Bea's name or agency. This woman had not got her job through Bea, either.

Bea said, 'Please don't hang up! Lord Rycroft is Kent's next of kin, isn't he?'

'What? Who are you?'

Bea tried to keep calm. 'My name is Mrs Abbot. I've been

called in to help Mrs Tarring and Miss Summerleys in an emergency. Hasn't Mrs Tarring been on the phone to you yet?'

And if not, what has she been doing all this time?

'I'm sorry, I can't answer any—'

'Kent Rycroft was attacked this morning and taken to hospital. I'm afraid the news is not good.'

'What do you mean? *Who* did you say you are?'

'Mrs Abbot. A friend of Miss Summerleys.'

'Who?'

Bea refrained from grinding her teeth. Didn't the Rycroft housekeepers ever contact one another, or was this forbidden by their code of discretion? 'Lord Rycroft's son is in hospital. The hospital needs to contact Lord Rycroft, urgently. So, if you could persuade him to come to the phone?'

'He's not here.' A trace of uncertainty. 'He left his breakfast on the table and called for his car to be brought round, even though it's supposed to be going in for a service, which I did remind him about. I didn't even have time to pack a bag for him. He said he'd be in touch. He's at the London house, I assume.'

'They say not. He didn't tell you where he was going?'

'No. Who are you, and what do you mean by—'

'He had a phone call, I suppose.'

'Well . . . yes. He took it on his mobile, which only accepts calls from a few people. I assumed it was Mr Kent ringing, but . . . you say Mr Kent's in hospital?'

'This is important. About what time did Lord Rycroft get this phone call?'

'I . . . I don't think I should say any more.'

'He breakfasts late? It was about eight thirty, perhaps?' That would tie in with the call Lucas had made when his breakfast had been interrupted.

'No, His Lordship doesn't rise until much later.'

So it wasn't Lord Rycroft whom Lucas had rung at half past eight. 'How much later? Nine, ten?'

'Nearer to ten, but I . . . no comment.'

'Has Mrs Tarring called you?'

No reply. The phone clicked off.

Magda looked as if she were about to dissolve into a puddle. 'It's a black hole. Everyone's disappearing!'

Bea straightened her own spine. 'I think we can assume Lucas was asked by someone he trusted to get the jewellery from the bank. I don't know why but, from what you say, he wouldn't have fallen for the usual sort of scam which parts a fool from his money. No, he's too intelligent for that. He checked that it was genuine, didn't he? He took delivery, and when in the taxi afterwards, he arranged to hand it over to someone he trusted.

'Meanwhile, he had an appointment to have his hair cut. He had plenty of time to have that done before he met . . . whoever . . . at Piers's place, so he gave you the jewellery for safekeeping and took the taxi on to the barber's. He never arrived there. He had a working cell phone. Perhaps he had second thoughts on his way there. Perhaps received another phone call which caused him to change his plans. Or he might well have double-checked with Lord Rycroft or Kent about the disposal of the goods? If that was the call which Lord Rycroft received, then you can construct a scenario in which the two men decided that, in view of the strange circumstances concerning the removal of the jewellery from the bank, they would forgo their plans for the day and arrange to meet.'

'Yes, but Lucas should have phoned me to tell me . . . ah, he couldn't, could he? My phone was in pieces on the studio floor by that time.'

'So if he'd tried to phone you and didn't get through, what would he think?'

Magda drew in a sharp breath. 'That I'd gone off with the goods? Oh, no! He knows me better than that. He can trust me to keep them safe.'

'In spite of the attentions of Tweedledum and Tweedledee?'

Magda made swimming motions with her hands. 'I don't know! I don't know! There's something else that's been bothering me. I know I didn't have time to make the beds this morning before we left, but . . .' She steadied herself. 'My bed's been made. I am not going to have hysterics. I must have forgotten that I'd made it.'

Bea started for the stairs at a run.

Magda followed, saying, 'No, no . . . it can't be!'

Bea threw open the door which led to Magda's bedroom. Sunshine shone through the window, lighting up the bed.

It was an old-fashioned double bed, made of pine. Solid and welcoming. Four ruffled pillows were arranged across the headboard, two on two. A double duvet, printed with pink flowers, had been spread across the bed. The duvet had a ruffle round it, too. It was a deep, expensive duvet, under which one could snuggle.

Magda had her fingers to her mouth. 'I left the duvet over the back of a chair, airing in front of the window. I always leave the window open at the top, to air the room. That's the way I was brought up.'

The window was still open, but the duvet was back on the bed, neatly fluffed up.

Bea twitched the duvet back, and gasped. She took a step back.

Magda screamed, soundlessly.

The body of a man lay on the bed with his head under the pillows. Not a big man. A truncated man. A headless man in good jeans and a cashmere sweater over a shirt. Black socks and brown brogues on his feet.

No sign of blood.

Bea steeled herself. She lifted the pillows off his face, one by one.

A fair-haired young man with a good tan. Eyes closed, lips slack. Asleep? No, he couldn't have slept with those two pillows over his head.

Bea touched his neck. 'No pulse. He's quite cold.'

She had jogged the bed. His hand moved.

Magda screamed again.

This time Bea joined her. Bea put both hands over her heart and stilled her breathing. She told herself that the corpse's hand had shifted because she'd jogged the bed. She touched the hand. It was cold and limp. Rigor mortis had been and gone so he hadn't died that morning. Last night? Some time yesterday?

What else could she see?

The man was white, Caucasian. Quite young. Possibly in his late teens or early twenties? Those reddish marks . . . check his eyes? Could she bear to touch him? She forced herself to do so. Yes. Nasty.

He'd been smothered. She thought.

Magda said, 'Oh, how could you? Ugh . . .' And dived for the bathroom.

Bea inspected the underside of the pillow which had been placed over the man's head. There were no marks on it. He'd been killed elsewhere and then dumped in Magda's bed.

Why in Magda's bed? To scare her away because she was protective of Lucas?

Bea felt for her mobile phone in her pocket. No mobile. Where had she left it? Downstairs on the kitchen table, that's where.

Magda was throwing up in the bathroom. Bea reckoned she'd be throwing up, too, if someone had planted a corpse in her bed.

Magda emerged, patting her mouth dry. 'What are we going to do?'

Bea ignored that. 'Is this man Kent Rycroft?'

Magda shuddered. Didn't want to look. She forced herself to stand right by the bed and look at the man. 'No.' She didn't sound sure of herself. Then, more strongly, 'No, it's not him. No beard, and younger. But it does look a bit like him. Is he one of the cousins, perhaps? I don't think I've seen him before. I mean, I don't think it's Kent, though I only ever saw him once at the interview, and I've heard that when people die they don't look like themselves.'

'It could be another member of the Rycroft family?'

A shrug. 'I've only ever met Lucas and Kent. Oh, and the twins. I've heard that there are some other cousins floating about but I've never met them.'

Bea put her arm around Magda. 'Come on, let's go downstairs and ring the police.'

'Not the police. You know we mustn't!'

'We can't protect the Rycrofts in the event of a murder, and you know it.'

Magda gave a little sob. 'The Queen in *Alice in Wonderland* keeps saying "Off with his head!" When I saw a man with his head under the pillow, I thought he'd lost his head.'

'Yes, yes.' Bea urged Magda down the stairs. 'Apart from Kent, what other members of the Rycroft family are about the right age as the man on the bed? You mentioned some cousins?'

'I can't think. Yes, I've had most of them on the phone at different times, I suppose, but . . .! Someone called Shirley and another called Hilary. Unusual names. I can't remember which is male and which female, but I think they're siblings. Then there's the twins. And Kent. There's another cousin or brother or something, but I don't know anything about him. Wait a minute, I think Kent had a son. I think he was at uni.'

'A university student would be younger than your corpse, wouldn't you say?'

'I don't know. If we ring the police I'll lose my job. But you're right. The Rycrofts think so much of themselves. Pride, dreadful pride. Pride goes before a fall, they say. I'm rambling. Take no notice.'

'What's happened here is constructive dismissal, meaning you're out of a job anyway. We'll pack and get you out of here. I'll get you another job.'

'But Lucas . . . what will he do without me?' A wail. 'Oh, where is he?'

'More to the point,' said Bea, 'where is Piers? I haven't seen him since he vanished with the biscuit tin.'

The phone rang downstairs. No, two phones.

Magda scrambled down the stairs faster than Bea, who didn't intend to have a fall on a strange flight of steps, so took her time getting down.

Magda had gone for the landline. 'Yes . . . Yes, I understand that, but we can't just do nothing because . . .' She looked at the phone blankly, and replaced it on the wall. 'That was Mrs Tarring, saying not to do anything and she's on her way here.'

Bea picked up her own mobile, interrupting its wish to send its caller to voicemail. A voice with a purr in it. A woman. An alto. Self-assured and well-educated. 'Mrs Abbot? My name is Darlene. Bill Morton says I have to ring you straight away, to reassure you that I am not selling your ward on to white slavers or whoever.'

Bea had forgotten all about her ward's weekend escapade. How could she have been so remiss? 'I'm glad to have heard from you. I'm sorry you've been put to so much inconvenience—'

'None at all. I am so very fond of dear Billy's grandchild, and I gather the two little girls are inseparable at school.'

She calls him 'Billy' instead of 'William'! I wonder how he likes that?

The woman continued. 'So naughty of him not to have cleared the invitation for your little ward with you first. I shall have to scold him about that, won't I?'

Bea was seized with an impulse to have hysterics. She mastered it, with an effort. *How dare the woman talk like that! As if Bea had to be warned off 'dear Billy'! Which was not the case. No. It had been many months since Bea had decided that she was not going to allow William Morton a permanent place in her life. A nice man, but . . .*

'I quite understand,' said Bea, in her creamiest tone. 'Now, if you'll give me your address and phone number in case of emergencies? Oh, and what arrangements will you make for getting the girls back to school tomorrow?'

Bea listened, made notes, and put the phone down.

Magda was opening then shutting the fridge door in a distracted fashion. 'If Mrs Tarring's coming over, what shall we have for lunch? Or, do you think she'll have eaten?'

She's ignoring the corpse in her bed. She's lost her sense of proportion.

'No more dilly-dallying,' said Bea. 'We have to ring the cops.'

'No, no! Mrs Tarring said we mustn't!'

'Mrs Tarring doesn't yet know about the man in your bed. That's a pleasure in store for her. But before that, I need to find Piers. He wandered off somewhere ages ago.'

She told herself no harm could have come to him in a flat which was empty of all personnel except for her, Magda . . . and the dead body, of course. She almost ran back along the corridor into the entrance hall. All was quiet.

A listening quiet? There was nobody in the library . . . unless you had a fanciful imagination and thought that the bug under the desk was lurking, watching . . .

Nonsense! Piers had removed that, hadn't he? Nevertheless.

There was nobody in the sitting room next door. No.
Lucas's bedroom? No, why would he . . .?
Piers was lying, spread-eagled on the bed. Dead?
'Piers!' She shook his shoulder.
A groan. Which meant he was alive!
Thank the Lord! I couldn't have borne it if . . .
'What's the time?' Piers tried to sit up. Rubbed his eyes.
Yawned, and yelped as his jaw protested. His bruise was
developing fast. 'Must have dropped off. Been a busy morning.'

Bea felt weak. She sat on the bed next to him. 'I thought
for a moment . . . what with your having been hit and all, I
thought you might be, well, unconscious.' Or dead.

'Mm? Don't you ever have a nap in the afternoon? Forty
winks. Keeps me going.'

For two pins Bea would have lain down beside him, and
let him put his arms around her. She could do with a cuddle.

No! What on earth was she thinking of? She'd be going in
for pink blouses next. It was being in contact with Magda and
her romantic notions that was putting these ideas into her head.

She said, 'Lucas Rycroft is missing. Remember? So is his
elder brother. And there's a stranger in Magda's bed. Dead.'

'Really? How inconvenient. Why is he in Magda's bed?'
He put his hand on Bea's shoulder in a gesture of affection,
then swung his legs round to sit up properly. He touched his
cheek and winced. Yes, his jaw was swollen. He'd taken some
aspirin, which must have helped him to relax and even to fall
asleep. His little nap couldn't indicate anything more serious,
could it?

She tried to concentrate. Piers had made a good point. Why
had the body been put in Magda's bed? If Bea was any judge
of the matter, he'd died somewhere else, because there had
been no signs to indicate that Magda's pillow had been used
to suffocate him.

Magda stood in the doorway. Hovering. Wringing her hands
in distress. 'Yes, why would anyone put him in my bed?'

Bea said, 'I think it was a warning to you to keep away
from Lucas. Someone thinks you might want to be helpful to
him in his hour of need.'

Magda said, 'Oh, do you really think so?' And turned pink.

Someone turned a key in the lock on the front door.

They all heard it.

'Lucas!' Magda started for the hall.

Bea heard the front door open and close, and Magda's forlorn exclamation, 'Oh, it's you!'

Piers struggled to his feet. '*Not* lover boy, I assume.'

'Don't be coarse!' Bea shook her head at Piers in mock disapproval. 'I don't suppose it's ever occurred to Lucas to think of Magda in that way.'

'Absence makes the heart grow fonder—'

'As soon as he turns up again, she'll remember all his irritating little ways.'

He yawned, and clapped his hand to his yellowing jaw. 'Remind me not to yawn. Have you got any more of those aspirins, by any chance?'

'You shouldn't have any more for a while.'

Magda appeared in the doorway. 'It's Mrs Tarring. Isn't that good news?' Trying to sound positive.

Mrs Tarring was an older version of Magda. She was better upholstered, wore a pale lipstick and sported a gold pin on the lapel of her jacket. Also mock-pearl earrings. 'Mrs Abbot? I don't understand why . . .' She switched her eyes to Piers. 'And who . . .?'

Bea took the initiative. 'This is my friend, Piers, the portrait painter who was supposed to have met with Lucas this morning. Would you like to view our corpse, which has been laid out tastefully in Magda's bed?'

'What!'

Bea led the way. Mrs Tarring followed her up the stairs, across the landing and into Magda's bedroom.

Bea said, 'Who do you think this is?'

Mrs Tarring looked. Gasped. Reached for something to hold on to. Connected with a substantial chest of drawers, and leaned on it.

Bea said, 'Is it Kent Rycroft?'

A fervent shake of the head. 'No!'

'Another Rycroft?'

A positive nod. A hand went to her mouth. Bea guided her to the bathroom.

Retching sounds. Flush of toilet.

Magda had followed them up. 'How dare they put someone in my bed!'

Bea said, 'You think this is the twins' work? I doubt it. Yes, I can see them bludgeoning someone to death, but I don't see them neatly laying their victim out in your bed. That's too subtle for them.'

Piers appeared. 'Let's have a look, then.' He bent over the body, showing no signs of revulsion. Then straightened up. 'He's the same physical type as the chap I found at my place, but this one is younger. Much younger. Who is he?'

Mrs Tarring emerged from the bathroom, dabbing her lips. 'It's Owen Rycroft.'

'Who's he?' asked Magda. 'Oh, wait a minute. He's the one there's been all the fuss about, isn't he? I've never met him, but didn't someone say he was going to move into the flat below us? But we never see our neighbours, so I . . . No, I've never seen him before.'

'Quite likely,' said Mrs Tarring. 'He's not been on the scene for long and he's had no reason to contact you.' She looked at the body, and looked away. 'I can't believe this is happening.'

Bea said, 'Let's go downstairs, shall we, and call the police.'

'No, we can't!' said Mrs Tarring.

'Sorry, one body too many,' said Bea, leading the way out of the bedroom.

'But you don't understand! Lord Rycroft is adamant that—'

'Mrs Tarring, this is *not* the twins' work, if that is what you were thinking. Now, where was Lord Rycroft when you rang him this morning?'

'I am forbidden to ring him. He rings me every Saturday morning at some time convenient to himself. I was really worried that I might have to break his rule and contact him, what with everything that's been happening, but fortunately he did ring me a little while back.'

'So you don't know if he was in London or not when he rang you?'

'He rang on his mobile. He was in the car.'

'His housekeeper – or whoever it was who answered the phone at the country house – said he left home after breakfast.

Now, when you spoke to Lord Rycroft, you did tell him about Kent, didn't you? We've found out which hospital he's in, but—'

'He said it was impossible that Kent had been attacked. He said I was talking nonsense. He said he was coming up to town, and he'd contact me again later. So it can't be Kent who's in the hospital.'

Bea considered tearing her hair out but didn't. She had had a particularly becoming cut and blow-dry that week, and didn't want to upset it.

Magda pulled Mrs Tarring into the sitting room. 'Come and see. The cabinet!'

Mrs Tarring stifled a cry.

'Now do you believe me?' said Magda. 'I told you the jade was gone.'

Mrs Tarring's eyes switched from side to side. 'It's insured. I'm sure it's insured.'

Bea said, 'Now there's a nasty thought. The Rycroft jewellery was removed from the bank this morning. Is it insured if it's taken out of the vaults, or not?'

Mrs Tarring's eyes widened. 'No, I don't think it will be. Not if it's been removed from . . . who has dared to do this?'

'Lucas, apparently. Acting under instructions from someone.' Bea touched Piers on the arm. 'Can you bear to contact the police again? We can't sit on this. Here, take my phone.'

'No!' said Mrs Tarring, in a faint voice. But then she sat down on the nearest chair and blew her nose, resigning herself to the situation.

SEVEN

Saturday afternoon

Piers made the call to the police.

After identifying himself and giving the address, he said, 'I was in touch with you earlier today about a man who'd been assaulted at my studio in West London. No, not here. In my house in Ealing. The man was carted off to hospital. No, I'm not ringing about that. No, I can't remember the name of the inspector who dealt with the matter, but I'm sure you can find it out even if it's not in your patch. Yes, I do understand that London is divided up into different areas and each has its own police force, but if you check around . . . Yes, I understand that I ought to have taken down all the details but I'd been knocked out and wasn't exactly firing on all cylinders. The police did take me to the hospital to be checked out . . . no, I'm not pulling your leg and yes, I do agree that wasting police time with frivolous queries must seem . . .'

The phone quacked, and Piers's eyebrows rose. Twice he tried to interrupt. Finally he said, 'Is it my turn to speak now? I have to report another body, but unlike the one this morning, this one did not hang on to life till I arrived. He is definitely dead, and in someone else's bed, not his own. No, not with a woman. It's not that sort of death. I really think you ought to take a look. I gave you the address earlier. Do you want me to repeat it?'

Apparently they did. After that, he ended the call and handed the phone back to Bea. 'They'll be fifteen minutes, at least.'

Bea put her arm round Mrs Tarring's shoulders. 'Look, I realize you've had a nasty shock but we don't have much time. Can you fill me in on who's who in the Rycroft family, and how Owen fits in?'

Mrs Tarring made an effort to pull herself together, but her eyes switched this way and that and never met Bea's. Was the woman considering what to say and what to keep quiet about?

'Lord Rycroft married twice. Kent is his son by his first marriage. Kent is the one who runs the family trust. Owen is the product of Lord Rycroft's second, short-lived marriage. He was brought up by his mother in Australia, where she'd gone to live after obtaining a divorce from His Lordship. When she died a few months ago, Owen came over to see if we'd give him a job. And that's what we did.'

There was a subtext here which Mrs Tarring was not giving. Bea checked with Piers, who had taken a seat at the far end of the room. His eyebrows peaked, and he sent her a look which meant that he didn't buy that story as it stood.

Bea said, 'Was Owen something of a black sheep, by any chance?'

'I really couldn't say.' A repressive tone.

Magda was frowning. 'He looks like Kent, a bit. I get that.'

Bea said, 'I suppose he could prove that he was who he said he was?'

'Of course. Kent found him a job, and he was provided with accommodation. As you say, the family resemblance is remarkable.'

Bea said, 'How come the twins don't resemble Kent and Owen so much?'

'They take after their mother, Mrs Nicholas. She was a large woman. Rode to hounds, that sort of thing.'

Bea said, 'I wonder how the twins took to Owen's arrival? Did they object to another Rycroft demanding a share of the family fortune?'

'You'd have to ask them.' Mrs Tarring pinched in her lips in an expression of distaste and then relaxed. 'You're right, of course. They didn't like it. Owen's personality was . . . abrasive. He did not trouble to make himself liked by the family. Lord Rycroft asked us in the office to make Owen welcome. And we did. Of course we did. But there have been times when . . . Oh, I really don't see why I should cover for him. I caught him trying to force one of the office girls to have sex with him. She was distressed. She has a boyfriend who is of a jealous nature and if he had decided to take Owen to task, well, it might have been very nasty. I warned Owen to keep away from the girl. He laughed at me. I said I'd complain to Lord Rycroft. Owen threatened to get me dismissed. He didn't succeed, of course, but after that I kept out of his way. I told Kent what had happened, but he couldn't do much with Owen, either.'

Bea looked to Piers for a comment. He closed one eye slowly, and then opened it again. Was he winking at her? Or . . . no. He was just tired. Now he was rubbing his forehead in weary fashion. Just tired.

She turned back to Mrs Tarring. 'So was it Owen's arrival from Australia which sent the family into a tizzy, and not some rumour that Lord Rycroft was going gaga?'

Mrs Tarring bit her lip. She checked with Magda, who was frowning at some thought of her own and didn't meet Mrs Tarring's eye. 'I've never observed Lord Rycroft doing anything to indicate that he was suffering from delusions, though I did hear one of the others worrying about . . . no, I really have nothing to say on the subject. *You* say Kent is in hospital, but Lord Rycroft says he isn't. I don't know what to think.'

'You could visit Kent in hospital,' said Bea.

Mrs Tarring lifted her hands. 'I repeat, Lord Rycroft doesn't believe it's Kent in the hospital, and I have to go along with that. I have never had anything like this happen before. When Lord Rycroft hears that you've called in the police, I don't know what he'll do. I'll have to tell him it wasn't me who made the call. I don't want to lose my job.'

'If the different members of the family are so alike physically, could it be one of the more distant cousins who's landed in hospital? There are others, aren't there?'

'No, no. Ridiculous!'

Bea wasn't so sure. There was a ring at the doorbell. That would be the police. She said, 'Piers, will you answer that? I expect the police will want to interview each of us separately. Magda, you won't be able to stay on here afterwards. When they've finished with you, would you like to come back with me for a few nights till you can get yourself sorted out? Here's my card. I may be released before you in which case I'll probably have gone home. You can get a taxi and follow. Ring me on my mobile when you're on your way, right?'

They all three turned to the door but nothing happened, except that the doorbell rang again, twice. Meaning it. Bea saw that Piers hadn't moved.

Magda said, 'I'll go,' and disappeared into the hall.

Piers was lolling in his chair, eyes closed and limbs relaxed. Bea hesitated. There'd been a niggle at the back of her mind ever since she'd found Piers lying asleep on Lucas's bed that morning. He'd said he was just having forty winks, but . . . surely there was no need to worry about Piers, was there? Except, of course, he had been hit on the head.

And, he'd winked at her. At least, she thought that was what he'd done. Was he shamming illness, or did he need to be returned to hospital?

Magda let a couple of police constables into the hall. One man, one woman. Magda introduced everyone by name, saying that Mrs Tarring was her boss, and that Bea and Piers were just friends.

Bea kept quiet.

Magda waited for Bea or Mrs Tarring to say something, but they didn't, so she went on, 'Yes, well. We did find a body. In my bed. Would you like to see?' She led the way out of the room and up the stairs.

Bea checked on Piers. 'Piers?' She shook his arm, and he woke, slowly. And treated her to another wink. Then he washed his face with his hands. 'Can't a man close his eyes for a minute around here?'

'No,' she said, pushing his chin back so that she could check on his eyes. Were the pupils dilated? She couldn't be sure. 'You *have* been concussed. The hospital ought not to have let you go. You need to be monitored to make sure you're not developing any serious symptoms.'

He yawned. 'I'm perfectly all right. I am not, repeat not, going to go back to hospital. Have the plod arrived?'

Had he not heard the doorbell?

She looked at her watch. 'No argument. You ought never to have been discharged. I'm taking you back there, now.'

'No way!' He tried to get up, and made it at the second attempt.

She said, 'I insist. And, I'm coming with you, to make sure you get seen.'

Mrs Tarring rose from her chair, looking upset. 'Oh, the poor man. But really, you can't walk out now. You can't go anywhere till the police have finished with us.'

Bea said, 'Piers is suffering from concussion and I'm taking him back to hospital. You can tell the police what they need to know. You know far more about what's happening than we do, anyway. We're just unfortunate bystanders. Don't forget to remind the police of the tie-up with the assault at Piers's studio this morning.' She got out her mobile and summoned a taxi to take them to the nearest hospital with an A & E department.

Mrs Tarring took a few steps to the door, and back again in agitation. 'You can't go till the police have taken your statement. I won't let you.'

'Watch me,' said Bea again, putting her mobile away and picking up her handbag.

There were noises off as the police descended, also on their phones, calling for back-up and Forensics and goodness knows what else. They went out of the front door, and returned. And clattered up the stairs again.

Piers remained seated, head hanging, until Bea judged that the way out was clear. Then, over Mrs Tarring's protestations, Bea pulled Piers to his feet and steered him across the hall, down the stairs and out into the fresh air. The taxi drove up and she put him into it, asking the driver to take them to the nearest A & E department.

Piers sat with his eyes closed throughout the journey. She sat beside him, holding his hand till they were decanted at the hospital. She got him out, leaned him against the wall, and paid off the taxi.

'Now!' she said, turning on Piers.

He bounced upright, grinning. Fully alive and full of energy. He swept his hands back through his hair, and adjusted the collar of his shirt. 'Home from home. This is where they brought me this morning. The coffee bar is at the far end.

We can use the facilities and have a cuppa before we go off again. It's time we tracked down the elusive Rycrofts, don't you think?'

She had to smile. 'I do. Sorry I took so long to work it out that you were acting concussed, although,' she gave him a close look, 'I'm not entirely sure that you were.'

'I did hit my head, and I did feel dazed for a bit, but I'm not sitting around for hours in a hospital while I feel all right.' He led the way into the hospital, indicated where the coffee bar was, and said he'd have an Americano and a sausage baguette, which proved to her that his stomach was in order, even if his head wasn't. She had a latte and an egg sandwich.

Over food she said, 'You know something about the Rycrofts? Something you weren't prepared to share with Magda and Mrs T?'

'Correct. Oh, boy! What a can of worms! Look, when I was first contacted about painting Lucas, I didn't much want to do it. Another dull academic, I thought. I'd got enough on as it was. You remember I told you that the twins knocked a couple of my half-finished paintings about? I've enough work on to keep me busy for another year, maybe eighteen months. I could murder those twins! All those hours of work! Ah well. Anyway, I was grumbling to one of my old friends about being asked to fit Lucas into my schedule, and he said he'd heard some amusing gossip about the Rycroft family. He wouldn't say what it was and, when I asked, he clammed up. Naturally that intrigued me.

'So, I put my thinking cap on, and wondered who I could ask. People do tell me all sorts, you know. Mostly it goes in one ear and out the other. I believe hairdressers get exposed to the same treatment. That weekend I met an old friend at an exhibition and she, Lady Catherine – the one I was supposed to be meeting for lunch today – was happy to share what she knew with me. A delightful woman. I'm distressed that I had to stand her up for lunch today. She will be quite cross with me, and I shall no doubt come in for a scolding. She's coming up to ninety years old, by the way, so you needn't be jealous.'

Bea suppressed an urge to hit him. 'Go on. What did she know, and how did she know it?'

'Mrs T was discretion itself when talking about the Rycrofts, wasn't she? Or maybe she really doesn't know. Perhaps it was before her time? Lord Rycroft, descendant of generations of blameless landowners and shrewd investors in this and that, had done the expected thing in his twenties and married a suitable heiress. Between them they produced the equally blameless and trustworthy Kent. But upon his wife dying early, the old lord broke with tradition and fell for . . . wait for it . . . a dancer! Not that I have anything against dancers, you understand. I have known many, and painted a few. Admirable creatures, driven by their talent. They don't think about much else. However, Melisande – that's what she called herself – had only one talent, and that wasn't for dancing. Lord Rycroft was besotted. He married her, bedecked her with pearls, and took her everywhere.'

'Owen was the result of this second marriage?'

'You're going too fast. Lord Rycroft may have been a terror in the boardroom – though my friend indicated he was more of a pussycat than a tiger, hence his handing over the Rycroft estate to a trust fund – but it seems he failed to satisfy his new bride in the bedroom. She began to bestow her favours elsewhere, starting with her husband's two brothers, Lucas and Nicholas.'

'Lucas! You astound me! From what Magda said about him . . . Wait a minute! When did all this happen?'

'Twenty-odd years ago. Lady Catherine told me about it because I'd asked her if she knew anything about Lucas, and of course she did. She said that the liaison with Lucas hadn't lasted long and had soured him for life . . . hence he'd never married, nor had his name been linked with another woman. After she'd tasted and abandoned Lucas, Melisande had moved on to the youngest of the brothers, Nicholas. He already had a wife and twin boys . . . that's Tweedledum and Tweedledee. Oh, by the way, Mrs Nicholas is said to have knocked her husband about a bit before, during and after their marriage.'

'No!' Bea grinned. 'Good for her!'

'Mm. Well. Maybe. The dancer eventually got tired of Nicholas, or Mrs Nicholas warned her off, I don't know which.

The dancer moved on, and Nicholas turned to drink. This is all gossip, you understand. It may not be true.'

'It sounds true.' Bea smothered a laugh. 'Mrs T did imply that Mrs Nicholas was a hefty creature.'

'Quite so. But that's not all. Brace yourself, for there's worse to come. Melisande's next conquest was a playboy much younger than herself, who was found stabbed to death in his car at the races. You can imagine the scandal! She was charged with murder but got off on a technicality, though everyone believed she was guilty. After the trial she disappeared for a couple of months, only to reappear with baby Owen in tow. She said he was a Rycroft, but that she personally had no idea which of the three brothers might have been responsible. As the boy had been born before Lord Rycroft divorced her, the boy is technically – and maybe correctly – her husband's legitimate son.'

'His Lordship didn't ask for a DNA test to decide which brother had been responsible?'

'I'm not sure that scientists then could distinguish between the offspring of three brothers, could they? Anyway, he didn't. He was so shattered, so humiliated, that he paid her off. He became paranoid about publicity. He believes that the merest hint of scandal, a parking or speeding ticket, for instance, and the papers would rake up the whole sorry story all over again.'

'Hurt pride. So that's why Melisande went to Australia, to get away from the scandal?'

'With her son. She married again. Nobody here gave the child a thought until he reappeared some months ago, saying his mother had died and he was claiming his birthright. Lady Catherine made me promise to tell her what, if anything, happens next.' He rubbed his hands. 'She'll be thrilled to hear the latest instalment.'

Bea was thoughtful. 'It does rather look as if it were Owen's arrival which upset the status quo in the Rycroft family. Talk about letting the fox into the henhouse! Magda says one moment everything was sweetness and light, and the next, every member of the family was on to Lucas to do something. Lucas refused to take action. Magda said she had heard that the old lord was going gaga, but somehow I think that was a red herring and the real problem was what to do about Owen.'

Piers said, 'You know, I'd imagined, from what I'd heard of Lucas, that he was a somewhat weak character, a small-time academic who wouldn't repay my attention. I'd half decided not to accept the commission, but Lady Catherine said she thought Lucas had developed into an interesting man, and that I should meet him before I decided. So that's what I did. I wonder what he really is like.'

Bea mused, 'Owen doesn't seem to have been a very pleasant character, and what's more, whatever his ambiguous background, he must be considered, legally, as the younger son of the old lord. This means that on his arrival there would be one more claimant on the resources of the Rycroft purse. We know the twins were agitating for more money, even before he came. I suppose they might have thought that if Owen were out of the way . . . but no, I really don't believe that they would have laid him out on Magda's bed after they'd killed him. It would be more their style to bash him over the head, and leave him wherever it was they'd found him . . . or perhaps they'd dump the body in a dark alley and try to make out his death was a robbery gone wrong. No, putting it into Magda's bed was malicious and . . . and yes, it was sly.'

'Owen was suffocated, wasn't he?'

'It looked like it. Not recently. He was quite cold, and limp. There'll have to be an autopsy. I really don't understand what's happening. First Lucas disappears, and then Owen turns up dead. And Kent? If it wasn't Kent who's been laid out cold at your studio, then who is it?'

Piers shrugged. 'Mrs Tarring can identify him, I assume. Or his father.'

'But where is Lord Rycroft? Shouldn't he have arrived in London by now and have picked up his messages? What a mess.'

'Hang about . . .' He disappeared down a corridor, reappearing with a notebook and pen. 'Bought from the shop. I'll draw my victim for you.'

'That's no good. I've never seen Kent, remember?'

Piers ignored that. He concentrated, swiftly sketching the head of a youngish man with a short beard. His eyes were closed, his hair dishevelled. 'His face was untouched. Only the back of his head was . . . you know. Shall I draw you the twins as well?'

Bea shuddered. 'What for? I mean, I've met them. Once seen . . .'

'Mm.' He turned a page and sketched them in, saying, 'I looked Lucas up on Facebook at one point. An academic of some standing. Belongs to this and that revered art institution. Publishes papers. Is asked to go on committees. I could only find his likeness in a group photograph, taken somewhere in Italy. Big man, standing at the back. Indistinct features. Clean-shaven. Fair hair. That's as far as I could go.' He threw the notebook onto the table.

Bea said, 'We have to find someone who knows the family and can identify your body.'

With some difficulty Piers extracted pieces of a smashed phone from his pocket and laid them on the table. 'If I could resurrect my phone, we could start asking around. Have you any idea how to extract a SIM card from one phone and put it in another?'

She picked up her handbag. 'Let's find a mobile phone shop and let them do it for us.'

Bea's phone rang.

It was a woman's voice on the phone. Bea thought she knew it but couldn't put a name to the person for a moment. 'Bea? Are you there? We've been waiting and waiting. Have you had an accident? Is my little daughter all right? We're worried half out of our wits.'

It was Bernice's mother, in a state! With a start, Bea remembered that she'd planned to take Bernice over to see her mother, stepfather, and delightful but noisy baby half-brother that afternoon. When Bernice had rung to say she was on her way down to the south coast, Bea had told the child to ring her mother and make her apologies. Bernice had failed to do so?

'I'm really sorry,' said Bea. 'Bernice rang me this morning to say she was on her way down to the Isle of Wight with her best friend, as they'd been invited to go sailing this weekend. I was not best pleased, as you can imagine, as we had made plans to visit you and we have tickets for the theatre tonight. I asked her to speak to you direct to apologize. She ought not

have altered our arrangements without permission, and I'm
going to have to have words with her about that. Do I take it
that she hasn't rung you?'

No, of course she hadn't.

'Oh dear, oh dear. She can be so very headstrong.'

'Too much so.' Bea would very much like to wring the
child's neck. Well, not exactly that, but . . . 'Trust me, she
won't do this again.'

'We stayed in all afternoon, waiting for her.' Bernice's
mother was a sweetie, but she did tend to whinge rather than
shout and scream when upset.

Bea said, 'Lord Morton has taken her down to the south
coast with his granddaughter. They're staying somewhere on
the Isle of Wight. I've spoken to their hostess for the weekend.
She promised to take good care of them.'

'I'm afraid Bernice just doesn't think! Which is all very
well, but—'

'I agree. It doesn't excuse her behaviour. I'll get her to ring
you as soon as she gets back. Also, I think she should write
you a note of apology.'

'Oh, I wouldn't want you to go to extra trouble. I mean,
she is a lovely girl, if a bit wilful. I mean, I wouldn't want
her to be punished or anything.'

Bea set her teeth. Letting Bernice act as she pleased was
no way to show her how to get along with other people. 'I'll
let her decide her own punishment. All right?'

'You won't be too harsh on her, will you?'

'No, I won't.' Bea clicked off her phone.

Piers seemed to find the situation amusing. Bea said, in her
sharpest tone, 'You try bringing up a lively youngster who
knows she's got more brains in her little finger than most
people have in their whole bodies—'

'And the knowledge that when she grows up she could buy
up half of Mayfair without feeling it? A fearsome prospect
for any parent. I gather her own mother can't cope.'

Bea sighed. 'No, she can't. She'd let Bernice walk all over
her.'

Piers said, 'I must meet this ward of yours one of these
days.' He didn't mean it.

'It is a relief,' said Bea, feeling disagreeable, 'to recall that you have never been interested in children.'

His eyebrows peaked. 'Touché.' He'd never been particularly interested in their one and only child until the boy had grown up and gone out into the world. 'Shall we go?'

EIGHT

Saturday late afternoon

They took another taxi to the nearest shopping centre and, while Piers busied himself selecting a new phone and getting the SIM card transferred, Bea found a seat in a nearby coffee shop, ordered a drink which she did not need and delved into Lucas's address book which, surprise!, had somehow found its way into her capacious handbag.

Soon enough Piers arrived, scowling at the price he'd been asked to pay for his new phone. The first thing he said was, 'Shouldn't you have turned that book over to the police?'

Bea put on her most innocent face. 'I forgot I had it.'

'In your dreams.' He wasn't in a good mood, was he? He looked at his watch. 'I'm afraid Lady Catherine is going to be annoyed. I don't make a habit of standing women up, but perhaps she'll forgive me when I bring her up to date on the Rycroft affair. May I use your phone to find Lady Catherine's number and then ring her? I've left my new phone charging in the shop. Remind me to collect it before we leave.'

She handed hers over. He growled to himself as he navigated the systems. 'Why don't you get yourself something more modern?'

She ignored that. Finally he got through to his elderly friend, and brought her up to date. Piers enjoyed giving her the juicy bits and, from the little shrieks of mock disbelief Bea could hear as Piers held her phone loosely to his ear, Lady Catherine evidently enjoyed hearing them. When he'd finished, Piers drew Bea's coffee towards him, and made inroads on that.

'Feeling better?' said Bea. 'Now, it's really lucky that Lucas's address book fell into my bag when I wasn't looking—'

'I said that you should have given it to the police.' He didn't really mean it. He produced his notebook and pen and began sketching again. This time it was Magda, all prettied up with a more becoming hairstyle and attention to eye makeup.

With a sweet smile, Bea said, 'I'm sure Mrs Tarring will be able to tell the police what they need to know. Now, pay attention. It's clear Lucas has had this book for years and years. As is usual it's printed in alphabetical order, but there's a section at the back which Lucas has used solely for family addresses. Fortunately for me, he's allocated one page to each person. When someone dies or moves, he crosses out the first address and puts in an arrow to the new one. With a bit of care, you can follow someone's life history this way.

'The first page is devoted to George, Lord Rycroft, who is Lucas's elder brother. Two addresses are given: one in London and one in the country. Complete with landline numbers which have remained the same throughout and several mobile numbers, all of which except the last have been crossed out. So far, so good. According to Mrs Tarring, Lord Rycroft is travelling back to London from the country as we speak, so there's no use trying him at present.

'The next page is for Kent, who is Lord Rycroft's eldest son. Now, I assume he was married at some point because a couple of people have referred to Kent having a son, but—'

'What happened to Kent's wife?'

'There's an entry here for a woman called Elsa, which has been crossed through a couple of times. No new entry has been given. I surmise that she's either divorced and out of touch, or dead.'

'Unlucky in their marriages, the Rycrofts.'

'You can talk.'

He protested, 'Come on; I've only been divorced once. You're carrying on as if I were Bluebeard or Henry the Eighth.'

'The fact that you didn't actually marry the women you've romanced over the years is irrelevant.' She stopped. 'We're quarrelling. Why?'

'Sex rears its ugly head,' said Piers. 'Also, you're worried about Bernice. You're using the Rycroft business to avoid thinking about her.'

Bea ignored his reference to sex. She was afraid he was right, as she could still feel the pull of sexual attraction in his presence, but she could not, really could *not* deal with that at the moment. As for Bernice, he was right about that, too. What was she to do with the child?

She brought her mind back to the present. The Rycrofts. Well, there was a puzzle which she might as well try to solve. 'Returning to the page for Kent, there's only one address and landline number for him, but a number of mobile phones. Then there's a series of addresses and phone numbers, which seem to chart the progress of a boy called Ellis from one boarding school to the other, then to a college in Cambridge. Finally, in one of the very last entries in this section, Ellis is to be contacted at a flat in an exclusive street not far from where his great-uncle Lucas lives. I think that's where he's living now. This must be Kent's son. Agreed?'

Piers was sketching again. Was he even listening? She noted the phone number for Ellis, and rang.

A man answered. A young man in a hurry. 'Yes?'

Bea said, 'Am I speaking to Ellis Rycroft?'

'What?' An educated voice. Noise of phone being put down. A shout to someone in the flat. 'Anyone know somebody called Ellis?' A second voice said something in the distance. The first man's voice returned. 'Sorry. I'm new here. Only moved in a while back. There's no Ellis living here.'

Bea said quickly, 'Don't put the phone down! Look, this is really urgent. We think his father's been taken to hospital—'

'What? Hold on a mo. I'll get someone . . .' Down went the phone again.

More voices offstage.

Phone picked up. A different voice, deeper. 'Ellis doesn't live here any more. You say his father is in hospital? But he'd know, wouldn't he?'

'A man answering the description of Ellis's father was found at the studio of a friend of mine this morning. He'd been attacked and was in a bad way. The police and an ambulance were called and he was taken to the hospital. We are trying to find a member of the family to confirm his identity and take charge.'

'If what you say is true, then shouldn't it be the police asking for Ellis?' An intelligent response.

'It should be. Yes. But they are relying on the Rycrofts' administrator to help them sort out the question of his identity, and she's otherwise engaged. My name is Mrs Abbot. The artist is a friend of mine. Neither of us knows any of the Rycrofts by sight. I've been called in by one of the Rycrofts' housekeepers to see if I could help. We honestly don't know if it's Kent Rycroft in hospital or one of his cousins. That's why we're trying to contact Ellis.'

A long moment in which the man thought about how to reply. 'Look, I can't help you. Ellis is dead. He died in an accident on his bike, nearly three months ago. He was a mad cyclist, out all hours of the day. Cycled to uni and cycled back. London traffic did for him. It was a shame. We miss him.'

'You shared the flat with him?'

'Yes. The flat is owned by his family. They allowed us to stay on and we pay them rent. There's four of us now. It works out pretty well. Look, I'm on my way out now. I have to meet someone in half an hour, so—'

'I'd be grateful for any information you can give me about Ellis's death. If I give you my phone number, do you think you could ring me back when you're free to talk?'

He had been well brought up. He huffed and puffed a bit, but took down Bea's number. And rang off.

Bea clicked her phone off. Maybe he'd ring back, and maybe he wouldn't. She said, 'Kent's son Ellis is dead. Lucas ought to have crossed his name off in his address book, but hasn't. Perhaps because he cared for the boy and didn't like to strike through his name? It was a traffic accident. That's the third member of the family to have gone missing. I can't think why, can you? What is wrong with the Rycrofts? The black sheep Owen is dead, the twins are on the rampage, and we're running out of names to pin on the man in hospital. It must be Kent, mustn't it? What on earth is that you're drawing?'

He turned the notebook so that she could see.

He'd drawn himself sitting on a pavement, holding up a placard saying 'Homeless'.

Bea's lips twitched. She'd been waiting for him to make a move on her, and here it came. Bea had asked Magda to move in for a few days, but she hadn't asked Piers to do the same although, yes, he was also technically homeless at the moment.

If he moved back in with her, how soon would it be before he wanted to move into her bed?

She'd kept him at a distance for years. Did she really want him back in her life?

She'd got used to being on her own. Well, except for her ward Bernice, of course. Bea enjoyed eating *when* she wanted, and *what* she wanted. She could get up and go to bed when she liked. She could read in bed and turn the light off when she wished. She didn't have to pick up men's socks or smelly shoes from the floor and deal with them. She had control of the television remote. She didn't have to guard her tongue or fit in with anyone else's timetable.

She was lonely.

Yes, but how lonely?

In some ways it would be good to invite someone else into her life but . . . yes, but. Piers was a tom cat. He couldn't help himself. Even in his sixties, he was attractive to the opposite sex.

He was drawing, again. Her face leapt into life on the page. He said, 'You've worn well.'

She knew that. So had he.

He said, 'I'm not penniless. I have investments. A couple of houses which I rent out. I could go to a hotel, or rent another flat, but I'm tired of living out of a suitcase. I've lived all over the place, in penthouses and garden flats, but I've not been able to make a home for myself since the day you threw me out.'

She knew that, too. She considered her options; she could offer him the tenancy of the mews cottage she owned at the end of her road. She garaged her car on the ground floor, but the upstairs rooms formed a self-contained flat, which she had been letting out on lucrative short-term holiday lets. The flat was vacant at the moment.

He said, 'I can't beg. I *won't* beg.'

No, she knew that, as well.

If she invited him back into her life, there would be fireworks now and again, but they knew one another so well that – on the whole – it would be, well, fun. Though 'fun' was not usually a term you would apply to a marriage between people who were verging on retirement. On the other hand, would Piers ever retire? Probably not. He was at the top of his game so there'd be no money problems with him around . . . not that she had any money problems herself, as the agency was going well, and she had no need to retire either.

Bea admired his talent, brains, his honesty, and his wit. But she knew him all too well. After a period of good behaviour, he'd start to take notice of other women and the cycle of love and betrayal, which had crucified her when they were married, would start up all over again. She'd married within a year of leaving school . . . too early, yes. He'd been still at art school and she'd just secured her first office job. At first it had been bliss. But soon after their son was born, he'd started to fret at the boundaries of family life and to respond to other women's lures.

She'd been so badly hurt by his infidelities that it had been years before she could allow herself to look at another man. Then her dear Hamilton had come along and swept her and her son into his arms and they'd had a comfortable and comforting marriage for so many years. She'd ached and grieved when Hamilton eventually died.

Could she bear to suffer so much again? Or, would she not mind so much if history repeated itself? After all, she was much older and wiser now.

He set his notebook aside. 'So, what's next?'

She was grateful that he had changed the subject. She stood up. 'Next, we visit the address Lucas has written down for Kent, who is his nephew, right? There's only one address for Kent so it doesn't look as if he's one to move around. Bring that notebook of yours. We may need it for identification purposes. You probably noticed there weren't any family photographs in Lucas's flat. He wasn't much interested in the family, was he? However, Kent did have a son, Ellis, so hopefully we'll find he had taken photographs of the two of them together.'

'Then we'll know if it's Kent or Lucas in the hospital, right? You're good at this, aren't you? Remind me to come back for my phone later.'

*   *   *

Kent lived in a three-storey mid-terrace early Victorian house, narrow but elegant, in a road not far from Lucas's home. As in Bea's place, there was a basement flat reached by an outside staircase, and steps up to a pillared porch on the ground floor. The window-boxes had been filled with spring bulbs and ivy, and everything from windows to paintwork looked as if it had been polished. The plane trees in the street outside were beginning to shoot forth green buds.

They mounted the steps to the front door, which was ajar. Not by much. The householder might have left in a hurry and failed to close it properly as he left, or someone had just gone in and failed to slam it shut behind them.

Bea rang the bell and waited, listening hard to see if there might be movement inside. Piers watched a 'yummy Mummy' walking her little dog on the other side of the street.

'Yes? What is it?' A woman in her late thirties appeared in the doorway. Another Rycroft? Straight blonde hair tucked behind her ears, no eyebrows to speak of, a sleeveless, cotton-mix dress drooping around a bony body. No makeup. Flat ballerina shoes. She seemed to be both wary and bothered about something.

Bea said, 'Forgive us for calling unannounced. I'm Bea Abbot of the Abbot Agency and Mrs Tarring has asked us to help her locate Kent Rycroft. This is his house, isn't it?'

Piers gave Bea a look which meant, 'Leave this to me.' He stepped into the hall, pushing the girl back before him. He said, 'I'm so glad we found you at home. You are . . .?'

She didn't want to let them in. Only, Piers had already managed to get in. 'I'm Shirley Rycroft, but . . .'

There'd been a telephone message from someone called Shirley in Lucas's waste-paper basket, hadn't there? Was this one of the distant cousins?

Piers bestowed a Grade V smile upon Shirley and, despite herself, she twitched a smile back. 'There's been a spot of bother. Mrs Tarring suggested Kent might have returned home. This is his house, isn't it?'

Bea shut the door on the outside wall, so that they were all three standing in a close group. The hall was of a reasonable size with doors open to a sitting room to the right and a kitchen further back. Light poured down from a tall window at the head of a flight of stairs ahead.

The woman said, 'If Mrs Tarring sent you, I suppose that's all right. But Kent isn't here. I don't know where he is.' She gestured to the sitting room. 'I've only just arrived. Someone's been here, searching for something. I was thinking I ought to report it to the police, but Kent hates publicity so much that I was waiting for him to decide whether to or not. I've tried ringing Mrs Tarring, but there's no reply. I don't know what to do.' She did indeed have a mobile phone in her hand.

Bea brushed past Shirley into the sitting room. No family photographs were on display, so that was a dead end. The furniture was comfortable without being fashionable. The Rycrofts didn't seem interested in fashion, did they? Drawers had been pulled out, the contents of a bookcase tumbled over. Yes, someone had been searching here, in the same way that Lucas's flat had been searched.

Shirley sniffed. 'I've tried ringing Kent, but he's not answering his phone.'

Bea explained, 'That's the problem. A man who might be Kent was attacked at my friend's house this morning and taken off to hospital.'

'Hospital?' Huge eyes, with tears in them. 'Kent has been mugged? Oh, that's terrible. Is he all right?'

Piers leafed through his notebook and held it out to her. 'Is this Kent?'

She looked, and recoiled. Colour flooded her face and left. 'That's not Kent. It's Owen! Where . . . why . . .?' She staggered. Sat down. Put a hand to her mouth. Was she going to vomit? She was pale enough. Shock.

'Are you all right? Do you want some water?'

Shirley shook her head, dumbly.

Piers said, 'Sorry to have given you such a fright. I'm an artist. Call me Piers.' He produced one of his slightly crooked, charming smiles. 'I paint portraits for a living. I was expecting Lucas Rycroft to call on me this morning but he didn't turn up.' He leafed through the book again and held up another drawing. 'Is this Lucas?'

Shirley frowned. 'No! No, that's Kent. Why have you drawn him?'

'It's not Lucas?'

Wide eyes. 'No, no! Uncle Lucas ties his hair back. And he's really old.'

'And these two?' Piers turned pages.

She peered at the drawings. 'That's the twins. They're cousins. I mean, we're all cousins. Why have you been drawing them?'

'Your twin cousins came to my studio demanding that I produce Lucas who had got delayed en route to meet me. They seemed to think I was hiding him, and were rather rough in searching the place.'

'Searched like this, you mean?' She gesticulated to the mess behind her.

Bea didn't think the twins had searched the studio in the same way. They'd overturned things, torn things off the wall. This was a comparatively genteel effort.

Piers produced his smile again. 'I have no idea of their real names, but I gather the twins are known in the family by the nicknames of Tweedledum and Tweedledee.'

'Yes, that's true.' Colour was coming back into her face. 'I think that sometimes they're a bit . . . naughty. What was that about Owen?' Her hands closed convulsively, and sweat stood out on her upper lip. Her eyes switched this way and that.

'He's dead.'

She jumped. Put her hands to her mouth, stared into the distance. And said . . . nothing.

Shock.

Bea tried for a gentle tone of voice. 'We're worried about Kent. You do know who we mean?'

She nodded, hands still over her mouth, eyes wide with fright.

Her reactions seem extreme. Or am I being unkind?

Piers said, 'After the twins left my place, I went looking for Lucas, who'd failed to turn up at my place. I didn't find him. On my return home, I found a man lying in the hallway. He'd been attacked and was unconscious. And you say this is Kent?' He held out his notebook to her.

She took one look, shrank back within herself and began to rock to and fro. 'Yes, that's Kent.' Her voice sounded rusty. She cleared her throat. 'Is he badly hurt?'

'He's in hospital. I gave the police the name of Lucas because that's who I was expecting to visit me, but I couldn't be sure of my identification. You've confirmed that it is Kent who was attacked. Have you any idea why?'

'I haven't the slightest.' Wide eyes, hands that trembled.

Uh-oh. I think you know all right. There was a flash of knowledge in your eyes just then. Piers may have missed it, but I didn't. Whatever it is she knows, she's decided not to say. What on earth is going on here?

Piers said, 'The police and the hospital need a member of his family to identify him.'

'Oh.' She looked around her, without focusing. 'I see what you mean. Someone ought to go, but . . . who would be best? When I arrived this morning and found the place empty, I did wonder where he was, but—'

'Yes,' said Bea. 'Why were you here?'

'What? Oh, I deal with the maintenance on the Rycroft houses in London. I don't do anything about the country house, of course, but—'

'You don't cover Lucas's place, do you?'

'No. He's so pernickety; if he even sees a maintenance man, he throws a strop. Mrs Tarring got his new housekeeper to look after all that for him. I haven't been there for ages.'

The way her eyelids skittered around when she said she hadn't been to his place for ages makes me think it was a lie. And, she hadn't needed to say that she hadn't been there. We hadn't asked her if she had. Why should she lie?

Piers said, 'Look, it's not up to us to decide, but you really ought to report the break-in here to the police.'

She made a despairing gesture with her hands. 'The door was open when I arrived.'

'Which means someone had a key?'

Shirley produced a hankie and wiped her eyes. 'If you tell the police, Uncle Rycroft will only say it was boys being boys.'

Her 'uncle' Rycroft would be Lord Rycroft, wouldn't it? She's referring to the twins?

Shirley blew her nose. 'Uncle Rycroft lets them get away with murder.'

Interesting choice of words.

Shirley tottered to her feet.

Piers put his arm around her, and she subsided gratefully into his care. 'Piers, isn't it? Tell me what to do.'

Bea wasn't having any of this missishness. 'You think the twins came here and searched this place? That they could get a key from the office, or borrow your key? Is it right that you have access to keys to all the Rycroft accommodation?'

'Well, yes. In a way. The keys are all kept in a cupboard at the office and the cupboard is kept locked, but I suppose anyone could borrow them, really.'

'You think the twins not only searched this place but also knocked Kent out?'

'Of course.' She shuddered. 'They give me the willies, those two. If you don't mind, I'd better lock up here and get round to the hospital to see Kent. Do you know which hospital?' She ushered them out of the house and locked the door behind her.

So Shirley had gone to the house armed with keys to get in? She said she'd found the front door open. Really? Do I believe her?

Piers said, 'You'll find him at Hammersmith Hospital.'

Shirley nodded, got into an unobtrusive car parked at the kerb and drove off.

'That's a nice girl,' said Piers. 'She has style.'

'You've told me often enough that when you draw someone, they reveal their true nature. Would you like to draw Shirley for me?'

Bea phoned for another taxi. Piers sat on the doorstep and sketched. When he started, he was humming to himself. By the time he finished, he was staring in disbelief at what he'd done. He handed his notebook to Bea.

First he'd drawn an accurate, even flattering portrait of Shirley. On the next page he'd drawn a caricature of a little monkey, with huge eyes. 'I really don't know where that came from.'

'A monkey. Mischievous, but out of her depth in a land where lions and tigers roam.'

Piers was annoyed. With himself for being taken in by Shirley, or with Bea for pointing out that Shirley was no sweet innocent? 'Why did you doubt her?'

'She had keys to the flat. She says she found the front door open. I don't know that I believe her. Why didn't she shut the door after herself when she got in?'

'She was in shock because she found the place had been ransacked.'

Bea reflected that men often give women the benefit of the doubt. Her expression must have told him to think again.

He rubbed his chin. 'You think she was expecting to meet someone there?'

'Why was she there in the first place? She said it was because she was responsible for the maintenance of the place, but I'm not sure I believe her.'

'You think she left the door ajar so that someone could get in after her? Someone who hadn't a key but was going to help her search the place. What for?'

'The jewels.'

'Nah. I expect the door sticks and she didn't close it firmly enough. Then it edged itself open again.' The taxi arrived. 'Where to now?'

'Your place. Give them the address.'

'Oh, good. I can grab a few essentials. And then what do you propose to do with me?'

She had been wondering whether or not she'd dump him in the mews cottage. That would be the appropriate thing to do. But, for some reason – perhaps because he'd championed Shirley, which wasn't a good reason, was it? – she'd decided against doing so. She said, 'I don't know. Have you a friend who'll give you a bed tonight?'

He gave her a Look. He turned his head away from her and said nothing. She smiled to herself. If he wanted to sulk, so be it.

NINE

There was no sign of the police outside Piers's house.

Piers's key let them into the hall. Doors had been left open on the ground floor. A suggestive bloodstain had spread itself across the floor of the hall but the cast-iron cockerel which had been used as a blunt instrument was nowhere to be seen.

What a pity. I liked that cockerel.

She said, 'Kent – or whoever it was – must still be alive, or the police would have taped this off as a crime scene and we wouldn't have been allowed in.'

Bea looked into the living room, which stretched from front to back of the house. As Piers had said, the place had been torn apart. Roughly. Not only had drawers been pulled out but the contents had been dumped and stirred around, possibly with a foot. The television had been levered off the wall and lay on its face on the carpet. An old-fashioned Bakelite telephone lay on the floor, its wiring torn from the socket on the skirting board.

The twins had been thorough, hadn't they!

Piers picked up the pieces of his laptop, which looked as if it had been stamped on. 'You carry on from day to day minding your own business and then this happens. I'm not staying here. I don't care where I go but I'm not staying here.' He hesitated. 'Bea, I hate to beg, but . . . look, can I leave my easel and canvases with you? I can go to a hotel or something, I'll only need a suitcase or two, but I'll need a Man with a Van for the big stuff, and I haven't got a working phone yet. Can you use your mobile to magic me up some transport? And as to where I should go . . .?'

She softened towards him. 'All right. You can have the mews cottage at the end of my road. I keep my car down below but there's a separate entrance to the flat above. Bedsitting room, k and b. The bedsitting room is not really big enough for you to use as a studio, but you can always rent somewhere else for work, can't you?' She got out her phone. 'Do you use any transport firm in particular?'

'Any one will do. Bless you. I'll stack everything that can be saved in the hall. No, perhaps not in the hall. In the living room. It shouldn't take me long to pack.'

She located a removal van company prepared to work at a weekend, and paid for it with her credit card. They were charging double time for a Saturday afternoon, needless to say. After that, she explored the rest of the house. In the kitchen everything had been swept off the surfaces and dumped on the floor. Cupboard doors had been wrenched open. One had even been torn off its hinges.

Piers didn't do much cooking, did he? There was a packet of cereal, a hand of bananas, some ready meals. There was some frozen food in the freezer and some milk and bread in the fridge. Bea found a cool bag, turned off the fridge and freezer and rescued their contents.

In the living room she picked up the broken laptop and all the paperwork that had been strewn around and dumped it beside the bag.

The garden? Bea didn't think he'd ever been out there. What had once been a lawn was now a sea, knee-high, of unkempt grass. A lounger at the far end was almost completely submerged.

Piers bumped and banged around on the top floor. His idea of packing was probably to swathe the tools of his trade in bubble wrap and thrust a few clothes into any old supermarket bag.

She took the stairs to the bedroom floor. More chaos here. She'd guessed correctly; he hadn't even started to pick up his clothes. Not that he had many. What he did possess had been torn out of the built-in wardrobe and left in a pile on the floor. The mattress had been stood on end beside the bed. The bedhead had been broken off from the base. The bed linen was strewn on the floor.

Piers hadn't used the back bedroom, but had dumped some empty boxes and an overnight bag or two there. Bea supposed

they were the ones he kept for his not infrequent flits from
one place to another. Good, the boxes and the bag would come
in useful.

The bathroom was spartan but adequate. The bathroom
cabinet had been opened and some over-the-counter remedies
had been tossed into the basin. Someone had used the toilet
and forgotten to get rid of the evidence. The bathroom stank.
Bea left it as it was. If Kent died, the bathroom might provide
evidence for the prosecution.

Piers came stumbling down the stairs with a portfolio under
one arm and some canvases under the other. As Bea had fore-
seen, his first concern had been for his paintings. He wasn't
bothered about his clothes or his shaving kit, was he? 'Did
you manage to get a removal van? When will they be here?'

'Give or take, an hour.'

He nodded and went past her down the stairs while she
went on up to the studio. To what had been his studio. He
didn't really care much where he lived, did he?

The mess in the studio was even worse than downstairs.
The destruction was thorough. Bea visualized the twins,
wreaking havoc. Stamp, stamp! Tear down! Frustration! Anger
out of control!

Searching the place was one thing, but pulling the blinds
down off the window, and overturning the table where Piers
kept his paints and brushes was mindless destruction. Did the
twins really think they were above the law? They had been
protected by their uncle Rycroft from the results of minor
transgressions for ages. Perhaps they felt that as their search
for the jewels was a family matter, they would still be
protected? Or perhaps they were notching up another gear
from bluster to bludgeoning?

Piers dragged a couple of empty boxes up the stairs and
proceeded to rescue what he could of his paints and brushes.

Bea went back down to the bedroom, took a travel bag from
the spare room and began to pack up his clothes. And then
his bed linen.

Piers paused in the doorway as he toted down an unruly
armful of canvases long enough to say, 'You shouldn't have
to pack for me.'

'The sooner we're out of here, the sooner I'll be pleased. I don't fancy coming up against the twins again and they haven't found what they've been searching for yet, have they?'

He shuddered. 'I've been wondering how many times I've hired a removal van to take me from one rented place to another. I usually dump anything which I can't get into the van. It's not much to show for a life, is it?'

'Except,' said Bea, 'your paintings hang in museums and galleries all round the world. You have painted a generation of worthwhile people.'

'And some thieves and scoundrels along the way as well. I'll paint those twins one day.'

One of the canvases under his arm slipped to the floor. He abandoned the rest to pick it up and show it to her. 'Look!' Someone had put a boot through this canvas. 'This is a portrait of a man who has done a lot of good in his life. Why would they want to destroy it?'

Bea shrugged. 'Evil can't stand the sight of excellence?'

He passed his hand over the ruined surface, mourning.

Bea's phone rang. She abandoned her packing to answer it as Piers went on down the stairs.

It was a man's voice on the phone. 'Mrs Abbot, that you there?' A deep man's voice. One she couldn't place at first. Then she could. 'This is Ellis's friend, from the flat. You rang me this morning, asking for details of his death. It was almost precisely three months ago. The sixth, to be exact. He was unconscious when they found him and he died on his way to hospital. He had a key with a tag on it, so the police knew where he lived. It fell to me to phone his father and break the news. One of the hardest things I've ever had to do. I liked Ellis. He was all right. You don't expect friends of your own age to die, do you?'

'No, you don't.'

'There was an autopsy, but it was clear he'd been run over by a car that hadn't stopped. They never found the car, unfortunately. The cremation was a fortnight later. We, his flatmates, were not invited. The family said they wanted to grieve in private. We sent a cheque to the Salvation Army. Ellis thought they were wonderful. We took his clothes there and a member of the family came and collected everything else. We'd have attended a memorial service but there wasn't one, so we had a bit of a wake here ourselves.'

Bea felt like sitting down. The mattress had gone, but she perched on the side of the bed frame. 'Do you know who came from the family to take his stuff?'

'No. I was out. Someone who had a key.'

'Did you ever meet his father?'

'No, everything was done through the Rycroft office.'

She tried to make sense of this development. 'Ellis's car? Did he have one?'

'Yes. He parked it in a dedicated space at the back here. It's gone. I suppose the man from the office took it when he collected Ellis's bits and pieces. If that's all . . .'

'Thank you. You've been most helpful.'

He switched off. And so did she.

She said, 'The heir and two spares.'

'What?' Piers was climbing the stairs again. She followed him up to the studio. He'd put a second ruined portrait back on his easel, and was teasing at the surface with a palette knife.

She said, 'Kent was the heir to Lord Rycroft. He's been attacked and left for dead. He may be dead by now, for all I know. Then the interloper who'd been brought up in Australia has been killed and left in Magda's bed. According to the law, he had to be treated as the old lord's heir, whether or not Lord Rycroft actually sired him. Now I hear that Ellis, who was Kent's son, died last year, too. It's an unlucky family.'

'How come?' He wasn't really paying attention.

Bea tried to make him understand. 'Look, the heir and two spares to the throne have all three been attacked and two of them are dead. Don't tell me that's a coincidence.'

'Mm? I wonder if I . . . no, mending the canvas won't work. It would always show.'

Bea persevered. 'So who gains from killing off the heir and the two spares?'

He woke up to that. 'You think the twins did this so that they can inherit when the old man dies?'

Bea rubbed her forehead. 'I'm not sure. I don't think that's right. All I know is that I'm way out of my depth and I need to get back to the safety of my own home as soon as possible, but I don't want to leave you here by yourself with the twins still hanging around, looking for the family jewels. You have ten minutes before the removal men arrive. How quickly can you dismantle that monster of an easel and get it down the stairs?'

Her phone rang again. 'Yes?' Through her teeth.

'Oh, Bea, I'm so worried!' It was Bernice's mother, in hysterical mood. 'My darling daughter hasn't rung us! We've kept off the phone so that she could get through, but she hasn't rung, and then I thought I could ring her mobile and I rang her number and it's switched off! How could she switch it off when she knows how anxious I must be to—'

'She's off sailing,' said Bea. 'Of course she's got her mobile switched off.'

'Yes, but you said she was going to ring us and—'

'I'll wring her neck when she gets back!' said Bea. 'She has no right to upset you like this.'

'Oh, I don't think . . . I wouldn't want you to punish her for—'

'She has to understand that promises are of importance.'

'Oh yes. I know that. And she is, I know, she can be very wayward, but we do understand, obviously, that it's not very interesting for her to have to spend time with us at home, as compared to going sailing.'

Bea almost snarled. 'It's called "SBO", which means, "Subject to a better offer". Which is totally antisocial and self-centred and won't win her any prizes in the popularity stakes. So yes, somehow or other, this is a lesson she has to learn.'

Silence. Piers was grinning. But at least he had started to dismantle his easel.

Bea stalked off down the stairs, trying to reassure Bernice's mother, who turned into a fluttery butterfly when under pressure. 'Look,' Bea said, 'I'm out of the house at the moment but going back in a few minutes. I'll try ringing Bernice's hostess. I'll leave a message for her to remind young Bernice of her manners, and I'll ring you back as soon as I hear from her. All right?'

'Oh, I wouldn't want to put you to any trouble. It's just that . . . are you still coming over for tea yourself? Only we usually eat a little early and—'

'No, that's very kind of you,' said Bea, hearing the front doorbell ring, and continuing down to the ground floor. Was it the twins? If it was, she was not opening the front door. 'I'm running late, I'm afraid. Speak to you later.'

There were two men silhouetted against the light in the window at the top of the door. Two thin men. Tall. Not the twins. Phew!

Bea opened the door to the removal men, and talked them through what needed to be done. Piers appeared with sections of the easel over his shoulder, and he took over the loading of his stuff.

Bea got out her phone again while calling instructions up to Piers. 'I'm off in a minute. Needed back home. Drop in at my place to collect the key to the mews cottage on your way, right, and don't forget to pick up your mobile? I'll take a taxi . . .'

Before she could key in the number, her phone rang again.

A woman this time. 'Is that Mrs Abbot? It's Magda here.' Her voice was high with tension.

Magda. Lucas's housekeeper, who'd got Bea involved with the twins and the vanishing jewellery and corpses galore. Had Lucas been found?

'Yes, Magda? How are things?'

'Oh, all right, really. Well, except . . . we've been with the police, and they've taken the body away, but they said I can't stay here, especially since it's my bedroom, if you see what I mean. You did say, didn't you, that I might be able to stay with you for a couple of days until I can find another position . . .?'

'Yes, of course,' said Bea, mentally giving herself a slap. What on earth had possessed her to offer this lightweight woman some hospitality? Magda reacted to difficult situations like cardboard in a downpour. Bea said, 'I'm not at home at the moment, but am taking a cab to get back there as quickly as possible. It will probably take me about half an hour. You remember where I live?'

'Oh yes, of course. The police were ever so kind but they

wouldn't let me take anything from my room.' She tried on a laugh for size. Not a success. 'I'll need to drop in to a supermarket some time. I haven't as much as a toothbrush to my name.'

'Well, I might be able to—'

'No, no. I couldn't think of it. I'll manage. You've been so kind. I couldn't put you to any more trouble.'

No, of course you couldn't think of it. Only, someone is going to have to make up the spare-room bed and supply towels and find some food, and prepare a meal for you. It will be no trouble at all!

Bea told herself not to grind her teeth. Her dentist had warned her it destroyed the enamel. 'Before you go, Magda – is Mrs Tarring with you?'

'Yes. She's ever so upset. She's going straight home to have a nice hot bath and watch the telly in her dressing gown.'

Which is just what I'd like to do. Unfortunately I can't duck responsibility for other people. Not like some!

Bea said, curbing impatience, 'That sounds sensible. Would you like to put her on the line for a moment?'

'Well, I would, but she's just on her own phone at the moment. Shall I get her to ring you when she finishes?'

Bea lost it. 'Just tell her that it's definitely Kent Rycroft who's in hospital. Not Lucas.'

'Ow!'

A clatter. Magda had dropped the phone? Muttered imprecations. A sharp voice telling someone to pull themselves together. Then Mrs Tarring picked up Magda's phone. 'Yes, Mrs Abbot? You have some news?'

'We've checked around. We spoke to Shirley Rycroft, whom we found at Kent's place – which has also been turned over by someone. Shirley says she found the front door open and the place ransacked, but she had keys to the place in her hand. She didn't want to inform the police, though I do think someone ought to do so. Shirley's manner was . . . evasive. I'm not sure what she was doing there. Anyway, when we told her that Kent had been attacked and taken off to hospital, she said she'd go there to see him. She said she thought it must be the twins who'd attacked Kent.'

Long, slow breathing. 'The twins? She really thinks . . .?'
A crack in the voice.

'Yes. Are you thinking what I'm thinking?'

'Why would the twins attack him?'

'How many billions do the Rycrofts have?'

'Yes, I suppose money might be a motive, but Kent does
what Lord Rycroft decides . . . who gets what, and so on.
The twins wouldn't automatically benefit if Kent were out of
the way. You say his house has been burgled? Oh, my God!
Who knows how . . . I mean, why would anyone want . . .
the insurance people must be informed, but how would I know
if anything has been stolen? This is . . . it's all too much!'
Her voice rose in panic.

'Surely the police ought to be informed about the break-in,
or whatever it was?'

'It's not my job . . . if only Kent were here. I don't know
what to do.' In a sober tone, 'I can't deal with this.'

'I don't know who can,' said Bea, 'but I do know that Lord
Rycroft needs to be informed of what's happening. Has he
arrived at his town house yet?'

'I've left messages. He hasn't responded. I even gave the
police his phone numbers. I had to. I know I may lose my job
but . . .'

'You did the right thing. Have you any idea where he
might be?'

'None. I wish I had. This is just too much.' The phone
clicked off.

Bea agreed. It was all too much.

She dialled for a cab, helped carry some of Piers's belongings
out to the van, reminded him to call in for the key before he
went to the mews and departed the scene with a sigh of relief.

Oh, for a nice, quiet cup of tea and a biscuit.

The taxi was able to park almost directly outside her house.
The relief, to be back on home ground! She paid the taxi off,
and he drove away.

Something was wrong, but she couldn't work out what it
was. And then she did.

The alarm on the wall above her bedroom window was
yammering fit to deafen everyone in earshot. One of her

neighbours had a key to her house for use in emergencies, but he must be away for the weekend. The others would be furious at the noise.

She let herself into the house. She'd thought a couple of times about having a new alarm which connected to the police station, but had done nothing about it because the house was rarely empty . . . which wasn't really a good reason.

That omission might have been a mistake.

She turned the alarm off in the hall, and stood there, listening. And looking.

Nothing seemed amiss in the hall. She could see through to the kitchen from where she stood by the front door. The kitchen looked undisturbed. She took a couple of steps along the hall until she could see into the big living room, which ran from front to back of the house. All seemed well, there.

Something . . . someone . . . shuffled.

A rat? Bea started, and put her hand to her heart.

A weak cry. 'Anyone there?'

A man? Who . . .?

Downstairs in the agency rooms?

How could that be? When she left, hadn't she locked the door to the stairs that led down to the agency rooms? She couldn't remember. Perhaps she hadn't.

She ditched her handbag but took out her mobile phone. Her finger hovered over the speed-dial to the police station. The door to the stairs hung open.

'Who is it?' she said, keeping her voice level.

'Help!' A man's voice? One she didn't recognize.

Someone who'd broken in from the street? Who'd come down the outside stairs to the agency rooms?

She mustn't let her voice tremble. 'Show yourself!'

A groan. 'I can't. Help . . .!'

A burglar? Who'd hurt himself, breaking in?

She took the inside stairs, keeping to the wall. Slowly.

There was no one on the stairs.

There was no light on in the agency rooms. It might be a nice sunny spring day outside, but the rooms in the basement were not over-supplied with windows and they kept the lights on in the agency rooms during the day.

'Help!' the voice repeated. 'Help us!'

Us!

Bea nearly screamed. 'Us' meant . . . the twins?

No, surely not!

Down in the jungle, something stirred . . .

There was a huddle of men crouched down by the door which led to the area steps. The door hung open, partially off its hinges. Two men had come down the area steps, bashed in the door to the agency rooms, and got no further.

The twins were locked together.

One was supporting the other, holding his brother closely, arms tight around him. His eyes were wide, scared . . . of what?

The other had his eyes closed. His mouth hung open.

His tie was off, his shirt open.

His legs sprawled, loosely.

At least they didn't seem to be in danger of attacking her.

Neither of them shifted position when she appeared.

'Help?'

She peered more closely.

One of them seemed to be alive, all right. The other wasn't moving.

Bea hung back, well beyond the reach of the twins' powerful arms. 'What's the matter? Why are you here?'

'Get an ambulance, bitch! Don't argue! Do it!'

Cautiously, 'Is this a trick?'

'No trick. Get moving!'

The second twin appeared to be unconscious. Bea rang for an ambulance. That done, she asked, 'What happened?'

'Dunno.' The twin who was conscious drooped, then pulled himself upright. 'Something in the bottle of drink we found in the car. We were on our way . . . can't remember where now.' His brow corrugated. 'Where was it? To see Lucas and that bitch of his? She'd lied to us, hadn't she? But we couldn't remember which number it was, so we went back to the office to check. Only there was no one there, was there? Saturday and all. Bro said you'd know which number it was, so we came round here, only you weren't in, and we tooled around a bit, thinking, like . . . and I was driving, it was my turn. We shared the drink. It was a warm day . . .'

He slumped over his twin, his eyes closing.

Had they been drugged? One of them seemed comatose – if not dead – while the other seemed to be on the verge of falling asleep. She'd heard that it was best to keep people talking who'd taken drugs, so she said, 'I don't understand why you broke in here.'

He jerked awake. 'What?' He looked around him. Was he not sure where he was?

'We were waiting for you, weren't we? In the car. Where were you? Bro dropped off and I couldn't wake him. I got him out of the car and up the steps to your front door, and I rang and rang on my mobile till the battery ran down. Bro's phone fell out of his pocket when I was getting him out of the car and smashed . . . You should have been at home, bitch! Where were you?'

'I had to go out,' said Bea, deciding not to explain where she'd been. She glanced at her watch again. How long would the ambulance be?

'When you didn't come, I got Bro down the steps and bashed open the door here . . . what do you want with such a big door, eh? And the alarm went off, fit to kill, and I thought that was good, that'd fetch you, or a neighbour . . . but nobody came.'

Tears stood out on his cheeks. He snuffled. 'Why didn't anybody come? You should have come!'

'The neighbours who have a key must have gone away for the weekend. I was supposed to be in. Only, you set us looking for Lucas . . .'

'I'll kill him when I see him!'

Someone rang the front doorbell, hard. Bea fled back up the inner stairs, afraid that at any moment now the twins would rise up and attack her from behind, drag her back down to the agency rooms and . . .

But no, she made it, panting, to the hallway, without having been tackled.

'You took your time!' complained Piers, looking tired, leaning against the wall. She remembered that he'd been knocked out that morning. She thought he probably ought to be in bed, being nursed by soft-footed, soft-voiced, attentive nurses, preferably size eight with big boobs.

Which she'd rather fancy herself. Well, not the boobs
and . . .

I'm rambling. Do I tell him about the twins? No. The ambu-
lance will be here in a minute and will take them off my hands.

She tried to pop her senses back into their right boxes. What
did he need to know about the cottage? She said, 'I'll fetch
the key. I've been renting it out for holiday lets so the elec-
tricity and gas are on and there's a landline phone which I
don't suppose anyone will use, but it got left there and I'm
still paying the bill.'

She kept spare keys in a special box fixed to the back of
one of the kitchen cupboard doors. The keys for the cottage
were on a key ring with a list of instructions about this and
that. She snatched it up and ran back to the hall, only to realize
that a spare key to the front door had got tangled with it.

She dithered, wondering whether to remove that key or not.
Giving it to Piers would be tantamount to inviting him back
into her home, and that she didn't want to do.

Or did she?

She hesitated and was lost.

He grabbed the keys, said, 'Thanks!' and disappeared.

She watched him climb into the front of the removal van
and saw it pull away. She wondered what he'd done with his
car. He hadn't used it that day and hadn't suggested they use
it, either. Had he said something about selling his old car and
getting a new one? She couldn't remember. Lots of people
didn't keep a car in London nowadays, because of the problems
of parking and/or garaging it.

An ambulance drew up.

Thank God for that.

She waved the paramedics in.

TEN

Bea showed the paramedics the way through the hall and down the stairs. 'I've been out for some time. When I got back I found the alarm ringing and that two men had broken in to the agency rooms down below. Both are very poorly. I'm not sure, but one might be dead.'

The twins hadn't moved. They were clasped together in life as in death. One was still breathing, though his eyes were at half-mast. The other seemed to be out of it.

The paramedics were efficient. One took a sniff and looked resigned. 'Drunk, both of them.'

'I don't think so,' said Bea. 'I think they've been drugged.'

'Intoxicated. Believe me, missus. Can't you smell it?'

Now they mentioned it, yes, perhaps she could smell something. Oranges? She'd hesitated to get close to them in case they'd grabbed her.

The paramedics looked at the broken door and put their heads outside into the area to assess how to get the bodies out. 'Did they get drunk, fall down the steps and couldn't get up again?'

Bea shrugged. 'I got back to find them like this.'

One of the paramedics said, 'I'll get the chair.' He departed up the outside steps.

The other produced a clipboard. 'Names?'

Bea said, 'Rycroft. First names unknown. I'd never met them till today. They forced their way into my house earlier this morning looking for a relative of theirs, and were most unpleasant when they didn't find him. Eventually they left. I'd hoped never to see them again, but when I returned to the house this afternoon, there they were.'

The paramedic was checking vital signs. 'Binge drinking can do this to you. They're both still alive, but . . . well, we'll do what we can. Do you know what they've taken?'

Bea said, 'One of them was still conscious when I arrived. He talked about sharing a bottle of something they'd found in their car. A sports car, I think. It must still be outside. The bottle may be in it.'

'Vodka, probably.' He stood up. 'Flavoured with orange juice. They'll find out at the hospital.' He looked at the broken door. 'You'll need to get that fixed.'

'I'm fully aware of that,' said Bea. 'It's a Saturday afternoon and it's not going to be easy to find someone to sort it today. Any ideas?'

They hadn't. She thought of asking Piers to help. He did know one end of a tool from the other but had only a basic knowledge of electrics. He'd probably fuse everything in the house while trying to restore the broken connection. Besides which, she didn't really want to ask him for a favour.

While the paramedics went about their business, she retreated to her office at the back of the house and tried to raise someone, anyone, who might be able to put the door back into position and reconnect the alarm.

She failed. No one was free. They could come on Monday. They would charge a fortune. She worked her way down the list in the Yellow Pages. Without success. She tried the alarm company; ditto. She got some good advice, which boiled down to nailing up the door to repel boarders, and making sure the alarm was reconnected.

Which did bother her. If she couldn't restore the alarm, wouldn't the baddies all be beating a path to her door?

There were noises off as the paramedics strove mightily to remove her unwelcome guests. She tried to ignore them.

She remembered that the police must be told of the break-in because she'd need a report in order to make her case to the insurance people and the alarm company.

She could scream! She gritted her teeth and applied herself to the phone again.

More noises off. Bea was pretty sure one of the twins was past help, but the other might survive, if he were lucky. She did not watch their removal.

She got through to the police eventually. They took details of the break-in but said that as the miscreants were being removed, the case was not urgent and she should make a formal report on Monday.

'We're off, then.' The larger of the two paramedics poked his head round the door of her office. 'You might want to clean the floor where they've been lying.'

Ugh! She'd been afraid of that.

Finally she had explored all her options bar one. So she rang Piers on the landline at the mews cottage. Fortunately he was there and picked up. She explained the situation, and he said he'd be there in ten.

By the time Bea had cleaned the floor where the twins had been lying – about which the least said the better – Piers arrived, carrying a toolbox. Bea filled him in on what had been happening.

'Drugged, you think?' He sniffed the air. 'Oranges?' He heaved the door back into place. It teetered, threatening to fall back on him. She added her weight to his, till it was roughly back in its frame once more.

He said, 'They used some force, didn't they? The hinges have been partially wrenched off the door jamb, and the lock's been torn out of the woodwork. I doubt if I can mend that. How do you fancy getting a new door, steel-lined?'

'Heavens! Do I need to live in a fortress?'

He grinned. 'Well, you do get involved in some dramatic events. What about Tweedledum and Tweedledee?'

'They won't be back in a hurry.'

'Don't you still have something they want?'

'I think that if they survive, they're not going to be on form for quite a while, which gives us a breathing space. They may suspect that the jewels arc here, but they can't be sure.'

'You don't fancy them for putting Owen in Magda's bed?'

'I agree that they are a couple of thugs, but I don't think they're terribly bright. Much as I think they need their bottoms smacked – hypothetically, I mean – I can't see them putting a headless man in Magda's bed.'

Piers dropped his screwdriver. 'He wasn't really headless, was he?'

'No, of course not. When we went into the bedroom first, it looked as if the bed had been properly made up. It was only when we pulled the duvet off that it looked as if the body had been decapitated because the head had been hidden under the pillows. The twins wouldn't think of doing that.'

'Agreed. They'd have left the body wherever they'd killed it. The paramedics thought the twins had been binge drinking. Isn't that more likely than their being drugged?'

'Y-yes. But surely, in the middle of the day . . .? Why would they binge drink if they were on the trail of the jewellery? One of them told me they'd found a bottle of something in their car. What more natural than they should neck it down? And yes, I do think they were drugged. But why? I agree, they deserve something bad happening to them. They crash and bash around and hurt people and think they can get away with it, but I can't think they've caused all the confusion surrounding the affairs of the Rycroft family. And, why now? It doesn't make sense.'

With a mallet Piers tried tapping the door further back into place. 'How on earth can I get this to stay put? I'd be happier if you had a steel-backed door. You need a builder on the job.'

'I couldn't get one to come out on a Saturday afternoon. Can't you bodge it for me, somehow? We'll have to do without the alarm. I'll organize something on Monday.'

Piers stroked his cheek with his mallet. 'You can't be left over the weekend without a working alarm system. I wonder, maybe I could patch it up for now by taking off the damaged hinges and refitting them lower down. The lock's shot, but I could fit bolts top and bottom. I'm not hot on electrics, but with a spot of luck I might be able to reconnect the alarm system. Only, you wouldn't be able to open and close this door in the usual way for a while.'

'Where will you get the bolts from at this time of day?'

'I'll bet you've got a couple on your garden shed door. I'll use those for now, and you can get better ones on Monday.'

'Understood. I'll tell the agency girls to use the front door upstairs for the time being.'

'And I suggest you get the alarm system tied in to the police station.'

Would her insurance cover a steel-lined door? No. They'd only cover replacing what had been there, plus it was going to cost more to tie the alarm system into the police station. Another job to do. Bother!

Piers managed to lever off the damaged hinges. They came away with a screech of tortured wood. It was a big, heavy door. The early Victorians had built to last.

She wasn't so sure that she would. As she went back up the stairs, she tried ringing Bernice's phone. Again it went to voicemail. She tried the number of Bernice's hostess for the weekend. Again, it went to voicemail. She was about to try William's number when the front doorbell rang and she answered the summons.

There on the doorstep was not only Magda Summerleys but also Mrs Tarring, the Rycroft administrator, and a third woman whom Bea failed to recognize.

'I hope you don't mind,' chirruped little Miss Summerleys, who looked as if she'd been dragged through a hedge backwards and not enjoyed the experience. 'Such a terrible day. And here's me with just the clothes I stand up in. Mrs Tarring was so good, going with me to the hospital, and we found poor Kent . . . oh, poor, poor man . . . he's always so capable and well, in charge, if you know what I mean.'

Mrs Tarring fidgeted on the doorstep. 'Magda was so upset. Well, I was, too. I said I'd see her safely into your hands, and then . . .'

'I turned up at Kent's bedside and found them there,' said the third woman. And now Bea knew her. She was the droopy blonde whom they'd seen in Kent's flat that morning. Shirley Rycroft.

'We met this morning, didn't we, Mrs Abbot? At poor Kent's flat.' Shirley clutched her arms. The early evening had turned chilly as the sun waned in the sky, and Shirley was still clad in the sleeveless summer dress she'd worn earlier, without a sweater or jacket to keep her warm. 'Mrs Tarring and Miss Summerleys were singing your praises and we wondered, we realize it's an imposition, but if we could all get together and talk through things, we might be able to work out what's going on, and what to do about it?'

Mrs Tarring was not so keen. 'Yes, Shirley, I know you said that, but it *is* an imposition, and Mrs Abbot has other things

to do today. Now that Magda is in safe hands, I do think
that—'

Magda broke in, 'If anyone can sort this, I'm sure Mrs
Abbot can. I mean, the police are . . .' She gestured helplessly.
'There's one lot for this and another lot for that, and the ones
who came to Lucas's place didn't want to know about Kent's
being struck down, which is terrible, and I really don't know
what I'm to do. I mean, I had to tell the police that I'm going
to be staying here tonight, but what happens tomorrow? Do I
have a job or don't I? When can I get my things from my
room, and what will happen if Lucas comes back and finds
the place locked up? And if he doesn't come back, who is
going to pay my wages at the end of the month? And what
is to happen to the jewellery which I hid, and I'm not at all
sure who it belongs to but I suppose it is safer in the garden
shed here than anywhere else.'

She produced a pack of tissues and blew her nose. If ever
there was a woman ground down by circumstances, she was it.

'There, there. It'll all come out in the wash,' said Shirley,
putting her arm around Magda and urging her inside. 'I'm
sure you've behaved beautifully and so has Mrs Abbot. You've
got a place to stay tonight and everything's going to be just
fine.'

Mrs Abbot did not think everything was going to be just
fine. Mrs Abbot had more than enough on her plate without
taking in waifs and strays.

'Oh yes,' said Magda, dabbing her eyes. 'Mrs Abbot was
absolutely wonderful this morning when the twins came. They
tortured her but she didn't say anything!'

'How very courageous of her,' said Mrs Tarring. And perhaps
she meant it.

'Indeed,' said Shirley. 'We all know Mrs Abbot is quite
something.'

Bea thought that Shirley's tone of voice verged on the border
of sarcastic. Bea wondered why Shirley had really come. The
woman had managed to get all three of them into the house
and was now closing the door on the outside world.

Bea surrendered to the inevitable. She gestured up the stairs.
'Magda, the spare bedroom is at the top of the stairs on the

first floor, to the right. It's en suite. Would you like to go upstairs and freshen up? I think I can find you a toothbrush and a fresh pair of pants . . . or there's a big Marks & Spencer's on the High Street which is open till late and could probably supply all you want. I'll find some sheets and towels for you in a minute. Mrs Tarring and Shirley, would you like to go into the sitting room, first door on your left? Take a seat. I'll be with you in a minute. I've had a second visit from the twins, who busted the door downstairs in order to get in, and I have someone down there doing some first aid on it at the moment. I'll have to see to him before I do anything else. Builders, you know. They need constant refreshment.'

Shirley's eyes narrowed. 'The twins have been here twice? And busted in which door?' She glanced at the front door, which didn't show any signs of abuse. 'Don't you have an alarm?'

'We're hoping to get it fixed. The twins seem to have imbibed something that disagreed with them, and they left in an ambulance.' With a bright smile Bea hurried down the stairs. Piers had suspended operations on the door and had come to the foot of the stairs, listening to what was happening above.

Bea closed the door behind her so that their conversation couldn't be overheard.

'Piers, I'm not sure what to think. I did invite Magda, yes. But the other two?'

He grunted. 'They're after the jewellery. Magda came right out and said she'd hidden it in your garden shed. Is she mad?'

'She's on the verge of collapse. I don't think Mrs Tarring is after the jewellery, but Shirley? I don't know. Perhaps. It would be a good idea to shift it somewhere else, anyway.'

'Any ideas?'

'Maybe.' Bea led the way through the main room and into her office. She'd closed but not locked the French doors that morning when she'd finished interviewing people. Now she threw them open. Birds twittered softly in the trees, a breeze persuaded petals to drop from the cherry tree near the pool, but the solar-operated fountain had ceased to burble now that the sun had passed behind the steeple of the church nearby. She pointed to the shed in the far corner.

'The jewels are in there under a pile of pots. You said you needed to use the bolts from the shed. It might well be a good idea to find another hiding place for the loot at the same time. Not that I think the twins will be coming back for it, but I don't think they're the only baddies on the block. Where would you put the stuff?'

He gave the garden the once-over, and made a suggestion that caused her to smile.

She said, 'That would do nicely. Only an artist would think of that. Talk about camouflage.'

He nodded. 'Leave it to me. You want me to stay on, after I've fixed the door? My weekend's ruined, anyway.'

'Surely there can't be any danger from those three women?'

He shot her a keen look. 'If you say so. I'd better get on with it, then. You said something about a cuppa. That would be good. Herbal tea, if you've got it. No sugar or milk. Now, as I'm going to be in and out of the garden for a while, can you draw your guests away from the windows?'

'Tea and chat is what they came for, and tea and chat they shall have.' She looked at her watch. 'Or rather, we need proper food. I'll organize a take-away for supper.'

As she want back up the stairs her mobile rang, and she answered it. This time it was from Bernice's mother, who still hadn't been contacted by her errant daughter. Bea soothed and promised retribution. She tried to remember the name of the woman who had invited William and the girls sailing that weekend. And failed. In a moment she would recall her name, or ring William again. Or perhaps Bernice might have come to her senses and turned her mobile back on. 'Sorry, sorry. Yes, I'm on to it. I'll ring you as soon as I hear anything definite.'

Back upstairs she made a mug of herbal tea for Piers, and popped her head through into the sitting room to ask if anyone else would like a cuppa. Her visitors were not talking to one another. Mrs Tarring was sitting at one end of the settee, and Shirley was standing by the back window, looking out onto the garden below. She was watching Piers, who was working on the door of the garden shed . . . which was where Magda had stashed the loot.

Shirley was enthusiastic. 'What a pretty garden. Sheltered by all those high walls. Is there no way out except through the house?'

'Correct.' Bea switched on the side lamps, and both women started.

'Tea? Oh yes, please,' said Shirley, walking away from the window. 'I assume that shed is where poor Magda hid the jewellery?'

'I believe so,' said Bea, drawing the curtain to shut out the view.

'I really ought to be on my way,' said Mrs Tarring. But made no move to go. She leaned back and closed her eyes. She looked exhausted, too. If Magda were worried about her job, so was Mrs Tarring. She was a widow, wasn't she? If she didn't earn, she had no one to support her. 'If only Lord Rycroft would answer his phone! I've rung and rung.'

Bea also drew the curtains at the front of the house, treated her uninvited guests to a social smile and took the mug of tea downstairs to Piers . . . who was not there. He must still be in the garden. So Bea trod the stairs up and up to find bed linen and towels for Magda, who was sitting on her bed in the dusk, having a little weep.

'You've had a tiring day,' said Bea, drawing the curtains and switching the light on there as well. 'Come on down and join us for a cuppa and something to eat. I'll help you make the bed up later.'

Magda muttered, 'You'll think me awful when you've been so very kind, but I can't help worrying about Lucas. This is not like him, not at all. I'm so afraid . . .'

'I know,' said Bea. 'Have you made a list of things you need to get at the shops before they close tonight? Toiletries, underwear?'

'I can't think constructively, which is ridiculous and most unlike me. I really must stop being such a Silly Billy,' said Magda. She dried her eyes and followed Bea downstairs to join the others.

Bea found some take-away menus and took them into the sitting room. 'Mrs Tarring, I assume you would like to stay for a bit to eat, and then perhaps help Magda do some essential shopping? Shirley, I can see you are feeling the cold. No doubt you want to get back to your own place and warm yourself up.'

'I'd love a bite to eat, too,' said Shirley, plonking herself down on the nearest chair. 'I really do think it would be helpful for us to exchange information, Mrs Abbot. I understand you are a widow and live alone?'

'For the moment, yes. My ward is due back from school tomorrow.'

'No man about the house?' A teasing look. 'Such a big house for just one person.'

That's an inappropriate comment from a stranger. Is she trying to put me down because I've no man about the house, or was that a veiled threat? She's not wearing an engagement or wedding ring herself, so sucks to her!

Bea bared her teeth in a social smile. 'Do you fancy a pizza, or some Indian food, or what?'

The consensus was for Italian. Bea ordered straightaway, while wondering whether Piers would want to return to the mews cottage to eat or not. Had he found the cool box full of food, and worked out how to use the microwave? Probably not.

Mrs Tarring stirred herself. 'We're giving you a lot of trouble. Shirley, why don't you make yourself useful by taking Magda shopping for essentials while I help Mrs Abbot put clean sheets on the bed?'

Shirley didn't look pleased with the idea, but Magda smiled and said she really did need to get one or two things. Fortunately she had her cards with her. Should she go now?

'Splendid,' said Bea. 'Remind me to let you have a spare key to the front door from the kitchen before you go, and the code for the alarm . . . that is, if we can get it to work, which is arguable. Take your time. I'll keep your food hot for you.'

Shirley said, 'Couldn't Mrs Abbot go shopping with Magda?'

'No,' said Bea. 'Not with workmen in the house. Which reminds me, I must see how this particular workman is getting on.' She shot down the stairs, to find Piers screwing the second bolt into place on the broken door.

'It's not brilliant,' he said. 'You really do need to get it replaced, but it'll withstand anything short of a battering ram for now. I'll test the electrics in a minute.'

'Oh, my goodness!' A bright, cheery voice. Shirley had followed Bea down the stairs and spotted Piers. 'Ah-ha, we meet again, Mr Whatever-your-name is. You're the artist boyfriend, aren't you? And handy with a toolbox? That's nice. Is this where you have your agency, Mrs Abbot? What lovely big rooms. And access to the garden at one side and to the street at the other? Is this where the twins broke in?'

'It is,' said Bea, 'and set the alarm off to the disgust of the whole neighbourhood. I'll be getting complaints about that.'

'I'll try the alarm now, shall I?' said Piers, and took the stairs to the hall.

Shirley drifted to the back of the building. The door to Bea's office was open and she noted that Piers had closed the French windows, and pulled the grille across. Bea said, 'We're very safety conscious, as you can see.'

Shirley said, 'So you are. Yet the twins managed to get in.'

Bea didn't reply to that. So what if Shirley was checking to see if she could break in to retrieve the jewels? Shirley wouldn't have the strength to get through the door, even in its present condition. Various noises off indicated that Piers was trying the alarm system out.

'Shall we join the others?' said Bea, smiling as she swept Shirley up the stairs again.

In the hall, Piers was shaking his head. 'Sorry. No can do. I can't make the alarm work. You'll have to get someone to look at it soonest.'

Did Shirley smile? Perhaps. Suddenly she was anxious to leave. 'Well, I'll be on my way, shall I? So good of you to take Magda in, Mrs Abbot.' Without waiting to say goodbye to the others she almost ran out of the house, pulling out her mobile phone as she did so. Was she going to let someone know that the house's alarm was out of order?

ELEVEN

Saturday, early supper

As soon as the door had closed behind Shirley, Piers grinned. 'I wasn't saying so in front of that little madam, but I've managed to reconnect the alarm, although it's a rough and ready job and may not last. You'll need to get it looked at properly on Monday. But there's no need to broadcast the fact, eh?'

Meaning that he'd more or less invited Shirley to break in tonight?

'Why, thank you, Piers. I'll know who to blame if we're burgled tonight.' Bea heard the sarcasm in her voice and was sorry for it.

He said, 'The thing is, better to have her attempt it tonight when we're on our guard, than to leave it till there's no one at home.'

He was right. In a way. And, he'd given up his time to help her. So she said, 'I'm sorry. Yes. You're right. And I am truly grateful.'

'How grateful?' He looked at her from under his eyebrows. She wondered why, and then got it. He was waiting for an invitation to stay on for supper. Should she invite him? Perhaps.

No, she wouldn't. Not this time. She was tired and he was pushing her too fast. She said, 'I hope you have a quiet evening. If you want to use the microwave, I've put all your ready meals in the cool bag. Now, if you'll excuse me, I've got guests to look after.'

He accepted that. 'I'll get my tools and go. But I'll be on call if you need me. Switch that alarm on when I leave and don't turn it off for any reason, right?'

She saw him off as the delivery boy arrived with their take-away food. Bea paid and Mrs Tarring came out of the sitting room to help her carry the food into the kitchen. Then Bea went back to the hall to switch on the alarm. It seemed to be working all right. Perhaps Piers was a better electrician than she'd thought.

Mrs Tarring was hovering, unwilling to settle. 'I must explain, we didn't want to bother you when you were so busy, but we remembered you said there was a spare key in the kitchen, and we found one so that Magda could go off shopping straight away. She said she'd be better off doing it alone. I didn't argue. I'm bushed. But perhaps I can help you with making up the bed for her?'

'And you thought it might be a good idea for us to pool our ideas? Shall we make up the bed now?' Bea led the way up the stairs. 'So, where do you think Lord Rycroft and Lucas have gone?'

Mrs Tarring said, 'I don't know where they are. It's been driving me crazy. I've even been wondering if Lord Rycroft has refused to respond to my calls because I'm not supposed to contact him at weekends. Perhaps he's so angry with me that he . . . I've been trying to work out where my loyalties lie. It's difficult. My predecessor in my job was sacked because he tattled to some tabloid journalist. His own fault entirely. He admitted it. He'd got drunk and talked about . . . well, you don't need to know about what.'

Bea extracted clean linen from the cupboard and took it into the spare room. 'I've heard one or two bits of gossip. Would that have been about Mrs Nicholas or the twins?'

Mrs Tarring grimaced. 'Neither. Lord Rycroft was married twice, and the least said about that second wife, the better.' She shook out a sheet and, with Bea anchoring the other side, tucked it over the mattress. 'What I have to decide is whether the situation is serious enough for me to talk about the family or not.'

'I don't have a loose tongue.'

'That's what I keep telling myself. But I also keep telling myself that as the police have taken over the killing of Owen and the attack on Kent, there is nothing that I can usefully say that would help.'

'Except find Lord Rycroft and Lucas? Did you tell the police about Lucas removing the jewellery from the bank and then disappearing?'

'No. It didn't seem relevant.'

'Come on, now, Mrs Tarring. You know it's all tied up in one untidy bundle; the twins need of money, Owen's bad behaviour, and his body being placed in Magda's bed. You know or suspect much more than you've told the police. Right?'

'They didn't want the background.'

'You mean that you didn't tell them how Owen's arrival started all this off?'

'I don't know that that is so, but I agree that . . . Mrs Abbot, I may be completely wrong. If I tell you the strange thoughts that have been passing through my head, it must be in confidence. One moment I think that if I don't tell the police what I suspect, Kent's assailant may never be brought to justice. And then I think that it doesn't matter because it couldn't have been Owen, because he was already dead when Kent was attacked. So now I don't know what to think.'

'Kent is not dead yet.'

'Thank God. I don't know what we'll do if he dies.'

'You don't feel the same obligation to find Owen's killer?'

Mrs Tarring pummelled a pillow into submission. 'Owen was a . . . I don't know how to describe him.'

'A scam artist? A hustler?'

'He was a genuine Rycroft. I know. The family checked. He really was the old lord's son.'

'But he was a slimy toad?'

Mrs Tarring barked out a laugh. 'Shall I do the duvet cover?'

'Owen wasn't content to be granted a place in the sun, but wanted to exclude others from it? The family was getting along fairly well until he came along and upset them, weren't they?'

'He was a liar and a thief. At least, I'm not absolutely one hundred per cent sure that he stole things, although I suspect that he did. He certainly stole reputations. He had a wicked tongue and could twist anyone's actions against them. I told you how he nearly got me the sack, didn't I? Did you know he managed to get the girl he'd assaulted sacked? He claimed she'd been filching from the petty cash. I didn't believe him, Kent didn't believe him, but the old lord said we had to take Owen's word for it and she had to go. Kent and I arranged for her to be given six months' pay and a good reference so that she'd leave quietly.

'When Owen found out, he was furious. He accused me of stealing the money and threatened to go to the police about it. Fortunately Lord Rycroft understood that Kent and I had acted that way to avoid publicity. It saddened him, but he was adamant that Owen had been misunderstood and was not to be blamed in any way. In fact, Lord Rycroft went out and ordered a new car for the lad to compensate him for what he called our "unpleasantness". The next day Owen strutted into the office and told me I'd better start looking for another job, because I was next for the chop! I told Kent what Owen had said and he reassured me that my job was safe, but if Owen had managed to persuade his father that I had been stealing from the firm or something, I don't know what would have happened. I suppose that gives me a motive for killing him. Only, I didn't.'

'No, you wouldn't have put him in Magda's bed.'

Mrs Tarring smoothed the clean duvet cover into place. 'No, I wouldn't. That was horrible.'

'Why do you think it was done?' Bea put some clean towels in the en suite, and checked that there were some toiletries on the shelf above the basin.

Mrs Tarring avoided Bea's eye as she tweaked the pillows into a better position. 'I don't know.'

'Yes, you do. Someone in the family thinks that Magda and Lucas might eventually get together—?'

'I don't think it's ever crossed Magda's mind.'

'No, I don't think it has. But she is very fond of Lucas, isn't she? Does he reciprocate, do you think?'

Mrs Tarring shook her head. 'I think he's too set in his ways to notice. He's something of an eccentric, is Lucas. Totally absorbed in his studies. I believe he's highly thought of, in his own way. But . . . how can I put it? Not one for social gatherings. He doesn't come on to women, isn't interested.'

'What would happen if Magda were to climb into his bed one day – not that she would, of course – but if she did, well, do you think something might happen? She's a pretty woman and fond of him. Don't you think someone might have been watching that situation carefully, and put Owen in Magda's bed to frighten her away?'

A tiny nod. 'Perhaps. She's a good girl, is Magda. She's a natural homemaker but no great intellectual prize, not up to his weight. After this is over, I think you should find her another man to work for, perhaps an older man who is looking for comfort in bed.'

A banshee wail shook the house.

Bea started for the stairs. 'Oh, no! It's the alarm. It must be Magda trying to get in.' She skittered down the stairs, looked through the door panel and saw that there was no one outside. She tried to silence the alarm. It wouldn't stop! The neighbours would be furious! She ran down to the basement. No, the door onto the street was still intact, securely bolted, just as Piers had left it.

The noise was appalling. She ran up to the hall again. Mrs Tarring was standing under the alarm panel, hands over her ears. She shouted, 'I don't think it's Magda!'

'I know!' Bea attacked the alarm again.

Silence.

Oh! My!

Bea leant against the wall. She felt quite limp. If the alarm was going to go off when no one had touched the door then . . . what could she do about that?

At that inappropriate moment, Bea's phone rang. It was Bernice's mother, enquiring if the girl had rung Bea yet, because she still hadn't been in touch with her mother.

Bea tried to switch her mind from one problem to the next. She soothed, and promised to ring as soon as William was back from sailing. Yes, she knew she'd promised to ring back before, but she was sure that there was nothing to worry about. No doubt Bernice was having a wonderful time and had forgotten to reassure people who ought to have been informed.

Someone turned a key in the lock and let themselves into the hall. The alarm didn't go off because Bea hadn't re-set it, had she?

This time it was Magda. 'I'm back!'

Bea finished the call to Bernice's mother and called out, 'How did you get on, Magda?' Then she reset the alarm.

Wouldn't you know, it went off again! Gritting her teeth, she cancelled the signal. Again. Better to have no alarm at all than for it to misbehave when it felt like it.

Magda was hanging about with packages. 'Is there a loose connection somewhere? My parents' alarm malfunctioned in the middle of the night once. It went on and on. It was awful.'

Bea summoned up a smile for Magda. 'No one can deal with it till Monday. Did you get everything you needed? Good.' And, including Mrs Tarring, 'Let's all go and eat, shall we? We can talk afterwards.'

Her mobile phone rang again. She answered it as she led the way to the kitchen. 'Yes?' She was terse.

It was Piers. 'I'm worried about you. Are you all right?'

'Sure. We're about to eat. Did you find the food in your cool box?'

'Yes, and I picked up my new phone which is now fully charged. But I can't settle. Shall I come round? Is the alarm all right?'

She couldn't cope with him tonight. 'It's fine. See you tomorrow sometime.' She clicked the phone off and started to unpack the food they'd ordered.

Magda was drooping with tiredness by the time they'd finished eating, and Bea suggested her guest might like to have an early night. Magda agreed. Bea made her a hot drink and filled a hot-water bottle for her to take up to bed. 'Sleep tight.'

Wanly, Magda pulled herself up the stairs and disappeared into her room. This left Mrs Tarring and Bea to clear the table and settle in the sitting room with a hot drink each.

'Now!' said Mrs Tarring.

Bea said, 'May I suggest we concentrate on one thing only, and that is trying to get in contact with Lord Rycroft and Lucas.'

Mrs Tarring threw up her hands. 'I'll try again.' She dialled different numbers, listened, shook her head. 'The same. Lord Rycroft's phone seems to be out of service. He's probably forgotten to charge it. And Lucas's is the same. Neither of them can be trusted to look after modern phones. I can't get through to Lord Rycroft's town housekeeper, either. Any ideas?'

'Let us think this through. You know Lucas and I don't. I think his actions today tell us a lot about him and his relationship with his family. So let's try to reconstruct what happened to him this morning. You've heard Magda's version which, for the moment at any rate, we'll take for gospel. At breakfast time this morning someone sent Lucas instructions to get the jewellery out of the bank, and included a key to the strong box. Who had access to the key for the safe deposit box?'

Mrs Tarring replied. 'Lord Rycroft used to keep the key, but I think he probably passed it over to Kent some time ago. He's been gradually passing more and more stuff over to Kent to deal with.'

'Is it just old age? Is it true that Lord Rycroft has been showing signs of Alzheimer's?'

'I really can't make up my mind. His housekeeper – not the one at the London house, who is really only a glorified cleaner and an awful fusspot, if you'll pardon my French, but the one in the country – she's been there many, many years, quite settled into the life there, and an excellent cook. Well, she's not one to tattle, but some time ago she called me to say she was worried about His Lordship. She said he'd been ordering stuff on the Internet, stuff he didn't need and says he didn't ask for. She said he'd become somewhat forgetful. He'd told the gardener to do such and such, and then couldn't remember why. I told Kent what she'd said and he went down to see his father. When he returned, Kent said His Lordship seemed perfectly all right to him, but had complained that someone was playing tricks on him, ordering stuff in his name and so on. He refused to see a doctor. Kent told me he didn't know what to think.'

'There are two possible explanations. One, Lord Rycroft might really be going doolally; perhaps getting paranoid, thinking someone was getting at him? And two, someone really has been playing tricks on him. Which?'

'I've thought and thought. I really don't know.'

'You think it was Lord Rycroft who authorized Lucas to take the jewellery out of the bank?'

Mrs Tarring was wretched. 'Why would he? That's what I don't understand. And, why did he ask Lucas – who hates getting involved in family business – instead of Kent, who's been wonderful, looking after everyone for ages.'

'How about this: if the old man really is paranoid, perhaps he's got to the point where he doesn't even trust Kent, but prefers to drag Lucas into the game? No. I prefer to think someone was playing tricks on him, for reasons which I'll explain in a moment. Let's follow the trail of the money. Lucas receives his instructions. He may not be streetwise, but he's no fool, so he double-checks. He makes a phone call to someone to check that this authorization is in order. Who did he ring?'

'Kent, of course. There's no one else. Or . . . his brother?'

'No, Lucas interrupted his early breakfast to make that call. He was going on to have his hair cut and meet the artist, remember? Lord Rycroft wasn't disturbed at his breakfast until much later in the morning. So it's Kent whom Lucas phones. Kent says he knows nothing about it. That throws them both into a flap. They consider the possibilities. In the first place, if the authorization is genuine and signed by Lord Rycroft in a fit of paranoia, then His Lordship is no longer fit to be trusted with important matters and it would be best to remove the jewellery from the bank and put it somewhere he couldn't get at it. If it's some joker – and I suspect they were both thinking it might be Owen – then the sooner the assets are placed elsewhere, the better. Do you agree?'

Mrs Tarring nodded. 'Yes, I do.'

'Now Lucas already had an engagement that morning. He decides he can fit in getting the jewels and meeting Kent if he takes Magda with him to hold onto the loot while he gets his hair cut. So he agrees to follow instructions. His mind must have been in a whirl. Was his elder brother really going bonkers or was someone trying to get hold of the family's jewels for some nefarious reason? He retrieves the jewellery and gets into a cab with Magda on his way to the studio. The next thing that happens, according to Magda, is that Lucas takes a phone call in the taxi. He confirms to his caller that he's got the jewellery and gives him the address of the studio. Can we make an educated guess who that someone was?'

'Kent, of course, confirming their arrangement. Lucas had arranged to meet him at the studio.'

'I think so, too. So Lucas, Kent and Magda are all on course to meet at the studio. The alternative theory would be that Lord Rycroft had phoned Lucas to make sure he'd got the jewellery, but that doesn't make sense because we don't think he heard about the removal of the jewels until he had breakfast later that morning. And it was a phone call he received – not one he made – which caused him to change his plans. He abandoned his breakfast and set out in his car for London. And we can guess why, can't we?'

'He'd just been told the jewellery had been taken out of the bank.'

'If he'd authorized it, then why would that be a surprise and why would it cause him to change his plans for the day?'

Mrs Tarring grimaced. 'That's true. So he didn't know about it, which means that we can discard the idea he'd organized it himself.' She thought about it. 'You think it was Owen who'd set up a plot to get control of the jewellery and that he intended to blame Lucas and Kent for stealing it? But wasn't he dead by that time?'

'He may have set up the scam only for someone else to take a hand in the game. Could Owen have got the old man to sign an authorization without his realizing what he was doing? Perhaps by sliding it in among some other papers?'

'I suppose he could. He did have permission to visit Lord Rycroft whenever he pleased. He was always down there, running little errands for his father. But, how did he get the bank key?' Mrs Tarring rubbed her forehead. 'Kent kept duplicates of the keys to all our properties in a locked cabinet in his office. Owen has been in and out of our offices every day, getting underfoot. It's true that the cabinet is often left unlocked during the day when maintenance men need access. The same goes for the safe. We are all in and out . . . any one of us could have taken the key, including me. Only I didn't.'

'All right, let's suppose for the moment that the scam was set up by Owen, who intended to use it to discredit Lucas, Kent and possibly, you. What stopped it going through?'

'Owen got himself killed.'

And you don't care who did it, do you? All you care about is Kent.

Mrs Tarring said, 'But Owen can't have attacked Kent because he was already dead. It must have been the twins.'

'No, that's not right. In the first place the timing is off, because the twins were here, trying to find out where Lucas and the jewels were, when Piers went out looking for Lucas at the barber's. Who else is there?'

Mrs Tarring didn't want to think about that. Her eyes switched right and left.

Bea prompted her. 'How did anyone else know Kent was going to turn up at the studio?'

Mrs Tarring shrugged. She didn't like this line of questioning.

Bea was patient. 'Look, we found a bug under Lucas's desk, which would have relayed his telephone conversations to another interested party. That's how the villains were alerted to the fact that Lucas was not going to play the role they'd assigned to him. I wonder if a similar bug has also been planted at Kent's place? Has he a full-time housekeeper?'

'No, he likes a bit of peace and quiet. He does have a housekeeper, of course. One you supplied. She doesn't live in, but puts in three days a week to clean, and to buy and cook food, which she leaves for him to heat up when he feels like it.'

'Magda told me that someone representing himself from your office managed to gain access to Lucas's study. From what you say, it wouldn't be difficult for him to run the same trick on Kent's housekeeper. One way or the other, one bug or two, I believe that's how someone knew where the jewellery was going to be, and at what time. But who planted the bugs and who was listening in?'

Still Mrs Tarring refused to play ball. Instead, she said, 'What I want to know is, who interrupted Lord Rycroft at breakfast and caused him to drive off in a hurry?'

'Someone he trusted. Not Owen, because he was dead by that time. I think it has to be either Kent or Lucas. Both of them would be worried sick about what was happening. They conferred; had Lord Rycroft really gone bananas and organized the removal of the family jewels? If so, he must be taken to a doctor and treated. Or, and I think this is most likely, both Kent and Lucas realized that Owen must be orchestrating this nastiest of scams, and they wanted to tear the scales from Lord Rycroft's eyes. Perhaps they decided that if they confronted Lord Rycroft together or alone, if they showed him the jewels, the old man would at last be convinced that Owen was a bad apple and must be dealt with. From what you tell me, it's likely that Lord Rycroft would have taken quite a bit of persuading. But, whether he'd been convinced of Owen's guilt or not, Lord Rycroft was sufficiently disturbed by what he heard to abandon his breakfast to meet them.'

'Wouldn't he have wanted Owen there, too? He'd have wanted Owen to prove his innocence.'

'Perhaps he tried to contact Owen, without realizing he'd been killed by that time. Owen was out of touch. I think Lord Rycroft would have tried to contact Owen, but when he failed, he asked Lucas and Kent to show him the evidence before he did anything else. So where did he plan to meet?'

'I don't know! I can't think!'

'You know the family well. You've observed all their comings and goings. You would have thought that Lord Rycroft would suggest they met at his London home, but his house-keeper is not answering the phone and neither is he, so we can't confirm that. Perhaps Kent and Lucas wanted to meet him on neutral ground somewhere? You say Owen had access to Lord Rycroft at his country house at all times. Did he by chance have a key to his London house as well?'

Mrs Tarring bit her lip. 'Yes, he did. You'll think security very lax, but when His Lordship asked us to give keys to Owen, we agreed. Naturally.'

'I can see how it was. Now where else would they meet? At Piers's studio?'

'Well, we know that Kent went there, but I can't think that Lucas or Lord Rycroft would have attacked Kent. That's unthinkable.'

'Agreed. So who do you think . . .?'

'I don't know. Don't ask me to speculate. I can't think!'

'All right. Let's get at it another way. Why did Lucas disappear? He dumped the jewels on Magda and said he'd be back after he'd visited the barber's. But he didn't turn up there. So where did he go, and why?'

'I don't know! I really don't!'

'What time did he set off for the barber's? About a quarter past ten, Magda said. His appointment with Piers was at eleven, right?'

Mrs Tarring nodded. 'You think it was Lucas who phoned Lord Rycroft and told him the bad news?'

'The timing fits. If we're correct in our assumptions, Lucas would think that at that point everything was under control. The jewels were in safe hands. Kent had been put in the picture. Lord Rycroft was steaming back to town to see for himself what had been going on and Owen . . . was dead. So what stopped Lucas from getting to the barber's?'

Mrs Tarring lifted her hands. 'I don't know.'

You suspect, but you don't know. So you won't talk. Mrs Tarring, are you friend or foe?

TWELVE

Saturday evening to Sunday morning

Bea said, 'Let's try again. His Lordship had got very fond of Owen. He wouldn't want to believe that he'd been deceived by the lad. Suppose, on his way back to London, he phoned Lucas and tore him off a strip. Suppose he said he didn't believe that Owen would deceive him, and that he was going to go straight to Owen's place to tell him what was going on. He didn't know Owen was dead. No one did. So where did Owen live?'

Mrs Tarring said, choosing her words with care, 'Kent had allocated him a flat in the Barbican but Owen hadn't liked it, and asked for something closer to the office, so he was in the process of moving into the apartment under Lucas's flat.'

Bea grimaced. 'That was adding fuel to the family's flames, wasn't it? Provocative, to say the least, if Owen was making trouble all round. Didn't Lucas or Kent object?'

'Lucas was surprised but said he didn't want to make a big deal about it. I believe Kent may have spoken to his father on the subject, but . . .' She gestured. 'Lord Rycroft hates to have his decisions questioned. Owen was having the place redecorated before he moved in.' Another gesture of despair. 'It cost a mint. I don't know what will happen to it now.'

'So, back to what Lucas did this morning. He's in the cab on his way to the barber's. Either he rings his elder brother, or his brother rings him. Lord Rycroft says he doesn't believe Owen has been cheating him. He says they must meet and sort it out. Lucas is presented with a difficult situation. He has taken the jewels out of the bank, remember. He sees that he could well be accused of theft on his own account. He believes that the stuff is safe with Magda. He agrees to abandon his plans for the day in order to meet his brother. He tries to ring Magda, to reschedule the meeting with Piers. He doesn't know that Magda's phone has been smashed by the twins. He can't get through to her. He directs the cab to take him to meet his brother. Where does he go, Mrs Tarring? To the Barbican to Owen's old flat, or to his new place in the same house as Lucas, or where?'

'Again, I don't know!'

'Kent, by that time, is on his way to the studio, where he meets up with . . . who, Mrs Tarring?'

'I don't know. I really don't.' Mrs Tarring rubbed her eyes. 'I'm exhausted. I can't think straight. It's been a terrible day, and tomorrow doesn't look any better. I must ring the hospital to see how Kent is, first thing in the morning. As for Lord Rycroft and Lucas, I'm sure they'll turn up when they're ready, and there'll be a perfectly good explanation for everything that's happened. I'm going home.'

Bea didn't stop her. She was tired, too. Almost too tired to get out of her chair. Her eyes switched to the clock on the mantelpiece. A pretty clock, with flowers painted on a wreath on its face. It was past ten in the evening.

Bea left Mrs Tarring ringing for a cab while she fed the cat Winston, who always swore he couldn't last through the night without a late-night pouch of food. Bea thought of ringing William Morton to ask how Bernice had got on, and decided it was too late to do so. The child must have been tucked up in bed hours ago.

She let Mrs Tarring out of the front door, and watched her walk slowly and stiffly down the steps and get into a cab. A fine night.

Bea hesitated to put the alarm back on, and eventually decided against doing so. It was too unreliable. She busied herself tidying the house, and then went upstairs to get ready for bed. All the time her ears were stretched to hear . . . what surely would not happen.

He still had not come by the time she had showered, got into her nightdress and shrugged on her dressing gown.

Only then did she hear his key turn in the lock.

She floated down the stairs, pleased that she hadn't put the alarm on. A shadowy figure slipped into the house, closed the front door and put his arms around her.

She was imagining things, of course. She'd been wondering what it would be like if he . . .

'I've been so worried about you,' he said. 'Are you all right? I had this fantasy of riding to your rescue, a knight on a white horse. The truth is I'm exhausted, I have a headache and I can hardly stand upright, but I couldn't stay away. I kept thinking someone would come and try to break in during the night, and you without a working alarm.'

'I can't trust it. What do you think?'

He said, 'I haven't a clue. You need a specialist. I'll try to raise one for you, tomorrow.' He was hollow-eyed, dishevelled. Too tired to be sexy . . . and yet . . . and yet . . .

She was comforted by his offer. 'Aspirin and a hot drink?'

'If you have them, yes. Probably nothing will happen but I'll sleep on the settee downstairs.'

He had caught her in a moment of weakness. She didn't want to be alone in the house that night.

She gave him a drink and some aspirins. She found him a duvet and a pillow. And with a firmness that slightly surprised her, she left him in the living room and went up to her own bed alone.

She told herself that she was too tired to sleep. She told herself that nothing would happen that night. She stretched out and found herself smiling. Had Piers expected to share her bed that night? In recent years he'd tried once or twice to . . . well . . . he'd even seemed to be jealous, slightly, of William Morton . . . who had behaved badly, taking Bernice off like that. In the morning . . .

In the darkest hour of the night, she half woke and started upright. What was that?

Her heart was beating far too fast.

She'd left her bedroom door ajar. There was a light on downstairs in the hall.

Yes, it was the alarm, yammering away. But she hadn't set it, had she?

She stumbled out of bed and made it down the stairs to the hall, holding on to the banister.

She met Piers coming up from the lighted basement. He shouted above the din. 'Someone bashed in the door again! Can you believe it?'

She shouted back, 'But I didn't turn the alarm on!' She fed the alarm the code and it took no notice.

Piers shouted something else, but she couldn't make out what it was. She tried the code again.

She was going to go mad! The noise went right through her head, shaking her body. She expected to see Magda running out of her room to see what was the matter, but no . . . perhaps she'd taken a sleeping tablet?

The third time Bea tried the code . . .

The noise died.

Bea leaned against the wall, breathing hard. She said to the alarm, 'You ought to be ashamed of yourself!'

Piers said, 'I thought you weren't going to set it.'

'I didn't.' She addressed the alarm box. 'You, mate, are for the chop!' And to Piers, 'Someone got in downstairs?'

'Looks like it. I can't see anyone in the agency rooms, but give me a torch and I'll search the garden for you.'

'No! Don't!' The thought of him meeting an intruder in the garden frightened her. 'Call the police!'

'Don't be silly! I'm only going to look. The alarm going off like that would have frightened any intruder away, but I'd better check.'

Suppose the intruder found the diamonds! But no . . . not at night. Piers had hidden them too well.

Piers said, 'I promise to be careful.'

Against her better judgement she found him a torch and, despite his orders to the contrary, she followed him downstairs. He'd left the lights on. She could see the rooms were empty of all but furniture.

Looking around, she could also see that someone had been in her office. The grille over the French windows had been wrenched back, and the French doors left open onto the garden. Her chair had been thrust back against the wall as the intruder plunged outside . . . or perhaps when they fled again on his, or her, return?

She watched Piers step into the garden and stand still, listening to the tiny sounds of the city at night and adjusting his eyes to the darkness. He said, 'Whoever it was, has gone.'

She leaned against the wall by the French windows while

Piers probed the shadows outside with the beam of her torch. There was some moonlight; not enough to be really helpful, and something could perhaps be lurking close under the walls . . . but no, nothing seemed to be moving, and no figure came crashing out of the darkness past her in an effort to escape.

Piers walked round the pool and shone the torch on the open door of the shed. Yes, someone had definitely gone in there and found . . . what?

She drew in a deep breath. They'd been looking for the jewels, right?

After a moment Piers returned, shaking his head. 'Whoever it was, has gone. They went straight to the garden shed, pulled everything apart, discovered the jewel cases, opened them, found them empty and left them scattered around. It's a good thing we took precautions.'

'Come inside.' Bea drew him in, closed the French windows and pulled the grille across. Thank heaven for small mercies because the grille still latched into place. Her mouth was dry. Her heart was still thumping with dread about what might have happened to Piers if he'd found the intruder in the garden. He was stupidly, criminally rash!

Piers went straight to the damaged door, which now hung askew again. The hinges were still in place, more or less, but the bolts had been torn away from the door jamb.

He considered the problem. 'I can't mend that. I'll have to shove it back into place and place a desk against it. Can't think how else to make it secure. Build a barricade of furniture around it, perhaps?' He began to do just that.

Bea said, 'Was it Shirley, after the jewellery?'

'Dunno. I didn't actually see anyone. The alarm woke me. I shot down here to find the French windows to the garden ajar, and the door to the area stairs as you see, levered open from the outside. Perhaps they used a tyre iron?'

'They'd been and gone by the time the alarm woke us?'

'I don't understand it. The alarm didn't go off when the intruder broke in or I'd have heard it and caught them in the act. When whoever it was found there weren't any jewels in the boxes, they must have fled and, pushing the door further open in leaving, they must have set the alarm off again.' He stood back, eyeing his furniture barricade with dissatisfaction. 'If anyone tries to get in through that, we'll hear them soon enough.'

He brushed his hands one against the other. 'You can go back to bed now.'

Should she ring the police? And tell them what? That an alarm, which hadn't been switched on, had repelled boarders? She shook her head. It was all too much. Tomorrow . . . she'd deal with it tomorrow.

She climbed the stairs to her bedroom. She was beyond taking any further action. Beyond thought.

She sank back onto the mattress. That alarm . . .! It had a mind of its own. Suppose someone came back again tonight? No, they wouldn't do that, not now they knew the jewels had been taken out of their boxes. Not when the alarm had gone off when they fled.

Except that it shouldn't have gone off, because she hadn't switched it on. The words 'intermittent fault' swam into her tired brain and swam away.

She turned over. It was all too much.

The light went out downstairs, and she closed her eyes. And soon enough, she slept . . . lightly . . . and then, deeply . . . and woke with the memory of being enclosed in strong arms, lying 'spoons' . . . or had she imagined it?

She flung out one arm but the bed was empty and cold beside her. Had he ever been there? No, of course not.

Birds were singing outside in the garden. Loudly. Birds had no consideration for people who needed a good eight hours' sleep.

She slept again, only to be woken by the chink of china as Piers put a mug of tea on her bedside table. She woke slowly, considering various options.

He said, 'I've always liked your early morning face.'

He meant, without makeup.

He kissed her lightly, first on one eyelid and then on the other.

Did she kiss him back? Surely not. The years unravelled and they were back in the first few months of their marriage, in the grotty little basement flat which was all they could afford, with her in a dead-end office job and him raging like a tiger with the need to paint and taking odd jobs here and there to make ends meet. Their loving had been oh, so sweet!

They'd married in church and divorced in a civil court. Once or twice he'd reminded her that they were still married in the eyes of the church. But then . . . his tom-catting around . . . their poverty . . . their child, now grown up and with a family of his own . . . she had moved on to marry again and although her dear Hamilton had died some years ago yet . . . no, she couldn't go back. Too much had happened in the years between.

She shook herself back to the present. 'Did the intruder leave any clue as to his identity?'

He shook his head. One side of his jaw was swollen and yellow under the stubble. He wouldn't be shaving today. Would he grow a beard? Wouldn't he look like a pirate of old, if he did grow a beard? She thrust such frivolous thoughts away.

He said, 'No. I went outside and down the stairs to the agency entrance this morning. Nothing. The visitor was anonymous. Could have come from anywhere. No fingerprints that I could see. My rough-and-ready repair is holding, and the alarm is still not switched on.'

She sat up in bed. 'You said "he?" It was a man?'

'I have no idea, but I can't see those thin arms of Shirley breaking down the door . . . although, of course, if she'd used a tyre iron . . .? No, it still requires more muscle than she's got. It might have been some opportunist burglar chancing his luck. I may be assuming too much but yes, I'd say it was a man.'

Bea thought about that. Shirley had told someone the alarm was not functioning, and someone had forced their way in. If it wasn't Shirley, then who could she have been working with? Some other member of the clan entirely?

He said, 'Changing the subject, are you going to church this morning? I could stay and provide breakfast for you and your guest if you like?'

She'd forgotten Magda. She'd forgotten today was Sunday. And yes, she did like to go to early morning communion on a Sunday when the world was less frantic than on a weekday.

She'd also forgotten that Piers had always got up before her, and that he liked to cook a big breakfast on a Sunday morning, ready for her return from church. He was rearranging his life to suit himself, and for some reason she was allowing him to do so. She sipped tea, hot and strong, just as she liked it. Ugh! He'd put sugar in it. She couldn't abide sugar in tea. She'd stopped taking sugar in her tea years ago, but had never thought to tell him. Why should she?

She replaced the mug on her cabinet.

'After breakfast,' he said, yawning, 'I'd better get back to the mews and find some clean clothes, try to put my easel together, ring the clients whose portraits have been spoiled and give them the bad news. You don't need me for anything else today, do you?'

A dash of cold water. Of course he wasn't going to hang about. He'd been sorry for her last night and had stayed downstairs to look after her. Now he was returning to his everyday life. She'd allowed herself to think . . . she'd imagined that he still loved her, after all these years. Of course he didn't.

And of course she didn't love him, either.

She swung her legs out of bed and reached for her dressing gown. 'Magda! How on earth did she manage to sleep through the racket last night? And Bernice, horrid child! She's upset all our family arrangements, deciding to go off on her own this weekend. And the door downstairs! Where do I get a new one? And the alarm! And the jewels! I suppose I'll be targeted again until I can get rid of them, and how am I supposed to do that? And I ought to check on the various members of the Rycroft family who may be alive, or dead, or in hospital.'

'That's my girl!' And he went off, with a smile, looking at his watch. No doubt wondering how soon he could get back to work.

She dressed, made up her face, snatched up a jacket, and stole out of the house as quietly as she could. She didn't want to face Magda. She didn't want to face anyone.

The air was fresh. A little breeze played with the bright new leaves on the trees in Church Street. Often enough she walked a short distance away to a different, not so high church for an early service, but today she hurried across the road and turned into the one on the corner. It was dim in there. Everything was hushed. Even the traffic noises were muted.

She sank into a chair at the back and tried to block out all worrying thoughts. She tried to pray, but could only manage the odd snatch here and there.

Bernice . . . Magda. The horrifying violence of . . .

Piers.

She found a hankie, and blew her nose. She wasn't going to cry.

What did she need to cry for? Everything was fine.

And if it wasn't, then it could soon be fixed.

The service began, and she tried to concentrate. It wasn't long before the age-old words of confession and praise took hold of her, and she was drawn into worship.

Afterwards, she sat on for a while, talking to God.

Dear Lord above, you know everything, all the secrets of our hearts. You know all our weaknesses, and because you are not only God but also man, you understand us better than we ourselves do.

I need help, Lord.

Every now and then, people in trouble come to me. I try to help them, but sometimes . . . it's so hard, always to be giving. Usually I don't mind. I recover quickly enough, working, seeing my friends, looking after Bernice . . . and please Lord, look after her for me. She's so wilful, and yet so vulnerable.

This time, Lord . . . Piers coming back into my life . . . I feel wounded.

I know that's stupid. I haven't really been wounded.

Well, yes. I have. It's an open wound. He's torn it open again, after all these years.

He's been hurt, too. Concussion. Knocked out. But he still came to my side. That's worth something. I must remember that, when he leaves again.

It was quiet in the church, between services.

Once she'd stopped battering away at God for help, she began to listen to what He was saying to her.

I will never ask you to do something beyond your ability to deal with. Why do you try to do things in your own strength, instead of asking for mine?

After a while she left the quiet of the church, emerging into the traffic and the buzz of the High Street. There was a flower stall outside the church. Bea bought a huge bunch of spring flowers: hyacinths white and blue, daffodils and narcissus. Their scent was almost too strong to be borne. They were symbols of hope in a world which was filled with creatures great and small: well-meaning and good-hearted; sometimes vicious.

All sorts. Both weak and strong.

Rycrofts: missing, in hospital and dead.

Those who mourned them.

Bernice! Why was she behaving so badly?

Bea let herself into the house and took the flowers straight through into the kitchen where Piers was busy at the hob, Magda was patting tears from her eyes, and Winston the cat was giving himself a post-meal wash and brush-up.

Piers gave Bea a look which said, 'Rescue me! Woman in tears!'

Bea ironed out a smile. 'How wonderful to have breakfast cooked for me. Magda, did you sleep well, my dear? Look at these lovely flowers. Don't they lift your spirits?'

'Yes, yes. They're beautiful.' To do her credit, Magda did make an effort to smile. 'Sorry to be such a cry-baby. I took a sleeping pill and yes, your bed is very comfortable, but when I woke up and realized . . .' She mastered her tears with an effort. 'Of all the people I've worked for, all these years, I do think Lucas was the nicest and kindest of men.'

'Jolly good,' said Bea, knowing it was an inappropriate response, but not sure what else to say. She took a couple of vases out of a cupboard, and pushed them towards Magda. 'Are you any good at arranging flowers? I'm sure you're much better at it than me.'

Piers said, 'Orange juice all round? Do you want cereal? If not, I've got bacon and eggs, tomatoes, baked beans and mushrooms for you. All right? And I've fed your cat. Can't remember his name, but he pointed out which sachet of food he wanted and it's all gone, so I imagine that was the right one.'

'Oh, you are good! When men can cook, they really are something, aren't they?' said Magda, deftly placing flowers in the vases. 'I don't usually bother with breakfast for myself but today is an exception.'

Piers hadn't met Bea's eye after that first plea for help with Magda. Now he poured boiling water into the big teapot, the one Bea didn't normally use. He said, 'Bea, you'll like to serve yourself?'

She understood, then. She'd not drunk the mug of tea he'd brought her in bed, and it had seemed to him like a rejection. She said, 'Thanks. Shall I pour for you as well? Do you take sugar nowadays? I don't.'

'What? Since when?' A sharp tone.

'I don't know. Some years ago.'

He frowned but made no further comment. He dished up and they got down to the serious business of setting themselves up for the day. Then, while Bea cleared away the breakfast things and Magda finished putting the flowers in water, Piers said he thought he'd best be on his way.

Magda managed to smile. 'You've been wonderful. I don't know what I'd have done without you.'

Bea was going to roll her eyes but Piers caught her by the arm, saying, 'A word,' and rushed her out into the hall, kicking the door to the kitchen shut behind him.

He kissed Bea. Hard.

She didn't resist.

Neither spoke.

He rubbed his swollen jaw. Kissing her might well have hurt.

She tried to smile. 'We can't just pick up where we left off.'

'Why not? You gave me the key to your front door.'

She could feel herself blush. She didn't reply, because she had done just that, possibly not meaning it. By accident. She could ask for it back. But she didn't.

He touched the tip of her nose with his forefinger, and left by the front door.

She shivered. Should she switch the central heating back on for a bit?

Someone rang the doorbell.

Mrs Tarring, looking harassed and ever so slightly unkempt. 'Is that girl still here? Magda, I mean?'

Magda appeared in the doorway to the kitchen. 'Did I hear my name?'

'Listen, girl. There's no easy way to say this, but . . .' Mrs Tarring took a step towards Magda, stumbled and nearly fell. 'Bad news!'

THIRTEEN

Sunday morning

M rs Tarring saved herself from falling by reaching out to the chest in the hall. She leaned on it, panting.

Bea got her arm under Mrs Tarring's and helped her through into the sitting room, where she sat her down on the settee.

Tears were running down Mrs Tarring's cheeks.

Magda cried, 'What is it? Oh! It's Lucas, isn't it?' She wept, too, hands over her mouth, awkwardly gulping. 'He's dead, too?'

Bea wished Piers had stayed for this tear-fest. He would have loved it. He'd have said it was 'real', two women with mouths awry, eyes shut, shoulders humping forward. Their legs had been thrown akimbo, regardless of the decencies. Oh, the amount of water that flowed from the two women! If they were living in *Alice in Wonderland*, this would be the pool of tears.

Mrs Tarring shook both her hands in the air, trying and failing to speak.

Magda sank into a chair, and let herself fall back till her head rested on the back.

Bea clapped her hands. 'That's quite enough, ladies! Time to stop crying and do something to sort this mess out. I am going to make some good coffee while you both dry your eyes and get yourselves sorted. Right?'

She didn't wait for a reply but went to the kitchen to make some extra-strong coffee. Her phone rang. It was William Morton, presumably ringing from the Isle of Wight.

'Sorry to ring you so early, Bea, but there's been a little problem here.'

With a catch in her voice, Bea said, 'Bernice? Has something happened to Bernice?' She envisaged a mishap at sea . . .

Bernice being washed overboard . . . an accident in the car in which she was a passenger . . . or a bout of poisoning, some food that . . .?

'No, no. Nothing to alarm. It's just that she's had a bit of a spat with Alicia, you know what kids are; one moment they're best friends and the next they're mortal enemies.' He tried a laugh on for size.

This was serious. Bea sank onto a stool. 'Tell me.'

'They quarrelled – you know what girls are like. Bernice can be very . . . very. You know?'

Bernice knew. 'Yes?' Putting iron into her voice.

'In fact, she has behaved rather badly. Our hostess is quite put out. She knows that the child has had a dysfunctional family and that you are trying to teach her manners, but she says Bernice has been, well, rude.'

'Really?' Even more iron in her voice.

'I couldn't get her to apologize. I was at my wits' end, what with Alicia being so upset, and Bernice . . . well, you know how impossible she can be.'

'Get to the point.'

'We're booked to take part in a regatta today, something our hostess has been planning for ages. Bernice has decided not to take part. You can imagine what a difficult situation this puts me in.'

Bea could imagine it very well. 'So . . .?'

In a rush of words, 'The child has stormed off. I caught up with her on the road. She insisted on being put on the ferry and says she'll make her own way back, if you please. I couldn't stop her.'

'So you let a twelve-year-old child, for whom you're responsible, go off by herself on public transport?' Bea let ice drip into her voice.

'What else could I do?' Almost whining. What a weakling!

'Bring her back yourself.'

'You must see I couldn't do that, not with all the arrangements that had been made for us this weekend. Anyway, Bernice insisted she didn't want anything more to do with me. Stalked off, in fact. I saw her onto the ferry and now I have to get back.'

'You're responsible if anything happens to her.'

'No, I'm—'

Bea shut off the call.

Dear Lord, please! Please keep her safe!

She tried Bernice's phone. The call went to voicemail. She left a message for the child to ring her, immediately! Straight away! Now!

Moving with care, she carried the tray with coffee, mugs, milk and sugar through to the sitting room, where her guests were patting their faces dry and adjusting their skirts. Bea's hands didn't even shake as she dispensed coffee and handed round milk and sugar. Her mind had split into two; one half was following Bernice on the ferry back to the mainland, while the other was trying to deal with the problems represented by these two irritating women. She would very much like to scream and howl, to lie down on the floor and have hysterics, but of course she couldn't do that. Not till she was alone, anyway.

She could do nothing about Bernice until the girl rang. Meanwhile, she had to solve the Rycroft problem. 'Now, Mrs Tarring,' said Bea, sipping her own coffee. 'I assume you have some news for us?'

'Yes.' Mrs Tarring rattled her cup back onto its saucer. 'I wish I hadn't. I don't understand why . . .' She made an effort to control herself. 'I had a message on my landline phone when I got home last night. From His Lordship's housekeeper here in town, to ring her on her mobile. I was so tired, but I did ring her and she said . . . Oh dear, she was in such a state. It took me ages to understand what she was saying. I knew she was inclined to be superstitious, but this was something else! She went on and on about fate and death and bad luck and how she wasn't going to stay to be a part of it . . . all nonsense of course! I offered to go round to her but she said she was giving in her notice and in fact had already packed up and left and gone to her brother's, because there was no way she was going to stay in that house of doom any longer, and I was not to ring her back because she was turning her phone off to get a good night's sleep. And she switched off.'

Mrs Tarring blew her nose and wiped her eyes. 'I tried to ring her back. No luck. You can imagine how worried I was.

The houses are never left unoccupied. The pictures, the silver, the antiques! I couldn't believe that she would have let us down at such a time. I hardly slept at all and this morning I made up my mind to go round to see her at her brother's . . . and then I realized I hadn't his phone number or address and that they would be at the office. Just as I was preparing to leave, she rang me again to say I should send her money on to her brother's house, plus two months' extra for her pain and suffering. I couldn't believe it. I said she couldn't just have abandoned the house like that, and she said it was more than flesh and blood could stand and someone else could put the dishwasher on, which was full at the time, but she wasn't going back even though she might have left a window open upstairs in her toilet and it wouldn't shut properly and it was my problem and I must get someone round to see to it.

'I told her, I said, "You can't leave without giving us notice," but she said it was already done and nothing would make her go back and I could find out about Lord Rycroft's death by ringing the police in Oxford and she wouldn't be going to the funeral, no matter what!'

'Oh!' cried Magda. 'Lord Rycroft's dead?'

'I couldn't believe it, but after she'd rung off I found the number of the Oxford police, and rang them. Yes, it's true. I'm still in shock. He'd driven off the road straight into a tree. A witness said he'd seen the car coming down the hill far too fast, tooting his horn, and he, the witness, wondered if the brakes had failed. No doubt the police will check. His Lordship was alive but unconscious when they got to him, and he died on the way to hospital. The police couldn't find his phone. They think it flew out of his hand in the impact and someone trod on it or it got damaged when they cut him out of the car. They identified him from cards in his wallet. His diary gave his contact details, next of kin and so on.'

Magda's face twisted. 'It definitely wasn't Lucas?'

'No, it was Lord Rycroft. They gave me the registration of the car. It's the one that's registered to him.'

Magda whispered, 'Thank God.'

Mrs Tarring said, 'I'm not sure I can thank God. What a mess!'

Bea concentrated. 'After the accident the police would have tried to contact his next of kin. First they would have tried Kent, whose mobile is missing and who is also in hospital. Then they'd try Owen's number, but he's dead. Lastly, they'd contact the London address, which is where, finally, they made contact with his housekeeper?'

Mrs Tarring said, 'I hope Kent agrees with me that that woman gets any back pay that's due to her and not a penny more. Leaving without notice and at such a time! Abandoning the house with a window upstairs open! And dirty plates in the dishwasher. Appalling behaviour.'

Bea said, 'Mrs Tarring, I realize this is a difficult situation for you, but as of this moment you represent the trust. The police and the hospital will want to know who is going to make arrangements for Lord Rycroft's funeral.'

'Kent decides everything like that. How do I know what to do? I rang Hammersmith Hospital to see how Kent was doing, and they wouldn't tell me anything because I'm not a relative, even though we visited him there yesterday. All this red tape!'

Magda dabbed her eyes. 'Oh! It's all too much.'

Bea tried to bring her mind back from the horrors that might even now be enveloping Bernice . . . white slavery . . . being picked up by a strange man . . .

Mrs Tarring sniffed, richly. 'I thought perhaps the family solicitor might be able to help, but it's a Sunday and there's no one at his office. I tried. I think he goes out of town at weekends. I don't know which funeral directors the family would like to use. Then, the newspapers ought to be informed, obituaries need to be prepared, and what about His Lordship's housekeeper at the country house? I did ring her to let her know what has happened, but she was no help. She said she'd stay on for a while if I personally guaranteed her wages, and I said I would, although I didn't think it was an appropriate time to . . .' She blew her nose. 'I'm afraid I may have been rather terse with her.'

Bea took a deep breath. 'Mrs Tarring, why did you come here this morning?'

Her two guests looked at her in astonishment. 'Why . . .?'

said Mrs Tarring. 'Well . . . I thought you might have some idea about . . . and I thought Magda ought to know that . . .'

Bea said, 'The two of you could solve this matter quite easily if you were only honest about what you know. Mrs Tarring, you came because you really know what this is all about but are afraid to admit it.'

'What! No, I don't! How could I?'

'And you, Magda,' said Bea, 'may not have been privy to what Lucas has been up to, but you know him well enough to say what he would or would not have done in different circumstances. Together you two could sort this. Alone, you are wasting time weeping and wailing. I could bash your heads together, I really could.'

The two women gaped. Bea told herself that she must not take out her problems on others. She wasn't angry with them, but with her wretched ward, Bernice. Letting loose her anger on these two helpless women would do no good. She said, 'Sorry. Got out of bed the wrong way this morning.'

Two pairs of eyes rounded. They'd thought of Bea as being Mother Hen, and Mother Hen had turned into a bad-tempered Eagle and snapped at them.

Bea took a deep breath. A very deep breath. Forget Bernice for the moment. Deal with the Rycrofts and their stupid, stupid play-acting. 'Mrs Tarring, you know perfectly well what all this is about.'

Mrs Tarring shook her head over and over. 'No, I don't. I swear I don't.'

Bea counted on her fingers. 'Lord Rycroft: a car accident. His son Kent: bashed over the head. His second son, Owen: killed and left in Magda's bed; his grandson Ellis: killed in a hit and run; his brother Lucas: disappeared. The twins: doped with a bottle of some drink left in their car. Six or seven mysteries over a weekend. What are the odds of that happening?'

'I don't know! Do you think I haven't thought and thought . . .?'

Bea said, 'It's quite simple. Who benefits?'

Mrs Tarring licked her lips. 'What? But . . . no one! The death duties are going to be . . . whoever died first: Owen, I suppose?'

'No,' said Magda, frowning. 'If Mrs Abbot is right, then it was Kent's son, Ellis, who died first. But that was a traffic accident, wasn't it? The same with Lord Rycroft's death. That witness must be wrong, saying that the car's brakes failed, and even if they did . . .' She thought about it. 'It's just an accident, isn't it?'

'Of course it is,' said Mrs Tarring. 'And, in any case, nobody benefits from their deaths. Not really. Because none of them owned anything. Their accommodation and living expenses are paid by the trust fund. That was done to reduce death duties.'

Bea reflected that however clever the trust's solicitors might have been, there would be some way that death duties would be demanded. First Ellis, next Owen, then Lord Rycroft. Oh yes, there'd be death duties all right. And what about the rest of them – the twins, and Kent? And Lucas? Sorting this lot out was going to keep the accountants happy for years.

Mrs Tarring sniffed. 'No individual benefits from what's happened. I can't believe what you're saying, Mrs Abbot. It's not true.'

Magda said, 'Surely, it's just a series of tragedies? I can quite see why Lord Rycroft's housekeeper thinks the Rycrofts are jinxed. Not that I believe it, of course.'

But she's not ruled it out, has she?

'Mrs Tarring knows what's behind all this,' said Bea, 'but she doesn't want to admit it. Follow the money trail. Who benefits if six members of the family are knocked out of the running? Magda, if Mrs Tarring won't tell me, you can, right?'

Magda frowned. 'Well, I suppose each of the remaining members of the family would be better off because there'll be a smaller number of people sharing the same pot of money. But Lucas isn't bothered by money. He really isn't.'

Bea said, 'I wasn't thinking of Lucas. Who else is left? Mrs Tarring, you made a reference to the Rycrofts having an extended family. Is Shirley one of them?'

'Well, yes. But her brother Hilary . . . I mean, he's not exactly . . . and they're from a junior branch of the family. Lord Rycroft's uncle had a son who produced three children. All three of them work for the firm in one capacity or another, but they're not important.'

'Three of them? Their names?'

'Shirley, whom you met yesterday, and Hilary. But you can count Hilary out.'

'That's two. Who's the third?'

'Ferdy. Short for Ferdinand.'

'So Shirley, Hilary and Ferdy are all minor members of the family, who have become major players with the deaths of senior members, right?'

'Well, yes. I suppose you could put it that way.'

Bea turned to Magda. 'What do you know about them?'

'It's true that someone called Shirley rang Lucas a couple of times, wanting him to do something about the family's problems, but I never met her before yesterday. Hilary? Is it a man or a woman? I've heard it can be either, but . . . Did I ever take a call from someone of that name? I don't think so. Ferdy?' She tested the name out, and shook her head. 'No.' Yet a slight frown remained on her forehead.

'What did Lucas say about them?'

A shrug. 'Why, nothing much. He read the messages, screwed them up and threw them in the waste-paper basket.'

Bea said, 'Mrs Tarring, what's wrong with Hilary?'

'He's, I don't know, but if I say he's retarded, then the thought police will come down on me, won't they? But that's what he is. He's got some kind of personality problem. I don't know that they've ever worked out exactly what it is. Down's syndrome, perhaps? He's a big lad, well grown, but he's not up to taking any kind of job. He gets into terrible rages some-times. It's the frustration, I suppose. He knows he's different from everyone else, but he's stuck where he is. His sister – that's Shirley – looks after him at home. Poor girl, she hasn't had much of a life, has she? That's why she's only part-time in the office. He used to come into the office with her. We kept some boxes of games for him to play with while she attended to this and that, but nowadays he refuses to come. Kent was talking of some residential accommodation for him but Shirley didn't like the idea and it came to nothing. The trust pays all expenses, of course.'

'What about Shirley? Is she on the payroll, too?'

'Well, yes. She helps manage some of the rented

accommodation for us, arranging and checking on maintenance jobs.'

'She has access to the keys and any paperwork that passes
through the office?'

'Yes, I suppose so. But it's ridiculous to suggest that she
could be involved in anything untoward.'

'How did Owen get on with Hilary?'

'All right, I suppose.'

'I very much doubt it. Mrs Tarring, you really have to tell
us what you know, or the killings will continue. You tell me
Owen was not a nice man. How did he behave to a relative
who had Down's syndrome?'

Mrs Tarring threw up her hands. 'You're right, of course.
Owen wasn't kind to Hilary. Perhaps because he hadn't been
brought up in this country and taught how to behave to people
less able than himself, he objected to Hilary's occasional presence in the office. Owen made fun of him. Shirley tried to
talk to him about it, but that was like a red rag to a bull. Owen
couldn't bear criticism. He blew up and shouted, raved . . .
said some horrid things. And because she'd defended her
brother, he also threatened her with the sack. But of course
Kent wouldn't have let her go, or cut off her allowance. I
mean, no way! Owen was out of order there.'

'No love lost?'

Mrs Tarring fidgeted. 'You're trying to make out that Shirley
could have been trying to get rid of all the other Rycrofts?
That's ridiculous. It's far more likely that Lucas might have
wanted the title, but that's ridiculous, too. He wouldn't.'

'That's outrageous!' Magda puffed herself up. 'How dare
you! Lucas wouldn't!'

'No, I don't think he would. Not really.' Mrs Tarring was
conciliatory.

Bea thought about it. 'Mrs Tarring, you mentioned another
brother. Ferdinand. Called Ferdy. What's he like?'

Mrs Tarring shrugged. 'Ferdy's all right. It's ridiculous to
think that he could have had a hand in what's been going on.
There are more Rycrofts in the background. I've been told it's
quite a big family. In Victorian times they thought nothing of
having ten or twelve children, you know.'

'How many more Rycrofts are being supported by the trust fund?'

Mrs Tarring reddened. 'How should I know? Several, I suppose.'

'You of all people should know.'

Mrs Tarring shook her head. She was not going to play Bea's game.

Bea thought there were more ways than one of skinning a cat. She turned to Magda. 'You remember telling me about a man who came to your place one day when Lucas was out. He had some papers for Lucas to sign. You took him into Lucas's study, and he caused a diversion by dropping his papers, which is probably when he planted a bug under Lucas's desk. He made a phone call, told you he'd mistaken the date or the day or the address or something, and left. Can you describe him?'

Magda said, 'But why . . .? Oh, if you think it's important.' She closed her eyes, an upright line forming between her eyebrows. 'He was in his early or mid-forties, perhaps? He wasn't fair-haired, like the other Rycrofts I've seen. He didn't look like Kent, or Tweedledum and Tweedledee, or Shirley. He'd not be any taller than me, and he wasn't very big.'

'Were his manners good?'

'Oh yes. He was courteous, perhaps a bit old-fashioned.'

'A leader or a foot soldier?'

A tiny smile. 'Well, not a captain of industry. That air of success is unmistakable. The man I saw was not accustomed to giving orders, but competent in what he did.'

Mrs Tarring looked down at her hands. Did this description mean something to her?

Magda concentrated. 'He gave an overall impression of being brown. I don't mean that he had a tan.' She gestured helplessly. 'What I mean is that his hair was brown and smooth, and brushed straight back. His suit was brown and his shoes were brown. He had a red waistcoat, though. A very dark red; perhaps you'd call it maroon?'

Bea was watching Mrs Tarring and saw her eyes stretch wide. Yes! She knew him.

Magda screwed up her face in an effort to remember. 'I

suppose he gave me his name, but if he did, I didn't take it in. He said he'd come from the Rycroft office with some papers for Lucas to sign. I saw the Rycroft crest and name on the folder he was holding, so I assumed he was who he said he was. No, I'm sure he didn't give me his name. I'm so stupid! I ought to have asked, but I was in the middle of cooking something and it didn't seem to matter because he said it was a mistake and left straight away.'

Bea said, 'Mrs Tarring, you know him.' She didn't make it a question.

Lips thinned. 'No. How could I?'

Bea said, 'Mrs Tarring, was that your "Ferdy"?'

A shrug. 'I don't know. It could be anyone.' A lie.

'Why are you protecting him?'

'Because . . . because he's a decent man, and if Owen hears that he made a silly mistake and went to the wrong place . . .' She caught herself up. 'But Owen's dead and can't do any more harm, can he? Well, yes. I suppose the man that Magda is describing might be Ferdinand Rycroft. He's been in the office for years, keeps everything going. Never minds staying late, or dealing with the most tiresome jobs. I'm really surprised that he made a mistake by going to Lucas's place instead of . . . wherever it was he was supposed to be. But I'm absolutely convinced he didn't do anything wrong.'

Magda gave Mrs Tarring an old-fashioned look. Had the almost-perfect Mrs Tarring a tender spot for Ferdy? It rather sounded like it.

Bea, however, tried to be reassuring. 'Of course. So what relation is Ferdy to the rest of the family?'

Mrs Tarring relaxed now her favourite was not under attack. 'He's Shirley and Hilary's much older brother. It's a junior branch of the family, descended from the old lord's uncle. Ferdy has his own little house out in the suburbs, out Ealing way, to the west. He's a widower. His wife died a couple of years ago, and there were no children, all very sad. But he's the one we can always rely on to turn up on time, and he's usually the last to leave the office in the evenings.'

Bea asked, 'How did he get on with Owen?'

Mrs Tarring raised both hands. 'Owen really was very

naughty. He called poor Ferdy "Robin Redbreast" because he likes red waistcoats. Owen used to tweak Ferdy's red hankie out of his breast pocket and wave it around. Poor Ferdy didn't know what to do. I thought one day he was going to cry, but he didn't, of course. I told Owen how good Ferdy was, and that he ought not to tease him, but . . .' A shrug. 'That was Owen, and no one dared stand up to him because the old lord made such a pet of him.'

Bea said, 'Can we take it that the Rycrofts were one big, happy family until Owen arrived and started to upset everyone?'

'Well, yes . . . and no. I mean, the twins – the ones you call Tweedledum and Tweedledee – they were always getting into debt and there was talk about them having beaten someone up, and Lord Rycroft kept saying that this was the very last time he'd help them out. No one thought he meant it, though, because he always gave in, in the end.'

'How did Owen react to that?'

'He said there was no point throwing good money after bad. He was trying to stiffen the old lord's resolve to stop supporting the twins. He said the money could have been better spent, by which I suppose he meant that he could do with it himself.'

'Owen didn't make himself popular, did he?'

Mrs Tarring compressed her lips, and shook her head. 'Well, he's gone now. Don't let's speak ill of the dead.'

'No, let's talk about the living. If I'm right, the Rycroft family has been decimated over the last few days. Who's still on the active list?'

'Lucas,' sighed Magda. 'Wherever he may be.'

'Kent, if he survives,' said Bea. 'Also Tweedledum and Tweedledee – ditto. If they survive. Also Shirley, Hilary and Ferdy. Anyone else lurking in the shadows?'

Mrs Tarring shook her head. 'There are some distant cousins somewhere, but you're right, there's no one else that the trust is supporting.'

Bea's phone rang. She excused herself and shot out to the kitchen to take the call. Would this be Bernice? Hopefully . . .

FOURTEEN

Sunday morning

Bea snatched up the phone.

'Is that you?' A small voice, restrained in tone. Angry? It was Bernice! At last! 'Bernice? Where are you?'

'I'm perfectly all right.' Definitely cross. 'There's absolutely no need to go ballistic just because I didn't want to go sailing again. It made me sick to my stomach.'

Bea held onto her temper. 'But you mustn't just rush off like that. Anything could happen to you.'

'I'm perfectly all right. I'm on the ferry and I'm sitting with some new friends and then I'll take the train to—'

'What new friends? Bernice, where did you meet—'

'I'll pass you over to them.'

Noises off. Then an older woman spoke into Bernice's phone. 'Mrs Abbot? Is that right? My name is Tinker. My daughter and I are returning home after a few days away on the Isle of Wight, and Bernice has attached herself to us. I asked her why she's travelling alone and she said there was some emergency and the people she was staying with couldn't spare the time to see her safely home. I said I didn't understand why not, and she said I'd better speak to you about it.'

The woman sounded sensible. Good. Bea told herself not to explode with rage. She modified her voice accordingly. 'Mrs Tinker, I don't understand why she's been left to travel alone, either. The people she was staying with rang me to say she was starting back by herself. As you can imagine, I've been worried sick about her. I'm so grateful that you can keep an eye on her on the ferry.'

'She says she's getting the train back into London and will take a taxi from the station to you. Is that right? I've checked, and she has enough money for the journey. We could see her onto the train if you like, but after that we're going east.'

Bernice was supposed to be going back to school that evening. Well, Bea would have to ring the school and explain. 'You are an answer to a prayer. If you could see her onto the train, that would be wonderful. I'll be waiting in for her this evening.'

'We'll do that then.' A pause. 'I'm not sure what exactly went wrong for the child this weekend. It's not always easy to tell, is it?'

'No, Mrs Tinker. It isn't. I shall have to find out. Would you let me have your phone number and address? I would like to write and thank you for looking after her. I am very grateful that Bernice found you.'

Numbers were exchanged, and then Bernice came back on the line.

'It's quite all right, you know. I chose Mrs Tinker because she looks like you.'

Bea stifled a scream. How dare Bernice! Before Bea could say anything else, the girl ended the call.

Bea controlled her fury and frustration. She must let William know the child was safe. She pressed buttons for William's phone. It went to voicemail. She left a message, 'Bernice has been in touch. She's on her way back to London. I'll let you know when she arrives.'

Presumably William would be out sailing with Alicia and his new girlfriend. Bea wished them luck. Well, she tried to, anyway. She told herself it was no good gnashing her teeth. It ruined the enamel.

She blew her nose and rolled her shoulders up and down and around, to ease stiffness. She had other work to do.

Back in the sitting room, Bea found the two women staring into space. Not talking to one another. Bea thought that it wouldn't take much to get them at one another's throats. Each knew something that the other didn't. And both suspected the fact.

Bea decided that she no longer trusted Mrs Tarring, or not very much, anyway. Would it be a good idea to separate her from Magda? Give the older woman something to do?

Bea sat down by Mrs Tarring. 'I've been thinking. We three know a great deal about the background to this affair which the various police forces don't. We need to tell them what we know. You, Mrs Tarring, have the skills needed to gather all the different threads of this investigation together. Consider this; Owen's body was found in Regent's Park and the Metropolitan Police are dealing with it. Kent was found in Ealing and a different police force is dealing with that. The Metropolitan Police know about Owen, but although my artist friend tried to tell them the two cases might be linked, they really didn't want to know about Kent. Lord Rycroft's accident took place near Oxford, and the police there will know nothing about Kent or about Owen . . . unless you told them?'

Mrs Tarring nodded. Instantly, she was bright and alert. 'No, I didn't. It never occurred to me. I see what you mean: each police force is acting independently and they won't be sharing information, although there is no connection that I can see.'

There's none so blind as those who refuse to see.

Bea continued, 'If I found you a desk, a phone and a computer, do you think you could find out which police force is dealing with which incident, and who is in charge of each one?'

Mrs Tarring leaped to her feet. 'I could do that. Yes, of course I could. Something positive to do at last! I feel so much better already.'

Bea got to her feet, too. 'I'm going to put you in the inter-view room downstairs. The coffee machine is broken, but I'll show you the loo and kitchen and leave you to it.'

Mrs Tarring was raring to go. 'I can get the local police phone numbers from the Internet, can't I? Lead me to it.'

'Exactly.'

Downstairs, Bea showed Mrs Tarring the small interview room at the back of the building, switched on the computer, put in the password and left her to it.

She went back upstairs to find Magda looking out of the back window, down onto the garden. Down to the garden shed, where she'd left the jewels?

Bea said, 'Now, Magda, I realize you didn't want to talk in front of Mrs Tarring, but you and I have both guessed where Lucas has gone.'

'Have I?'

'Oh yes. You can't be sure, but you have been working out a scenario which satisfies you, and so have I. Lucas left the studio, on his way to the barber's. He received a phone call from his brother, saying that he was on his way in to London and would meet him . . . where?'

Magda shrugged. She still wasn't going to say what she thought.

Bea almost smiled. 'You're right to keep your thoughts to yourself. Who can you trust? But let me have my say. They probably agreed to meet at His Lordship's London house. Lucas would have tried to phone you to explain the change of plan. Your phone had been destroyed so he couldn't get through. What's more, when he got to the rendezvous, his brother wasn't there. He waited. And waited. He tried to phone his brother. No reply, because His Lordship's phone had been broken or otherwise lost in the crash. Remember that the police considered the car crash an accident . . . and maybe it was. What happened next?'

Another shrug, but Magda turned her eyes on Bea and kept them there.

Bea said, 'Lucas is no fool. He might not be worldly wise, but he has brains. What did he do next, Magda?'

'I don't know. I really don't.' She dropped her eyes from Bea's. She'd been thinking along those lines, too.

Bea said, 'For months, ever since Owen arrived, members of the family have been ringing Lucas, asking him to intervene in the arguments that had been raging about Owen's behaviour. Without success. Lucas knew all about the turmoil in the family. He can't contact you, or his brother, or his nephew Kent. Alarm bells ring. And rightly so, methinks. He could run away, but that's not his style. So I'm asking you again, Magda: what does he do?'

'I don't know.'

'I think you do. Let's go back a bit. Owen's body was cold when we found him. Rigor mortis had been and gone, which indicates to me that he wasn't killed on Saturday but probably on Friday. And not where he was found. What were Lucas's movements on Friday? Did he have any visitors? Owen, for instance?'

Magda felt free to talk about that. 'No, no visitors. He worked at home most of the day. He's writing a book on how you can date pictures by the paint that's been used. An expensive colour made from lapis lazuli was not discovered till such and such a time, so you can tell a fake picture if that particular blue has been used in a picture that's supposed to be from the twelfth century. It's very interesting. He is disciplined about taking exercise. After a light lunch he goes for a swim, Mondays, Wednesdays and Fridays. On Thursday afternoons he's been meeting a colleague to talk about some collaboration or other, I don't know where, but the details will be in his diary, I suppose.

'Every other day he reads or deals with correspondence in the afternoons and takes a brisk walk for half an hour in the early evening before supper at seven. Friday was much as usual. On Friday evening I served him a home-made chicken and mushroom pie with French beans, followed by an apple, cheese and biscuits, and coffee. He didn't go out that evening, but read in the sitting room, listening to a concert on the radio.'

'Did the police ask you about his movements on Friday?'

'No. They didn't.'

'They will, you know. Because you can alibi him for that day.'

Magda's face lost most of its colour. 'You think they'll suspect Lucas of . . . Oh, nonsense!'

'Anyone who disappears during the course of a police investigation is suspect. Where is he, Magda?'

She reddened. 'How should I know?'

'You're beginning to wonder if he's in danger, too, aren't you?'

No reply.

'If I were you, I'd be worried, too. He'll also be worried because he can't contact you.'

Magda turned her head away. 'I doubt if he'd care, much.'

'I have no idea whether he cares much or little. I think he's scared and has found himself a safe place in which to hide. You've studied him. You know where he'd go. You mentioned that he belongs to a club. He'll have gone there, won't he?'

Magda took a deep breath. 'Yes, I suppose he might have done.'

'Mrs Tarring will soon find out which police force is dealing with which assault or deaths in the family, and we'll help them to join up the dots. In the meantime, perhaps you'd like to reassure Lucas that you are still alive and kicking.'

'I don't have the number of his club and they wouldn't tell me if he were there or not. You know club rules. Complete discretion. Denial. The old gentlemen's clubs are like a sanctuary from daily life.'

Bea slapped Lucas's address book down onto the table. 'He'll have the number of his club in this book. Ring there and leave a message to say your phone is out of order, and please would he ring you at this landline number. Give him some kind of password so that he knows it's you on the phone. I think that's where he went, but if not . . . he'll have gone to a hotel, wouldn't he? Which hotel, Magda? He doesn't like visitors at the house, but perhaps he arranges for colleagues from out of London to stay in a London hotel occasionally? Wouldn't he have the number of those hotels in his little book?'

Magda picked the book up. 'He might. Yes.'

'You'll think me paranoid but, whatever you find out, don't tell Mrs Tarring.'

Magda's eyes narrowed. 'Why not?' But yes, she knew.

'You're right to be careful. You've decided to trust no one. Well, you can trust me because you know I have nothing to gain in this matter. But yes, you've noticed that Mrs Tarring has divided loyalties, and is not being open with what she knows. And, there's an awful lot of unexplained deaths around.'

Magda said, 'I told myself I was imagining things, but if you agree with me . . .? Do you really think Lucas may be in danger?'

'I would, if I were in his shoes. It depends how much he knows. Does he even know about his brother's death yet? And the attack on Kent? Probably not. There's three different police forces dealing with the Rycroft deaths, and none of them may be willing to share information. The sooner Lucas is back in touch, the better.'

Magda stiffened her spine. 'You'll want me to tell the police what I know, not only about giving Lucas an alibi, but also what I've learned about the other Rycrofts? Well, there goes my job. Mrs Tarring will kill me if I tell the police what we've learned about Owen and the twins and so on. But if Lucas is in trouble then of course I must do it. I hope you can find me another job, Mrs Abbot. I don't suppose I'll ever find another one I like as much as this, but . . . tough! That's life!'

'Good girl.' Bea looked at her watch. Lucas might have had the sense to keep his head down. Or, he could be lying dead in a ditch somewhere. 'I'll go and see how Mrs Tarring is getting on while you start leaving messages for Lucas, right?'

Magda began to turn over the pages of the address book. Bea was halfway down the stairs to the agency rooms when her mobile phone rang.

Piers. 'Are you all right?'

'Yes, of course. I . . . no, I'm not.' The words had shot out of her without her thinking what she was saying. She was annoyed with herself. She was miserable, and hurting and angry. But she didn't want Piers around. Or did she?

'I'll be round in five.' He cut off the call.

Bea was furious with herself. Why on earth had she said she couldn't cope? Of course she could cope. She always had coped, hadn't she? No matter what. She didn't need Piers. He'd only expect . . . well, more than she could give.

But it was done. She'd given him a key to the house. She hadn't meant to do so. She would have to make that clear at some point. Meanwhile, she supposed he could make himself useful, if he could prise himself away from his paints and his women for a while.

Mrs Tarring looked up as Bea walked in. 'I've remembered the name of the detective inspector who's dealing with Owen's death. Actually it's a woman. I'm trying to track her down at the moment, but it's a Sunday and I've had no luck so far. You're right. It's good to be doing something.'

'Excellent. Magda's working on another line of enquiry.'

Mrs Tarring swivelled round in her chair. 'Lucas has been missing for a day now. Ought we not to inform the police?'

'If he's any sense,' said Bea, leaving the room, 'he'll have left the country!'

'What!' Mrs Tarring couldn't take a joke on the subject, could she?

Before Bea could say anything else, someone rang the doorbell upstairs. Even as Bea started back up the stairs, Piers let himself in to the house . . .

. . . and, would you believe it, the alarm went off again!

Bea tried the code. Once. Twice. She screamed.

The alarm screamed back. And then, just as suddenly as it had started, the noise stopped. 'Thank God for that.'

'Are you all right?' Piers grabbed her upper arms and checked her over for signs of wear and tear.

'Yes, of course I am. Don't be silly.' But she was trembling. Shock. Anger. His proximity. His warmth. His strength.

He said, 'You're wound up so tightly you'll spin off into outer space if you're not careful.'

She tried to relax. Tried to smile. 'Yes, I know. I'm worried sick. Do you know what Bernice has done now? She didn't like sailing after all and decided to come back to town by herself. She found a nice woman to look after her on the ferry, who has promised to put her on the right train to London.'

'How old is she?'

'Old enough to know better. I know. It's got to me, rather. What's more, the Rycrofts have got themselves into the most dreadful mess. Can you spare the time to make some phone calls for me?'

'Lead on.'

She led the way down to the agency rooms, and into the room in which Mrs Tarring was working. 'You remember my friend Piers? He's come to help us, too. Piers, Mrs Tarring is helping us sort out which police force is dealing with which Rycroft death.'

Piers gave Bea a long, narrow-eyed look. And then he smiled at Mrs Tarring. 'Difficult circumstances. How are you coping?'

Mrs Tarring said, 'Oh, well. Yes, it is awful, isn't it?' And yes, the woman preened.

Bea reflected that there was no use getting at Piers for

flirting. He didn't mean it. It was something in the water. Charisma. Call it what you like. He didn't do it on purpose.

'What can I do to help?' he said.

Bea took him into her own office. 'There's a phone. Mrs Tarring is dealing with the police, so could you start ringing round the hospitals to see which Rycroft is where and whether or not they are likely to survive? Kent was taken to Hammersmith, possibly under the name of Lucas Rycroft, though that should have been corrected by now because Mrs Tarring, Magda and Shirley visited him there yesterday. The hospital wouldn't give Mrs Tarring any details when she rang this morning because she's not a relative. Can you say you're his cousin, or ringing for the Rycroft family trust? And then, it's possible that Tweedledum and Tweedledee were also taken there. I did give the name of Rycroft for them. I have no idea what their Christian names are, though "Christian" is hardly what I'd call either of them. One of them looked to me as if he were dying, but he might have survived and—'

Piers slid into her chair and reached for the phone. 'Who knows their real names? Mrs Tarring?'

'I'll ask her.' Bea scooted back next door to interrupt Mrs Tarring on the phone. 'What are the twins' real names?'

'Er . . .' For a moment Mrs Tarring was at a loss. 'Everyone always calls them . . . no, I do know!' She slapped her forehead. 'Tony and Timmy.'

Bea shot back to her office. Piers was already on the phone, nodding and taking notes. He was writing on the back of the interview sheets she'd been using yesterday. Oh well, so long as they didn't get filed under 'Forget this one!'

She said, 'Tweedledum and Tweedledee are really called Tony and Tim. Anthony and Timothy, I suppose.'

Piers suspended operations on the phone. 'Bad news. Kent didn't make it. They have him down as Lucas Kent Rycroft. There'll have to be an autopsy.'

'Oh dear. Yes, of course.'

Bea skidded back to Mrs Tarring, who was frowning and talking into the phone. 'Look, can't you just tell me who . . .? Yes, I understand. But it really is important.' And then, looking up at Bea, 'Yes?'

'Bad news. I'm so sorry, but Kent didn't make it.'

Mrs Tarring dropped the phone on the desk. She blinked once, and then again. Her shoulders heaved, and she reached into a pocket for a hankie. The phone made a quacking noise. She pushed it aside. She couldn't deal with it. Not yet.

Bea was annoyed with herself for breaking the news so baldly. She picked up the phone and said, 'Who am I speaking to?' But the line died. Someone considered their time was too important to waste, hanging around.

'Sorry,' said Mrs Tarring, blowing her nose. 'I suppose I half expected it, but . . . oh dear. Kent was such a good person to work for. So efficient. A bit distant at times since his son died, but fundamentally kind. And so soon after . . .' She shook her head, finding words useless to express her sorrow.

'I'm sorry,' Bea said. Really, that was all you could say.

Mrs Tarring said, indistinctly, round her hankie, 'It is all too much.' She wept. 'I can't be expected to cope. There's too much going on. Too many deaths. I don't understand any of it. It can't just be a coincidence that everyone's dying. Can it?'

'No, it can't. I suggest that you try to contact the trust's solicitor and break the bad news to him. Even if he's out of town, you must have a mobile number for him, yes? Good.'

Mrs Tarring put her hankie away. 'You're right. I must get on with the job. I'll allow myself to cry later. Oh, and I've just thought: can you find the Rycrofts another housekeeper for the London house? And we'll need to get hold of a security guard firm, too. Someone will have to live in until we can make a permanent appointment. The house cannot be left unoccupied.'

'I'll see to it tomorrow,' said Bea.

Mrs Tarring cleared her throat and picked up the phone again. Mrs Tarring could be trusted to get on with the task Bea had set her.

Bea checked next door with Piers. He waved a pencil at her. 'Bingo! Charing Cross Hospital has one dead and one live Rycroft. I assume they were the unpleasant duo who wrecked my studio, rendered me homeless and afterwards paid a visit to you. Have we any idea yet which police force is dealing with which incident?'

'Mrs Tarring is onto it. Where did you say the police took you after you found Kent?'

'Ealing Police Station. And then they dumped me at Ealing Hospital. I haven't a clue who's in charge there. Sorry. I wasn't exactly firing on all cylinders.'

'Mrs Tarring will find out. Meanwhile, can you discover where Lord Rycroft's body was taken? A mortuary in Oxford, I assume. There's going to be a post mortem, so I suppose he'll be there for a while. Mrs Tarring is trying to raise the trust's solicitor to help her deal with what's happening.'

She went next door. Mrs Tarring was on the phone, taking notes.

'Any news of the solicitor?'

'I've left a message on his mobile phone, which is switched off at present. He's probably out on the golf course somewhere. It's the weekend, you see. He'll ring back when he can, I'm sure. Meanwhile, I'll get back to tracing who is looking into the attack on Kent.'

Bea left her to it and charged up the stairs, slowing down as she reached the hall. Were the stairs steeper than they used to be or, perish the thought, was she getting tired? All this dashing about! She wasn't as young as she had been.

Magda was sitting with her knees together, her hands folded in her lap, and her head bent.

Bea pulled up sharply. Was Magda praying?

Magda heard Bea. She looked up, and tried to smile. 'Sorry, I was miles away. Trying to pray, actually. I haven't done that for years. I expect you think it doesn't do any good, but it seemed appropriate.'

'Yes,' said Bea, 'I pray, too. You've found out where Lucas is?'

'I think he's at his club, though they won't admit it. I left a message and a password. "Lapis lazuli", the stone that makes that wonderful blue paint.'

Bea picked up Lucas's address book. 'The police will want this. I'm thinking we should make a copy of all the Rycroft family's details before we hand it over to them. In particular we need to know where to find Ferdy, Shirley and Hilary.'

Magda's eyes didn't leave the book. She didn't like it passing out of her hands, did she?

Bea said, 'I'm so sorry. Before I forget, I have some more bad news for you. Kent didn't make it.'

Magda sighed. 'That's a shame. I only met him the once, but I was impressed. Mrs Tarring must be devastated.' She stood up, and ran her fingers through her hair. 'I must look awful.' She held up her hands. 'Look at me. Shaking!'

She was being brave, but she was a bit battered around the edges. It was then that Bea noticed Magda was wearing, not her old-lady-type pink blouse, but a rather becoming short-sleeved top in blue, pink and lilac. And lipstick. Oh-ho! Magda was fast coming out of her shell, wasn't she?

FIFTEEN

'Well,' said Bea, 'there is some good news; one of the Terrible Twins is dead, and the other has survived but is still in hospital.'

Magda nodded. 'Yes, that does make me feel better. But still terrified. Who's next for the chop? Is it me? Was Owen put in my bed as a warning to me not to have anything more to do with the Rycrofts?'

'If it was, you're going to ignore it. Aren't you?'

A shy smile. 'I suppose I am. I'm not going to hide myself away, but it doesn't stop me quaking inside. I just hope that Lucas gets one of my messages. Once I know he's safe, I can walk away and think about the Rycrofts no more.'

Bea hinted, 'Lucas might want to keep you on, no matter what Mrs Tarring says.'

Magda's lips tightened. 'Oh, no. He won't want me around after this. His family goes back to the Conquest, or something. I mean, he's a lovely man, and I've so much enjoyed working for him. When he explains what he's writing, and his research . . .' She shook her head, with a real smile, 'It's so interesting! And he's so kind, you've no idea. When I told him about my father's wanting a special high chair, he researched one for me, and he's even encouraged me to try new dishes out for him to eat, and he was talking about my going to an exhibition with him, something that he's particularly interested in.'

It sounded as if Lucas was taking an interest in more than an exhibition. It sounded to Bea as if he were coming out of a long period of non-interest in women – probably caused by his sister-in-law's messing up the family big time – and had begun to find Magda as interesting as she found him. Not only had he talked to her about his work and taken it upon himself to help find her father a suitable chair, but he'd also watched television with her.

Magda said, 'I know that nothing can come of it. Mrs Abbot, promise me you'll find someone good to be his next housekeeper?'

What could Bea say, except, 'Yes, of course.' Then her own worries drifted up to the surface. She said, 'I'm sorry if I've been a bit sharp. I have a young ward. She's at boarding school. She was supposed to spend the weekend with friends in the country, but she walked out on them and is making her way back to London all by herself. I must say I'm imagining all sorts of horrors.'

Oh, Bernice, am I going to take you apart when you get back here?

Magda said, 'Oh, that's terrible. You've been so good, helping us while you must be wishing us anywhere else but here.'

What excellent manners Magda had.

Bea said, 'If you've finished up here, would you like to join us downstairs? I'm going to try to work out a timeline of who did what, and to whom.'

So downstairs Bea and Magda went. Bea asked the others to join her in the main agency room, to see if they could sort out exactly what had been happening. They pushed a couple of desks together and settled around them.

Piers said, 'I've got this and that. And some thoughts which may be quite irrelevant. I haven't covered all the hospitals yet, but I think I've found out where most of the bodies lie.'

Mrs Tarring said, 'I'm nowhere through getting all the information about which police forces are dealing with which incident, but I have got some of it.'

Bea nodded. 'Then let's start by constructing a timetable of events, leaving lots of space around it, which we can fill in with our thoughts and whatever data we can find.'

Magda smiled politely but her thoughts were clearly elsewhere.

Bea found some sheets of A3 paper and handed out big pens to everyone.

Mrs Tarring was dubious. 'Wouldn't it be better to have a spreadsheet on the computer?'

Bea said, 'We'll transfer all the information we get onto the computer, once we've worked out some kind of timeline. Let's start by writing down who was attacked, in what order, if possible, with place and time. We'll put down everything we know about each incident. We'll start a second column for which hospital they were taken to, and what happened to them there. And lastly, we'll fill in which police force is dealing with each incident, preferably with contact names and numbers. Right?'

'I get it,' said Piers. 'We are the command centre for all information.'

Mrs Tarring gave him A Look. Such frivolity did not accord with her more serious view of life. 'I still think it would be easier on a computer.'

'Yes,' said Bea, 'but not when we have four people inputting data at once. We need something larger than a computer screen for this. Let's tape sheets of A3 together and work on them. Now, the first victim must be Owen. Do we all agree on that? Yes?'

'No,' said Magda. 'At least . . . I may be speaking out of turn, and what do I know about it, but do you want to consider the death of Kent's only son? I never met him, of course, but I do remember Lucas going to the funeral. A hit and run, wasn't it? Some time ago?'

'Irrelevant,' said Mrs Tarring.

Bea agreed. 'Possibly irrelevant, but let's include him down for the moment. He died three months ago, wasn't it? Which would be some time after Owen arrived and caused chaos?'

'Well, yes.' Mrs Tarring pinched in her lips. 'But you can't seriously believe that Owen killed Ellis. That's ridiculous.'

Piers was easy. 'Let's put him down in brackets as being a possible victim.'

Mrs Tarring would have objected, but Bea said, 'Go for it, Piers.' And he did. Then he wrote down Owen's name. 'There was some doubt as to his parentage, if we can trust the gossipmongers. Do we know whose son he really was?'

Mrs Tarring said, 'He was Lord Rycroft's. He had his birth certificate stating that his father was Lord Rycroft.'

'Not necessarily proof that he was,' said Piers.

Mrs Tarring bridled. 'How dare you!'

Bea said, hastily, 'Well, leave that for the moment. Piers, put his name down next. According to what we observed, he was probably killed – we don't know where – sometime on Friday. But he wasn't put into Magda's bed till the Saturday morning while she and Lucas were out of the house.'

'Weird,' said Piers. 'I mean, that's like two crimes. Killing him is one thing, but putting him in Magda's bed is another. That speaks of a personal grudge. Who would dislike Magda enough to do that to her?'

Magda started on hearing her name, and looked around as if to wonder where she was.

Mrs Tarring was magisterial. She even bestowed a look of approbation on Magda. 'In my opinion, Magda has a pleasant personality and, as far as I know, hasn't quarrelled with anyone. Not even with Owen. Magda, you never met Owen, did you?'

Magda shook her head. 'Not till I found him in my bed.'

'Which means,' said Bea, 'that that placement was really aimed at Lucas. Agreed? Let's get on with making the chart. Who murdered Owen? Any ideas?'

Mrs Tarring looked grim. 'Everyone. No one. Take your pick. He'd upset everyone, in and out of the office. Except for his father, that is. Lord Rycroft thought he could do no wrong.'

Bea wondered, 'Do you think we should include the removal of the jewels from the bank in our chart? That's a crime in itself . . . or is it? Mrs Tarring, do you agree with me that it must have been Owen who'd plotted to get the family jewels out of the bank?'

'Well, it wasn't Kent. Why would he do that? He could get them out any time he liked. And it wasn't Lord Rycroft, for the same reason.'

'Besides which,' said Bea, 'neither of them would need to use Lucas to do the deed for them. Whoever organized that caper selected Lucas to take the blame. They thought he would be too stupid to query an order on official notepaper. And there they made a mistake.'

Piers said, 'But why would Owen do it?'

'He wanted to get Lucas into trouble,' said Bea. 'Why? It's only a guess, but I think it might have been because Lucas wasn't afraid of him. Lucas ignored him, and Owen didn't like that. If everything had gone to plan and Lucas had taken the jewels out of the bank using forged papers, Owen could have screamed to the police that Lucas had stolen the jewels. And there they would be, in Lucas's possession. Mrs Tarring, can you think of any other reason why Owen might want to incriminate Lucas? There wasn't any bad blood between them . . . or was there?'

'Well, I suppose . . . though it's a poor reason, but Owen wasn't happy with his new flat. He'd liked it at first, but when he realized that Lucas's flat was so much larger and brighter, he wanted them to swap. Lucas didn't make a fuss; he just said he wasn't moving. So I suppose it is possible that Owen thought up that ploy with the jewels to bring Lucas down. And another thing, Lucas put in a good word for the girl Owen had got sacked. Owen heard about it, and made a lot of rude remarks about Lucas wanting to get into the girl's pants . . . Sorry, but he did! No one believed him. And we all hoped Lucas would never hear about it.'

Bea said, 'Yes, I can see that it would have amused Owen to get Lucas blamed for theft. We know Owen was in and out of the office. He had access to all the paperwork, and to the key of the safety deposit box. What do you suppose he intended to do with the jewels?'

Mrs Tarring was finding all this difficult. She didn't really have a flexible mind, did she? Or was hindered by her loyalty to the family name? She hesitated. 'He might not want to do anything with them except frame Lucas for their theft. I'm sorry to say, he did bear grudges. He spent a lot of time trying to get back at anyone he thought had injured him. Even if it was unintentional. He came in one day raving about someone who'd pushed past him in a queue at the bank, and how he had taken the number of their car and was going to follow them home and do them an injury. Kent tried to calm him down, but then he turned on Kent for not backing him up and, oh . . . he was a difficult man to deal with.'

Piers said, 'Sounds to me like he had an inferiority complex. He knew he wasn't measuring up to the Rycroft image, and so wanted to pull everyone else down to his level.'

Bea mused, 'Someone must have found out what Owen was planning to do. How did they find out, do you think? I mean, Owen was dead by the time Lucas went to the bank.'

No one knew the answer to that one. Bea thought of bugs placed beside telephones. Who was it who had been listening in on Lucas's phone conversations? Not Owen, who was dead by that time. Who could it have been?

Piers said, 'It would be interesting to know for certain where Owen was killed and when. Any ideas?'

Mrs Tarring said, 'How could we possibly know where he was killed?'

'That's easy,' said Bea. 'He was killed in his new flat, which was directly under Lucas's. All the killer had to do was wait for Lucas and Magda to go out for the day, and pop the corpse up the stairs.'

Everyone nodded. Piers said, 'Do the police know that he lived under the shop?'

Mrs Tarring made a note. 'I'll check.'

Magda stood up. 'I'm sorry, but I'm finding this all very difficult. I can't really contribute to what you're doing. Would anyone like a cup of coffee, or shall I rustle up some lunch for us all?'

And then she can be close to the phone upstairs if it rings . . .

'Bless you, my dear,' said Bea. 'More coffee would be good. And how about some cheese and salad stuffs for lunch? It's all in the fridge in the kitchen.'

Magda went off, taking the stairs at a run.

Piers put down his pen. 'I've put "Removal of jewels!" straight after Owen's death. We don't know what time Owen was killed, though we think it was on Friday, but we can estimate times for Saturday morning.'

Bea said, 'Magda said she and Lucas went to the bank about half nine. Then on to the studio about ten or ten fifteen.'

Piers wrote that in. 'The next victims were me and Magda. But at least we know who did that. The Terrible Twins roughed us up, knocked me out, wrecked the place, and departed. I'm writing down . . . eleven o'clock, twins visit studio, tear the place apart. Eleven twenty to half past, the twins leave. I return to consciousness. Magda leaves to come here and I go in search of Lucas, whom I don't find. I'm back at the studio about noon. Where did the twins go after they left the studio?'

Bea said, 'Yes, let's follow their trail. They told me they drove around looking for Magda. First they tried Lucas's place, where they failed to gain entry because they hadn't got any keys. Then they tried the office, which was all locked up for the weekend and finally came back here. I believed them when they said they couldn't get in to Lucas's place and I don't think they were responsible for stealing Lucas's collection of jade. They were still after Magda and the jewels at that point. Besides, their method of searching is destruction, and Lucas's place was tossed but not destroyed.'

Piers said, 'You've got a point there.'

Bea said, 'Their second visit to me ended in tragi-comedy. They had found a bottle of something to drink, which had been placed by someone unknown in their open-topped car, and by the time they arrived here they were in some distress. Several people have assumed that it was the twins who assaulted Kent, but I don't think they did. In the first place, they admitted roughing up Piers but didn't mention harming Kent. And I don't think they had time to return to the studio and attack Kent before making their return visit to me at noon.'

'It would have been close, almost impossible for them to have done that. And, why should they return to the studio? It makes no sense. I'd gone to the barber's, drawn a blank there and was back at the studio about the same time the twins reached you. And that's when I found Kent on the floor.'

'So, who did Kent in? It happened between the time you left at eleven twenty or half past eleven, and what . . . about noon?' Bea frowned down at the chart. 'And who knew that the jewels had been taken from the bank? Apart from Kent and Lord Rycroft.'

Mrs Tarring lowered her head.

Why? Why was the woman not taking part in this discussion? What did she know that she wasn't prepared to tell us? There was something the twins had said. They'd referred to a woman whom they had failed to contact. They'd called her not by her name, but by a nickname . . . 'Herself'. There were

*only two women involved in this affair, weren't there? Or three,
if you counted Magda. Mrs Tarring, Shirley, Magda. Eeeny
meeny miney mo.*

Piers said, 'Yes, how *did* the twins get to know the jewels
had been removed from the bank? Do you suppose it was they
who planned it, and not Owen?' He answered his own question. 'No. If they had planned it, they wouldn't have been able
to get the necessary paperwork and the key from the office.'

Bea watched Mrs Tarring play with her pen. 'Unless they
had an accomplice?'

'Ridiculous,' said Mrs Tarring. Half-heartedly.

Piers said, 'On the other hand, do you think the twins organized the bugging of Lucas's phone? Do you think they might
have done Kent's as well? Is that their style? Again; no. I
wouldn't have thought so.' He threw down his pen. 'Is some
madman going around knocking off anyone with the name of
Rycroft? And why? And now we come to the next question;
who poisoned the twins? At least, we assume it was poison?
One of them died, remember. So who had it in for them?'

'What's more,' said Bea, 'who arranged for Lord Rycroft
to die? Or was that really just an accident?'

Mrs Tarring cleared her throat. 'No, I'm sure that was just
an accident. He was a terrible driver, you know, and if he was
on his phone coming down a hill too fast . . . well, what can
you expect? Of course the police will look into the question,
but I'm sure there's nothing in it. Let me fill you in on which
police force seems to have been in attendance, and who we
have to contact there. Now, the police force dealing with Owen
. . . I have the details here somewhere.'

Bea watched Mrs Tarring at work, her lips tight, her eyes
on what she was writing.

The chart showed . . . something. Something that Mrs Tarring
didn't want to talk about? Bea ran her eyes down the timetable
again. She said, 'I'll just pop upstairs and check timings with
Magda.'

Bea went up the stairs and was passing the door to the
living room, when her landline rang. She saw Magda elbow
deep in salad stuffs. When she heard the phone, Magda
dropped her knife and dived to wash her hands at the sink

. . . which meant that Bea got to the landline first. She answered with her number.

'May I ask, do you have a password for me?' A deep voice. A man's. Lucas?

'Lapis lazuli,' said Bea. 'Are you all right?' *Silly question!*

'Perfectly. Is Miss Summerleys with you, and is she safe?'

'Yes, to both.' *He's going to ask about the jewellery next.*

'Good. I was concerned. May I ask who I am speaking to?'

'Bea Abbot. The head of the agency that arranged Mrs Tarring's and Miss Summerleys's jobs with the Rycroft Foundation. They are both here with me, and we are trying to work out what's been happening. Would you care to join us?'

His formality was beginning to affect her.

'If it would not be too much trouble. I would like to assure myself that Miss Summerleys has not suffered unduly from recent events.'

If Bea had a weakness, it was a desire to laugh hysterically at inappropriate moments. Lucas was too Old School for words! How Piers would appreciate the man! She suppressed her giggles as she gave her address, but couldn't resist adding, 'You are welcome to join us for a light luncheon, if you wish.'

'Thank you. That would be delightful.'

He rang off.

Magda hovered in the doorway, eyes shining with hope. 'Was that . . .?'

'It was. And he was most concerned about you. What's more, he didn't even ask about the jewellery.'

'No, well; he'd know I would look after it for him.' She ran her fingers back through her hair, coaxing it into a becoming frame for her face. 'I must look a sight.'

'You look great.' And indeed, with a little colour in her cheeks and her hair loose, Magda did indeed look fine. A little hope and a little lipstick had transformed her.

Magda went into housekeeper mode. 'He'll be hungry. Shall I make some soup for lunch as well? Or a fresh fruit salad for afters?'

'As you please,' said Bea. 'But while you're doing that, can you go over the timings for yesterday morning with me again? Starting with the interruption at breakfast time.'

Magda threw the ingredients for a mushroom soup together while she recapped on everything she could remember. Bea made notes. When she'd finished, Bea stroked her cheek with her pen.

'Mm. Magda, how did the twins know that Lucas was going to be at the studio?'

'I don't know. From the bug they'd placed under Lucas's desk? Except that we thought it must be the man from the office – Ferdy – who did that, didn't we? I don't think the twins had ever been to Lucas's place at all. I mean, he didn't care for them.'

'It's clear that anyone who had access to the office could get hold of keys to all the Rycroft homes, but the twins didn't, did they?'

'I really don't know. I was only there that once for my interview.'

'Do you think the twins took the jade?'

Magda thought about it. And shook her head. 'Now why don't I think they did? They've stolen other stuff, according to Mrs Tarring.' She paused while stirring the soup. 'I think, maybe . . . the twins smash and bash everywhere they go, don't they? But though I know someone searched Lucas's place, they didn't do any real damage, did they? Does that make sense?'

'Yes, my dear; it does. So who stole the jade?'

'I really don't know.'

Bea could see that she really didn't.

Mrs Tarring knew, didn't she? Or guessed.

And didn't want to say.

Why?

Bea went back down the stairs, to hear Piers muttering to himself, 'There's not enough time. Not nearly enough time.'

Bea gave them the new timings she'd got from Magda, and Piers conscientiously wrote them down. It was a case of five minutes here or there. There wasn't much in it.

Piers's frown was pronounced. He threw his pen down. 'Look, I don't care what you think. I'm convinced there's more than one person at work here. One person can't have been responsible for so many deaths, poisonings and assaults,

all so close together. The first one – Owen's – was on
Friday. All right. But there were three more on Saturday
morning; Lord Rycroft and his son Kent, plus one of the twins.
You can say that Lord Rycroft's death was an accident and
perhaps it was. Let's take that death out of the equation. That
leaves two more deaths – Kent's and one of the twins – to be
explained away. Plus, Owen's body had to be disposed of
during Saturday morning. It's just not possible that one person
could have done all that. The only question is, was it two
people acting together, or three?'

'What a ridiculous idea!' Mrs Tarring glared at Piers.
Mrs Tarring sounded so sure. Mrs Tarring knew something
that they didn't.

Following that train of thought, Bea said again, 'Who profits
from these deaths?'

Mrs Tarring lifted her hands in helpless fashion. 'No one
does, really. Death duties will be paid by the trust. All the
accommodation was held in the name of the Rycroft Trust
and allocated to each Rycroft at a peppercorn rent. Yes,
each one was given a hefty allowance for living expenses
and yes, there's more in the pot to share out now that
some members have died, but . . . surely this is not about
money!'

Bea said, 'Is it about revenge? I can understand why
Owen might have been killed. He was an obnoxious little
toad, according to everything I've heard. And the Terrible
Twins may well have made some enemies, the way they
carry on, but . . . Kent? And Lord Rycroft? Why were
they killed?'

'I am sure that Lord Rycroft's death was an accident,' said
Mrs Tarring, 'and perhaps whoever hit Kent didn't mean to
kill him, but just to knock him out—'

'With my iron cockerel doorstop?' said Piers. 'You don't
use a weapon if you're accustomed to using your fists. One
of the twins knocked me out with a single blow from his right
fist, but the cockerel was a weapon picked up and used by a
different sort of person, don't you think?'

Bea drew a box in one corner, and entered three names in
it. 'Any advance on those three for Villain of the Week?'

Piers looked over her shoulder. 'Shirley, Hilary and Ferdinand?'

'Ridiculous!' said Mrs Tarring, showing signs of temper. 'Ferdy wouldn't! That is just so . . .'

Piers put the point of his pen on Hilary's name. 'Who is he, then? Or is it a she?'

'A he,' said Bea. 'A distant cousin who has a bad temper. And was threatened with all sorts by Owen. And yes, I think he's been caught up in the family feud. Don't you think so, Mrs Tarring?'

Mrs Tarring was distracted. 'Impossible! I wish we could all go back in time and find that none of this has happened.'

Bea was gentle. 'You don't really wish that Owen was still alive, do you? Remember how he threatened your job?'

'Yes, but . . . Lord Rycroft wouldn't have allowed him to . . . it wouldn't have come to anything.'

'Lord Rycroft thought the sun shone out of Owen's behind, didn't he? Lord Rycroft didn't lift a finger when Owen wanted the girl in the office sacked, did he? And I think Owen is the likeliest candidate to have arranged the removal of the jewellery from the bank. That way he'd be getting back at other members of the family as well, wouldn't he? He meant to tangle Kent and Lucas in his scheme . . . right?'

'I don't know. I don't know!'

Bea sank back in her chair. 'I agree, nothing can be proved. We can only guess about all sorts of things. We know that people have died, but we don't know why or who killed them. We don't even know whether one or two of the deaths were accidents. We have pieces of information here and there, but we don't know how to join them together.'

'A patchwork quilt,' said Piers, looking pleased with himself. 'It's made of all different shapes and sizes and pieces of material but, when stitched together, it can keep you beautifully warm at night. I had one once, years ago. I wonder what became of it.'

Bea ignored that. 'Mrs Tarring, I know all this is very painful for you. You've worked for the family for so long, and you have strong feelings of loyalty to them. But I have a horrid feeling that if we don't work together, there will be yet more deaths. What is it you know that you are not telling us?'

Mrs Tarring looked as if she were on the verge of tears. 'Nothing!'

The doorbell sounded on the floor above.

Mrs Tarring started. 'Who is that?'

Bea said, 'Enter Lucas Rycroft, stage left. At least, I hope so.'

SIXTEEN

Sunday lunchtime

Bea ran up the stairs, expecting that Magda would get to the front door first, but the girl was still fussing in the kitchen by the time Bea let Lucas into the hall.

He was not what she'd expected.

For one thing, he was a big man; not fat, but big-boned, well over six foot tall and broad-shouldered. He was a striking-looking Viking type, not young but in his prime. He was not handsome, for he had an eagle's beak of a nose. He was clean-shaven, with plentiful long fair hair going grey, well-brushed and swept back into an elastic band at the nape of his neck. He was wearing a caramel-coloured suit of some light material over a good white shirt, no tie. Pricey, and becoming, even if not entirely appropriate under present circumstances. Bea had somehow expected him to be wearing some kind of mourning, until she realized he'd probably not been able to change his clothes since he'd left home yesterday morning.

And, he had a presence.

He inclined his head to Bea. 'Mrs Abbot, I presume?'

He extended his hand, and she shook it.

'Oh, Lucas! Are you all right? I've been so worried about you!' Magda flew into the hall from the kitchen, arms reaching up to touch him . . . until she remembered just in time that she was only his housekeeper. She stopped short within six feet of him. And blushed, painfully. 'I'm sorry. Mr Rycroft, I mean.'

Startled, Lucas's eyes widened . . . and then narrowed. He had heavy-lidded eyes, which were steel grey.

Oh. So Magda didn't usually call her employer by his Christian name? And he thinks of her as 'Miss Summerleys'.

Bea, who liked Magda, covered the girl's confusion, saying,

'As you can see, Magda's been badly shaken. The bruises the Terrible Twins inflicted on her are awful. They tortured her but she didn't tell them anything. She's a brave girl, and hasn't let them prevent her from preparing a nice lunch for us all.'

'Tortured her?' He looked from Bea to Magda. 'They hurt you?'

Magda put her arms behind her and blushed. 'It was nothing, Mr Rycroft. And they got nothing out of me.'

Lucas switched his eyes back to Bea. And nodded. He was a man of some intelligence, for he had received and understood Bea's message. He said, 'I am so sorry, Miss Summerleys. Or, under the circumstances, may I now call you "Magda"?'

Mrs Tarring appeared at the head of the stairs. 'Not "Mr Rycroft", Magda.'

'Not . . .?' said Bea.

Mrs Tarring's eyes were on Lucas. 'I am so sorry for your losses, my lord.'

Everyone switched eyes to Lucas, who inclined his head. 'Thank you, Mrs Tarring. I fear it will take me some time to get used to my new name.'

'What . . .?' said Magda.

Piers appeared behind Mrs Tarring. Grinning. He said, 'I've got it. Lucas's elder brother was Lord Rycroft. When he died, the title would normally have passed to his sons or his grandson, but they're dead, too. So, as Lucas is the next eldest, he becomes Lord Rycroft.'

'Oh!' cried Magda, and reached out for the wall to steady herself.

Lord Rycroft said, 'Under present circumstances, I think we can dispense with formality, don't you? "Lucas" it is. Thank you, Mrs Tarring. And,' to Piers, 'you are the artist I was supposed to meet yesterday? I see you've suffered some bruising, too. Was that also at the hands of my cousins?'

'Yes, it was,' said Bea. 'This is Piers, who happens to be my ex-husband. The twins wrecked his studio so he's had to find other accommodation. He's been trying to help us sort out who's behind the deaths in your family.'

Piers extended his hand to Lucas, giving him the once-over as he did so. 'Yes, I shall enjoy painting you.'

'When this is over.' Lucas had his priorities right.

Mrs Tarring was on edge. 'May I ask where you've been, my lord? We haven't known what to do, or where to turn. So many deaths! So many decisions have to be made! If you'd only kept in touch . . .!'

'Lunch is ready, I believe,' said Bea. 'Let's eat first and catch up afterwards.'

Magda was carefully not looking at Lucas. 'I haven't had time to lay the table for us in the big room.'

Bea was quick to scotch the notion of such formality. 'Let's grab a knife and fork each, take everything into the big room, and help ourselves. I'm dying to find out what's been going on.'

'Splendid,' said Lucas. 'Show me what to do.' He'd probably never had to set a table in his life before, but he was giving it a good try.

Bea rolled her eyes at Piers and he rolled his back. Mrs Tarring fussed about washing her hands before she ate, while Magda took her blushes to the stove to serve up bowls of her home-made soup.

Bea removed Winston the cat from the central unit, and set him down outside the back door before transferring bowls of soup to a tray. 'Don't let that cat fool you. He's been well fed already today but can't resist trying his charms on newcomers.' She grabbed salt and pepper and a bundle of cutlery to take through to the big room.

'I like cats,' said Lucas, to the surprise of all concerned. He took the tray off Magda. 'This way, is it? My brother Nicholas was allergic to cats, so we couldn't have them at home. I've always thought I'd like one to sit on my lap in my old age.'

As a conversation stopper, it scored high. Mrs Tarring and Magda gaped. Piers's eyebrows rose.

Bea threw some place mats on the table as she suppressed a giggle. She realized Lucas was trying to be sociable, and said hastily, 'Winston adopted me, rather than the other way round. He knows a sucker when he sees one. Now, grab a chair, everyone, and let's get down to it.'

'Excellent,' said Lucas, taking the carver and automatically becoming the Head of the Table. Magda hovered, holding a dish of hot rolls. Lucas pulled out a chair for her to sit at his right-hand side. Mrs Tarring inserted herself into a chair opposite Lucas. Bea thought the woman was being unusually quiet. Perhaps she was only too happy to have someone make decisions again?

Bea dispensed paper napkins, wondering where on earth her linen ones had gone. She hadn't thought of using the good linen ones for years, not since her dear second husband had passed away. She noticed with some amusement that Piers had pushed aside his plate of soup, and was busying himself sketching Lucas in his notebook.

She reached over to Piers and lifted the pencil out of his hand. 'Eat first. Indulge yourself afterwards.' She checked that everyone was into their soup, which they were. 'And now, my lord? What has been happening to you?'

'Where do you want me to start? I suspect with Owen. In case you've heard that there were doubts on the matter, he was indeed my elder brother George's son. When he first arrived in this country, he amused himself trying to set my brother George and me at odds.'

Bea prompted him. 'And . . .?'

He focused on her, then looked at everyone around the table. 'I suppose that now is as good a time as any to speak about it. There was a long gap between my elder brother George and myself. Our mother had several miscarriages before producing me and, finally, Nicholas. George fulfilled his duties to the family by marrying young and producing a son while I was still at school. I was slow-witted, a daydreamer, an introvert, hiding behind books while my younger brother, Nicholas, grew up like George, enjoying life; he was athletic and popular. Nicholas married a girl from a suitable family and produced twin boys by the time that George's first marriage met a tragic end; she contracted diphtheria and died young. Eventually George met Melisande and there was a whirlwind romance. She was exquisite. Pictures of her don't do her justice. And she seemed to find my company agreeable. I was flattered. And yes, I fell for her. I'd never met anyone like her before. Never will again.'

Magda's head drooped.

Did he notice? Yes, perhaps he did.

He said, 'She was ambitious. Amoral. I couldn't see it at the time, but . . .' A heavy sigh. 'After a while she began to confide in me how unhappy she was with my brother. She said he didn't understand her. She loved to have men competing for her attention. She used me to make George jealous. She told me, she swore to me . . . well, it was all lies, of course, but I believed her when she said she was going to divorce George and marry me. And so, yes, we ended up in bed for the whole of one weekend. George found us there and there was a terrible row. I was ashamed of myself, and yet I still wanted her . . . it was a bad situation.

'George took her away with him. I didn't speak to him for months afterwards, but we made up after she left George and moved in with Nicholas. She only stayed with him for a short time though, until his wife threw her out. And then, it was one humiliation after another. She went off with another man, he was found dead; there was a trial, all very messy. George paid her off in return for a divorce and she left for Australia with her baby. It was a dreadful time. Every day there was another story in the press. Mostly inaccurate, but hurtful.'

He sighed. 'We survived, but the episode left its mark. George became paranoid about gossip, I dedicated my life to art and Nicholas went to the dogs. Quite literally. He spent all his days at one racecourse or another. Nothing much changed over the years till Owen arrived, claiming his right to a seat in the sun. Like his mother, he tried playing us all off against one another, declaring one week that George was his father, and the next that I or Nicholas had sired him. I refused to play his little game so he turned on me, vowing all sorts of nonsense to which I paid no attention at the time. Afterwards, I thought over what he'd said and began to think he was right, and that I had turned into a human fossil. He did me a favour because he jolted me out of the rut I'd been in.'

Bea said, 'Let's be clear about this. Someone did take steps to discover whose son he really was?'

'Correct. You must understand that Nicholas, our younger brother, had died by this time. George asked me to arrange for tests to be made, and they were conclusive. Owen was indeed George's son. I must admit I was somewhat relieved to learn that it was so. But his words had set me thinking that I might well have been missing out by cutting myself off from society, so . . .' He fiddled with his glasses and looked self-conscious, 'I took a colleague's advice and for the last couple of months I've been seeing a counsellor once a week on Thursday afternoons.'

'Oh!' Magda drew back in her chair, her eyes wide.

Lucas smiled. Just a crack of a smile, but it was interesting to see how it changed his face. He no longer looked autocratic, but almost genial. There was charm there, now.

Lucas said, 'Life opens up, as it were. I suppose I have Owen to thank for that.'

'You know he's dead?' said Bea.

He inclined his head. He knew.

Bea cleared away the soup plates, stacking them on a tray. 'Will someone help me bring in the next course?'

Magda and Mrs Tarring sprang to help her, while Piers went back to his sketches, and Lucas got up to wander around the room, looking at this and that. When Bea brought in a big dish of mixed salads, she found him standing by the window overlooking the garden. He'd put on a pair of glasses to scrutinize the portrait Piers had painted of her second, much-loved husband, Hamilton, who'd died far from home.

Lucas flicked a glance at Bea. 'Your friend Piers painted this? I recognize the hand. His prices have been rising for some years. This is a good example of his work. Strong. The sitter was a "giver" and not a "taker", I assume.'

Unexpectedly Bea felt tears well up. 'That's Hamilton, my second husband. And yes, he was a good man. Piers and I married very young. Too young. We parted company after four years and went our separate ways. Then I met Hamilton, and we had many happy years together before he died. I miss him still.'

'You are good friends now with this Piers? The interaction between the two of you indicates it.'

'Yes. Come back to the table. Cold meats and salad.'

He inclined his head, put away his glasses and returned

to his seat, where Magda helped him to a selection of everything.

Bea was amused to see that Piers had gone back to drawing Lucas, instead of eating. Lucas didn't seem to have noticed. Bea wasn't sure how he'd react to being sketched, so tapped Piers on his arm, saying, 'Perhaps Lucas would like to see the chart we've been working on.'

Piers put aside his pencil with reluctance, but went off to fetch it.

Lucas poked at some salami. 'What is this? Do I like it?'

Magda said, 'Yes, you do. We had some last week, remember?'

Bea smiled to herself. Lucas was eating everything he'd been given. She finished off her own plateful as Piers brought up the unwieldy sheets of paper on which they'd been working. Lucas pushed aside his empty plate and held out his hand for the papers. Piers meekly surrendered the lot.

Bea, Mrs Tarring and Magda hastily cleared away the used plates as Lucas laid the timetable out on the table and, frowning, donned his glasses. He looked through them, blinked, and took them off again. Without a word, Magda took the glasses off him, cleaned them, and put them back in his hand.

Bea noticed he wasn't looking at Magda. And Magda wasn't looking at him. Bea wasn't sure what this meant. Possibly that they were now conscious of each other's presence in a way they hadn't been before?

Lucas studied the paper on which they'd been working. Everyone waited to hear what he'd have to say. Finally he put his finger on the 'box' that Bea had filled in. 'Who wrote this? It's in a different hand from the rest.'

'I wrote those names down,' said Bea. 'It's only a suggestion, but I do wonder if any or all of them are involved in what's been happening. Shall I make some coffee?'

No one seemed interested, so she took the remains of lunch out to the kitchen, helped by Magda, but not by Piers . . . who had gone back to his sketching.

When she returned, she found Lucas still studying the timetable. As she took her seat again, he said, 'Ferdinand, Shirley and Hilary. But not the twins? Why not? You have a good reason?'

Lucas was as dispassionate as a High Court judge, which made Bea nervous. 'You understand that a lot of what is written there is conjecture. Piers has been checking the hospitals to see where the bodies might have ended up, alive or dead. Mrs Tarring hasn't finished yet. She was trying to find out which police force was dealing with which crime.'

'Yes, I see. Thank you, Mrs Tarring.' He really had excellent manners. He took off his glasses, and sat back in his chair. 'Well, I can confirm that much of what you have written here is correct.'

Bea said, 'Owen upset everyone in the family, it seems. The question is, which of you retaliated?'

'Well, it's true that Owen persuaded George that Kent did not respect his father as he ought to do. Owen was always trying to portray Kent in a bad light. He hinted that Kent was trying to rush his father into an early grave, and that he, Owen, was the only one who really cared for him. Unfortunately my brother gave credence to some of the wild tales Owen spread around about Kent. No sooner did Kent disprove one lie than Owen thought up another. But Kent was too well grounded; perhaps I should say, over-confident? He didn't do anything about it for a long time.'

Bea said, 'Owen didn't like anyone very much, did he? We heard that he tried to pick quarrels with everyone, and that the rest of the family wanted you to intervene in the family squabbles.'

'I considered doing so, yes. But I decided there was no point. If my brother chose to make a favourite of his younger son, there was nothing I could do about it. As for the rest of the family, they were appropriately provided for. And I had my own life to lead.'

Did he give a sideways glance at Magda when he said that? Possibly. Hmm.

'Owen couldn't get at you in any way? I heard he coveted your flat for himself?'

A ghost of a smile. 'Owen was a bully, and if you stand up to bullies, they usually cave in. Yes, he tried it on with me, and I told him I was thinking of investigating what he'd been up to in Melbourne before he came to England. I wondered aloud if his past in Australia had, perhaps, not been as pure as driven snow. I said I was sure his father would be interested to know all about it. He assured me he wouldn't mention a swap again.'

'I like it,' said Bea. 'But his defeat over the flat probably made him all the more determined to bring you down.'

'Possibly. But I saw no reason to give in to blackmail, and I did in fact set various enquiries into his past in motion.'

Mrs Tarring said, 'That was well handled, my lord. Even Kent couldn't have done better.' And then, remembering, 'It will probably be you who runs the organization in future, my lord.'

'Only until we find a suitable candidate to take over. No doubt our solicitors will help us find someone appropriate.'

Mrs Tarring persisted, 'There are other Rycrofts. One of them, perhaps, might step up to the challenge?'

Lucas's eyebrows rose, but all he said was, 'We will discuss this some other time.' He collected the eyes of everyone round the table. 'Shall we move on? I see you have already prepared a rough timetable for yesterday morning. You believe Owen was killed on the Friday. I understand the police think so, too, since they asked me to give them my movements for the whole of that day.'

Magda said, 'You've been in touch with the police? You know I can give you an alibi for Friday?'

'Indeed. I informed them of that. Now: this timetable. May I add my tuppence-worth?' Without waiting for their consent, he said, 'On Saturday morning my breakfast was interrupted by a courier bearing a request on the Rycroft Trust paper, for me to remove certain items from the bank. A key was enclosed, together with an authorization. A typed covering note apparently signed by my brother George requested that I retrieve the jewellery from the bank and hand it over to Kent. The rest of the paperwork had been signed by Kent – or so it appeared.'

Bea said, 'You didn't accept this at face value?'

'Certainly not. Since when did Kent involve me in such an errand? I went to my study and rang Kent. As I had suspected, he knew nothing of the matter and had not signed any such papers. His father had not mentioned any such thing to him, either. We concluded that if someone could produce paperwork convincing enough to fool the bank, the jewels were in jeopardy. Even if we destroyed that authorization, a second set of papers could be produced by the swindler to remove the assets on another day when we might not have the opportunity to intercept them. Owen had shown himself to be without shame or morals in pursuing vendettas against various people whom he imagined had slighted him, and we assumed that this was just another of his little plots, which this time was aimed to incriminate myself and Kent. We decided therefore to remove the jewellery from a bank whose details were known to the office and to go together to deposit them in another bank, perhaps under a false name. To keep them safe.'

Bea said, 'What you didn't know was that your phone was bugged and someone was listening in to all your conversations.'

'What!' A long stare at Bea. 'Ah. That explains a lot. I couldn't understand how anyone else should have known what I was doing. Who installed the bug, and who was listening in?'

Bea said, 'We don't know for sure, though we have our suspicions. So you rescued the jewellery, put it in your briefcase, and with Magda took a cab to Piers's place. On the way—'

'Kent rang me. I confirmed I had the gems and that I was on my way to Piers's studio, which is where we had agreed to meet before going on to another bank. Kent said he was uneasy about not letting George know what was happening. He said he would contact him direct and fill him in before meeting me at the studio. I dropped Miss Summerleys, er, Magda, at the artist's place and took the cab on, intending to call at the barber's shop and return. But on the way—'

'George rang you to ask what was going on. He'd had a phone call from Kent while he was at his late breakfast, telling him about the plan to remove the Rycroft jewels from the bank. It threw him into a tizzy because he knew nothing about it. He got into his car and started back to London. And, on the way, he phoned you?'

'Yes. He was furious. Said Owen would never dream of

cheating him and that Kent and I had made this story up to damage the lad's credibility. He demanded we take the jewels back to the bank in which they had been lodged. I refused. He said he wanted a meeting straight away with Owen and Kent and me, at his London address. He said he was going to ring Kent direct and tear him off a strip. He said I should go straight to the London house and wait for him, that he'd be there in an hour or so. He rang off before I could demur. I rang Kent to make sure he knew about the change of venue, but he didn't pick up. I assumed he was out of touch because he was a careful driver and wouldn't take calls when in traffic. I left a voice message for him to ring me.'

Bea said, 'Clearly, Kent didn't get the message about a change of venue. What time had you arranged to meet him at the studio?'

'Eleven. I had planned to visit the barber's first, remember?'

'While you were en route to the barber's and before Kent arrived, the twins arrived at the studio in search of the jewels.'

Lucas said, 'How did they know the jewels had been taken out of the bank, and where they were going to be taken?'

'We know there was a bug under your desk which would tell the listener what you planned to do but . . .' Here Bea stopped to think. 'Did you say, in your breakfast call to Kent, that you planned to take Magda with you to the bank?'

He shook his head. 'No, I didn't. In the heat of the moment I'd forgotten all about the appointment with Piers. It was only when Miss . . . when Magda reminded me that I asked her to come with me.'

'Which means,' said Bea, 'that it wasn't only your phone that was bugged, but also Kent's. You spoke to him in the taxi after leaving the bank, and told him you had Magda with you and that she'd have the jewels with her at the studio. Someone was listening in to that phone call, which you made to Kent's landline, right?'

'There were two bugs? Who placed them?'

'We can't answer for Kent's, but yours was planted, we believe, by a man answering Ferdinand Rycroft's description.'

Mrs Tarring jumped on that. 'Unproven.'

'Ferdinand?' Lucas had trouble taking that in.

'His description matches the man who gained access to your study on a day when you were out. He created a diversion during which he might well have installed a bug and left, saying he'd got the address wrong.'

Lucas looked at Magda, who nodded. 'A slightly built man in brown, with a red waistcoat.'

Lucas tightened his lips. 'I find it hard to believe that the Ferdinand I knew would do such a thing. I've always thought him a poor sort of creature, defeated by life. He hardly raises his eyes from the floor when he speaks. You really think he was able to obtain and place listening bugs in our houses? Why? And how did he acquire such things?'

Bea said, 'I may be wrong, but sometimes worms turn. Owen not only made fun of Ferdinand, but threatened his comfortable lifestyle, and he wasn't the only one who felt that way. Your brother George was besotted with Owen and some members of the family feared that, if Owen had his way, they'd be cut off without a penny. Owen pushed people too far. They tried to get you to intervene; you declined. Some of them started to meet and to talk about what could be done to stop Owen. And that, I think, is where the twins' access to a different lifestyle came in handy. Through their contacts at nightclubs or on the Internet, they acquired pieces of listening equipment so that they could find out what Owen was doing. Perhaps they hoped to entrap him into some unwise comments which they could take to his father as proof that the lad was unworthy of the name of Rycroft.'

Lucas frowned. 'You think they planted bugs indiscriminately?'

'They didn't do it themselves. They got Ferdinand to do it, because he was unobtrusive and could furnish himself with sufficiently good paperwork to gain access to the different Rycroft houses. No one else could do it so easily. Shirley couldn't, because you didn't let her loose in your place. So yes, it was Ferdinand who put a bug under your desk. He got in under false pretences and did the deed without rousing suspicion. I think he also put bugs in Kent's house, and in Owen's flat. That way the conspirators would know exactly what was happening.'

Piers said, 'That's how they knew that Owen was planning

to have Lucas and Kent take the jewels from the bank on false papers, in order to accuse you both of theft.'

Bea continued, 'Fate played into their hands. They knew what Owen planned to do and then, phut! He was out of the picture, but the scam had been started and they saw that they could take it over for themselves. They adapted Owen's plan to divert the jewels into their own hands leaving Lucas and Kent to take the blame.'

Lucas said, 'You think the twins were in on it with Ferdinand?'

'I think they all saw pound signs, but I don't think they acted as one. I think they split in different directions. Take the twins; they saw an opportunity to grab the jewels while they were in your possession. So they turned up at Piers's studio thinking they could somehow bamboozle you and Kent into handing them over. But you weren't there, and neither was Kent. They lost it. They assaulted Piers and tortured Magda . . .'

Lucas dropped his eyes to Magda, whose eyes were on her fingernails. He touched her hand and said, 'I'm sorry.'

Bea continued, 'When the twins had gone, empty handed, Piers left in search of you, my lord, and Magda took refuge here. Only after they'd gone did Kent arrive at the studio to find the place empty. We don't know who he met there, but someone bashed his head in, took his ID and left him there to die.'

Lucas blinked. Slowly. 'Yes. Kent's death is perhaps the very worst of this affair. I was fond of him. He was the best of the family. What a waste. A criminal waste.'

SEVENTEEN

Sunday, early afternoon

Bea said, 'You knew Kent had died?'

'Yes. I'll come to that in a minute.' He narrowed his eyes. 'But if I'm following you correctly, you don't think it was the twins who killed him, because they were otherwise engaged?'

Bea nodded. 'They left the studio only to come here and confront Magda. They didn't find her, but they did find me. I didn't help them, either. So they left to look for Magda at your place. They didn't want to return to the studio because they'd roughed up Piers and thought he would have called in the cops.'

'You think the twins had an accomplice who killed Kent?' He looked down at the paper on the table, homing in on the box in which Bea had written three names. 'One of these three?'

'It's possible,' said Bea, looking hard at Mrs Tarring, who changed colour but made no comment. 'Now, your brother had asked you to abandon your plans for the morning to meet him at the London house. Did you not try to let Piers and Magda know of the change of venue?'

'Of course. No reply to either. I couldn't think what had happened. I was in two minds; I could return to the studio and explain what had happened or meet with George and make my excuses to Piers later. But if I went back to the studio I'd miss my brother and Kent, who should both be approaching the town house at that point. Or so I thought. I arrived at the town house and used my key to let myself in. The Rycroft family papers are housed there and I consult them every now and then so I've always had a key. George didn't mind, especially as he doesn't come up to town for weeks at a time. His housekeeper didn't like me arriving unannounced. She said she hadn't been expecting anyone, that neither George nor Kent had said they were planning to call in. I told her they were on their way and that I'd wait for them.

'I waited and waited. I kept trying to contact someone – Miss Summerleys, Piers, or George. Or Kent. I understood that there'd be no reply to Kent's landline because he'd obviously left home by that time and was on his way to meet me. But my messages to his mobile went to voicemail and he didn't ring back. I noticed the battery on my phone was dying and I hadn't my charger with me so I started using my brother's landline. I couldn't understand why there was no reply to Miss Summerleys's phone. I thought she might have gone home for some reason but when I rang my landline, a stranger answered. I think now that it must have been a policeman, but at the time I thought I must have dialled a wrong number, and put the phone down.'

'The twins smashed my phone,' said Magda. 'And Piers's. We couldn't contact you, and you couldn't contact us.'

'Eventually I thought of trying Mrs Tarring, but she didn't answer her phone, either.'

'By that time,' said Magda, 'we had gone back home only to discover the place had been searched and the jade collection removed.'

He passed his hand across his eyes. 'Yes, that is a blow, though trivial in view of everything else that has happened. The police asked me about that. They thought it might have been an opportunist thief, but . . .' He shook his head. 'Unlikely, I think.'

Magda continued her report. 'Then we found Owen's body. That was it. We had to call the police.'

'After that,' said Mrs Tarring, 'I couldn't take any calls.'

Lucas gave her a long, considering look.

Bea also considered what Mrs Tarring had and had not done. Why hadn't the woman taken Lucas's call earlier? Wasn't there another occasion on which she ought to have been in contact, and hadn't?

Bea said, 'How long did you wait at the London house, my lord?'

'Call me Lucas, please. About an hour and a half. George's

housekeeper brought me a sandwich, but I couldn't settle. My mobile had died. I used George's landline to keep trying everyone at intervals, but no one picked up. I checked with George's housekeeper in the country; she said he'd left ages ago. Finally I left a note for my brother and went home, only to find the police in situ. They were kind enough to inform me that a body had been found in my bed—'

'Not your bed,' said Magda. 'Mine.'

Lucas frowned. 'That's strange. They told me the body was in mine. I was afraid it was you, Miss Summerleys, er, Magda, though I couldn't think why. The police wouldn't let me in further than the hall. They knew nothing, would tell me nothing. At first I refused to cooperate until I knew what had happened to you. I kept asking, was it your body in my bed? It was a total nightmare. Finally they told me it was a man and that my housekeeper and a friend had called them in, and had subsequently left to make a statement at the police station. That was a relief, of sorts.

'They interrogated me up hill and down dale, wanting me to explain what had been going on. I told them I had no idea. They showed me pictures of the dead man, and I identified Owen. They said he'd been dead since the previous day and what had I been doing then. I'd been chasing around all that morning thinking Owen had set up some sort of scam . . . and yet, they said he was dead!

'I had difficulty believing it. And, where was everybody? The police wanted to know what I thought of Owen. I told them. I was open and frank in my answers. I got the impression they thought I must have killed him. They took me down to the station and I made a statement there. Then they told me I could go but not return home, and not to leave London. They wanted to know where I could be found. I said I'd be at my club. So many unanswered questions. Where was my brother and my nephew? And Miss Summerleys? I knew her parents lived somewhere up north. I assumed she must have gone there, but I had no idea of the address or how to contact her.

'I decided the first thing to do was to get another charger for my phone. At the shop they told me it would take some hours to get it working again. That didn't help. So I went back to George's place, hoping he'd have turned up there by now. I tried George's housekeeper in the country again. She insisted he was at the town house, but of course he wasn't. And his town housekeeper had vanished. The house was empty. Does anyone know what happened to her?'

'Yes,' said Bea. 'The Oxford police had rung her to say Lord Rycroft had met with a fatal accident, so she packed up and left to stay with her brother.'

He nodded, the lines on his face deepening. 'Poor George. Yes, I did hear, eventually.'

Bea said, 'Your London housekeeper let Mrs Tarring know about it but not till early this morning, so she couldn't tell you what had happened.'

'She couldn't get through to me, anyway. Once back at George's, I put my phone on charge and used George's landline to call another cab. I went round to Piers's studio, thinking that Kent might have mistaken the time or the day . . . which was absurd, but I was clutching at straws. Again, there was a policeman on the door. He wouldn't let me in, refused to answer my questions. I was half out of my mind by that time. I feared that Miss Summerleys must have been involved in some accident, but they said it was a man and he wasn't dead, and that he'd been taken to hospital. I assumed, wrongly as it turns out, that this was the artist himself.'

Bea shook her head. 'No, it was Kent.'

'I know that now, but at the time I imagined some weird scenario in which the artist had frightened Miss Summerleys away and she'd left. There was only one place to go and that was back to George's house. There wasn't a note, or a message on the phone. Nothing to tell me why it had been abandoned. It was like the *Mary Celeste*. But at least I had access to a phone. I left messages everywhere I could think of, saying where I was and asking for information. I made myself a sandwich – I left rather a mess in the kitchen, I fear – and started phoning the hospitals. By that time it was early evening. That's when I heard Kent had been taken in. I took a cab and went to see him. He was unconscious. They said . . .'

He blinked again, slowly. 'I stayed with him until he . . .

eventually . . . but at least they did let me stay. I talked to him, held his hand. They say hearing is the last of the senses to go. I remembered him being born and what a game little lad he used to be, climbing every tree in sight. He wanted to go into the army, you know? But he settled down to deal with family affairs when he realized that he was the only one who could do so.

'He married a girl . . . not a good choice. I think she married him thinking he'd inherit the title and the country house, but we're a long-lived family and George was only too hale and hearty. She went off with someone else. They divorced but he had custody of the child, Ellis. Kent didn't seem bothered by her leaving him, but he was very cut up when Ellis was killed. Again, such a waste.'

'Was Ellis killed before or after Owen descended upon the family?'

His eyes swivelled to Bea and narrowed. He became very still. 'You are suggesting that Owen was responsible for Ellis's death? No one has suggested it before. I think . . . not. It is true that Owen had arrived and started to make a nuisance of himself before Ellis died, but you must realize that Ellis was a demon cyclist, riding through London's traffic as if he were the only person on the roads. No, I think it was an accident.'

Bea nodded. 'Understood. It was just a thought.'

He inclined his head. 'Kent took his son's death hard. I was thinking, when I sat beside him last night, that at least he'd see his son again soon. He died about midnight. I went back to the town house. Returning to childhood, you might say. I slept in the room that had been mine when I was growing up. I didn't sleep well. And then, I overslept.

'This morning there was still no sign of anyone. I tried our solicitor, and the call went to voicemail. Finally I tried the housekeeper's brother's number, thinking he might know why she wasn't at work. She said she wasn't coming back and told me what had happened to George. She said she'd left the number of the Oxford Police Station on the pad by the phone. I'd seen it but not recognized it for what it was. So I rang them. Apparently he'd been on his phone while driving back to London; the brakes had failed as he'd descended a steep hill; he'd taken a corner too fast and run into a tree. It took my breath away. I tried to ring you, Mrs Tarring, but your phone was always engaged.'

Mrs Tarring said, 'Yes, I suppose it would have been. By that time I was trying to get details of which police force had been dealing with which incident.'

He nodded. 'Poor George. A kind and generous man.' His eyes went out of focus. Then he shook himself back to the present. 'He was much older than me. He'd been there all my life. My first thought was that I must tell Kent. And then I remembered he was dead, too.'

He turned back to Mrs Tarring. 'I'm afraid this will mean a lot of extra work for you. Our solicitors may be able to suggest someone to deal with registering the deaths, finding out which funeral directors should be asked to officiate, and so on. I didn't have their phone number on my mobile, but I suppose waiting till tomorrow won't be a problem. The police said that there will have to be an autopsy in both cases. No, in all three cases. Owen was a Rycroft, too. And then there will have to be notices to the papers, arrangements for the funerals, and so on.'

He shuddered, and closed his eyes for a moment. 'I really have very little idea of what is required, but I suppose I will learn. Meanwhile, Mrs Tarring, both his housekeepers must be reassured that they will be properly looked after. Do you think you could do that for me?'

Mrs Tarring nodded and made a note.

Lucas visibly turned his mind away from death. 'Anyway, when I'd pulled myself together this morning, I remembered I'd told the police I'd be at my club, and of course I wasn't. So I rang there to see if they'd been round looking for me, and they hadn't. But I was informed that Miss Summerleys had left a message for me to ring here. So here I am, and this might be an appropriate moment to find out what has been happening to other people.'

'Shall I begin?' asked Magda. 'You need to know that the jewels are safe.'

Lucas inclined his head. 'I never doubted it.'

Bea's mobile rang, and she answered it. A stranger was on

the phone. A man with a clear-cut, precise voice, holding back some annoyance. 'Is that Mrs Abbot?'

'Yes, indeed.'

'Would you be so kind as to confirm your address and email?'

'What? Are you the police?'

'Certainly not. While I was otherwise occupied, my wife foolishly agreed to chaperone a child on the train journey to London and deliver her to a Mrs Abbot who has an agency in Kensington. I have this address on my smartphone and would be grateful if you would confirm that you are she.'

'Bernice? You have Bernice?' For a moment Bea wished the child to the devil! Just as things were getting interesting with the Rycrofts! Then her anxiety for the child broke through. She took the phone through into the kitchen so that she could talk in private. She gave her address.

'Can you send me a selfie, so that I can check your details against your picture on the website of your agency?'

'Tell me what to do.' He told her. Bea was all fingers and thumbs. She'd never had to send anyone a selfie before. She knew youngsters did it all the time, but she really did not use the media that much.

Finally, the man seemed to be satisfied. 'Very well. You are who you say you are.'

'You have Bernice with you? I've been worried sick about her.'

'I understand you allowed her to go off to stay with a friend without knowing the host or hostess.'

'Far from it. I expected her back here for a family weekend. We had tickets for the theatre and planned to visit relatives.'

Oh, those tickets! She'd forgotten she was going to return them to the theatre. Ah well, it was too late to do anything about them now.

Bea continued, 'Bernice received what she thought was a better offer, and I checked with her friend's grandfather, whom I knew—'

'Who apparently allowed her to make the return journey on her own. What were you thinking of?' The man was a censorious pig! On the other hand, he was quite right.

'At the moment,' said Bea, 'I am only so pleased that she has managed to find good people to look after her.'

There were raised voices from the big room. Bother! She spoke into the phone. 'There has been a, er, complication at this end. I am extremely grateful to you for looking after Bernice. She was supposed to be returning to boarding school this evening, but I think I should inform them what has happened, and keep her here overnight. Would it be possible for you to put her into a taxi at the station, and give the driver this address?'

'Certainly not. I wouldn't dream of abandoning a child on the streets of London. Who knows what might befall her? And it is out of the question that you should ask me and my family to delay our own return home to the Midlands in order to deliver her to your door. No. Either you collect her yourself in forty-five minutes from the main ticket office, or I hand her over to the police to look after.'

Bea wanted to scream. In fact, she did so, silently. The man was right, of course. He was acting as a good citizen should. But talk about inconvenient!

'I agree,' said Bea. 'How shall I know you, and may I speak to Bernice?'

'I will recognize you, Mrs Abbot. You do not need to know me.' He switched his phone off. Bea pressed the buttons for Bernice's phone. It went to voicemail.

At that point she did open her mouth wide and screamed, semi-silently. Not enough to disturb the people next door . . . except that Piers hove into sight, looking worried.

'What's up?'

'That pesky child! She's found someone to look after her on the train coming back to London. I have to fetch her in forty-five minutes from outside the ticket office at the station while I've got the people next door in the middle of a crisis. I could wring her neck!'

She looked around for her handbag. Did she have keys, cards, makeup bag? Did she need a coat, or would a jacket do? She shot out to the hall to find something to wear.

Piers followed her, looking at his watch. 'I don't have a car at the moment. Shall I get a cab? But, London traffic is unpredictable. The Tube would be quicker—'

'Yes, it would. The Circle line is slow, but sure. You're right; I'll take the Tube.'

'Would you like me to come with you?' He sounded unsure of himself.

She told herself she was making a big mistake, but nodded. And shrugged herself into the first jacket that came to hand.

He said, 'I'll tell the people next door that they can stay here if they like, but we've got to go out. Right? You go on ahead. I'll catch you up.'

She nodded and half ran, half power-walked out of the house and along to the main road. The lights were at red. Traffic had stopped. She managed to get across one lane, then two . . . and down the street, past the church . . . and there was Piers, loping along at her side. He took her arm to cross the High Street. She did not know why she didn't object to his doing this. Into the ticket hall they went and through the barriers. Oyster cards are a wonderful invention. A train was due in one minute. Thank the Lord. Praise Be. And all that jazz. On to the train. They were lucky enough to get seats side by side.

Piers said, 'Why is the child doing this?'

A good question. Bea didn't know. But she'd find out, if it killed her.

Piers said, 'I know so little about children.'

It was true. He'd always said small children bored him. He'd shown little interest in their son until he was in his twenties, when Piers had looked him up and started to get to know him. Now that son was married with a couple of small children, Piers kept in touch now and then, but seemed to have no need for a closer relationship. He said, 'What makes Bernice tick?'

Bea had to think hard about that. 'She had a rotten childhood with a clever con man for a father and a doormat for a mother. She was rescued by her intelligent but aged great-aunt and travelled the world with her till the child decided for herself that she needed to go to boarding school to get a proper education. She knows that she's got twice the brains and strength of character of almost everyone she's ever met. She thinks for herself, sometimes without knowing all the facts, and so she has and will make mistakes. She is aware that she will inherit a stonking fortune, which gives her a certain sense of entitlement; other people can see this as arrogance.

'Her mother and stepfather are not up to her weight. She's fond of them and of her little half-brother, but they can't offer her anything but unconditional love. As yet Bernice hasn't worked out that such love has a price above rubies. For some years Bernice has looked after and protected a girl called Alicia, who befriended her when she first went to boarding school. I have a feeling that something has gone wrong there, precipitating her flight back to London.'

'She'd originally arranged to spend this weekend with you and see her family?'

'Yes. The theatre tickets I got for us have gone to waste. Annoying. And her mother is upset and complaining about it. That's going to take a bit of sorting.'

'How do you personally get on with the child?'

'I don't think of her as a child, but as a pre-teen. She infuriates me and she enriches my life. By the time she's eighteen and at uni, she will have left me far behind. She loves me, fiercely, most of the time. Some of the time she hates me because I'm her guardian and she doesn't like bowing down to authority. She is approaching puberty late. Some days she's a real Plain Jane, but other days you can see she's going to blaze into beauty. Not in a Beauty Queen style – although she has good bone structure – but with intelligence and wit.'

He was silent as the train trundled through station after station. Finally he said, 'Lucas is not going to enjoy being the titular head of the family, is he? My guess is that he'll settle down to look after them for a while and then find someone like Kent to do the nitty-gritty for him.'

She nodded, checking her watch. Were they going to make it in time?

He said, 'Little Miss Sugar and Spice is in her element, isn't she? Do you think Lucas is beginning to realize how lucky he is to have her? She's every old man's dream. Someone to look after him in his old age.'

Bea shook with laughter. 'Her name is "Magda".'

He repeated, 'She reminds me of a duvet. All warm and soft. She will feed him and pander to his every whim. Do you think he's too self-centred to have thought of bedding her? Or has the counselling turned his thoughts in a different direction?'

'I'm not listening,' said Bea. Although, of course, she was. And smiling.

'Mrs Tarring, on the other hand, is an enigma. I can't read her. Can you?'

'I am beginning to think she's protecting someone else in the family. But I can't think why.'

'Oh, I can think why. At least . . . ah, this is where we get off.'

They made it to the ticket office just in time.

Bea saw Bernice from way off; a stiff little figure exuding a force field. Bernice did not want to be in her present company, did she? A dumpy woman with a couple of unruly small children in tow was standing next to her, fussing with something in her handbag, while her husband – fleshy and pompous – had his smartphone out while double-checking the time by his wristwatch.

Bea swooped on Bernice to give her a hug. The child was rigid in her arms, not giving an inch. 'Bernice! Are you all right?'

'Mrs Abbot, I presume?' The man was annoyed. 'You are one minute late.'

'Apologies. The trains—'

'This whole affair has caused us to miss our connection—'

His wife broke in, 'No, it hasn't, Henry. You said it would be better to wait for—'

'Enough.' The man turned to Piers, who was hovering. 'And who is this?'

Bea started to say, 'This is my—'

Bernice interrupted. 'He's her first husband. He's a painter, supposed to be quite good. If you like that sort of thing.' The insult was intentional.

Piers grinned. 'Touché, my girl. Luckily for you, I don't paint children.'

Bea suppressed an urge to bang both their heads together. She said, 'Now, Bernice, thank the kind lady and gentlemen for looking after you so well, and we'll be on our way.'

'Thank you,' said Bernice, biting the words off. 'It was kind of you, even though I could have managed perfectly well without you.'

Bernice was in a snit, wasn't she! Bea decided to ignore it for the time being. They could hardly deal with whatever-it-was on the station platform. She thanked the man and his wife profusely. 'You have been so good. I really appreciate it. Come, Bernice; let's get home. The Tube station is this way.'

Bernice hung back. 'Didn't you bring a car?'

'No. Gridlock in the streets. It was quicker by Tube.'

Bernice's frown said it all. *Peasants! I'm worth more than this!*

Bea grasped Bernice's shoulder and, with Piers on her heels, walked her down to the Tube. Bea tried to explain. 'Bernice, we must talk, later. In the meantime you must know that a lot has happened at home this weekend. One of the agency clients found herself involved in a family dispute and has taken refuge with us.'

Bernice managed a complicated shrug. What did she care about that! She didn't look at Piers, but when they had got onto the train and found seats, she said, 'Why is he hanging around?'

'Piers. His name is Piers, as you very well know. Our client was in his studio when everything went haywire. A visitor was killed in his hallway, he was assaulted, and then the violence moved into our house. Piers has been helping me work out what's going on. I don't want you involved in any way. Somehow or other I'll have to get you back to school this evening.'

'Well, I'm not going back to that school. It's boring. I need better teaching. I've decided I'm going to live at home and go to day school.'

Bea closed her eyes. This was not good news. Even if the child were right in thinking she could do better at a different school – and she'd chosen this school herself because the maths teaching was exceptional – her decision raised all sorts of problems. What other school would take her in the middle of the spring term? And did Bea really want to have the child around twenty-four seven? Oh, dear! She said,

'What about Alicia? Isn't she your best friend? Doesn't she need you?'

'Alicia's stupid. All she thinks about is boys.'

Oh? Puberty has struck there, has it? But not yet for Bernice?

Bernice said, 'You don't need Piers any more, now. I'm back for good.'

EIGHTEEN

Sunday afternoon

'**D**rat!' said Piers, taking this in his stride. 'I'm being turned down by a pre-teen! I must be losing my touch.'

Bea said, 'That was very rude, Bernice. Also, wrong! We must have a proper discussion about your future, but not like this. I'm not happy about having you at home while I have another guest who's in trouble. Perhaps you could go to your mother's tonight? She's been ringing me, worried about you. I'll phone the school to say you'll not be back tonight, and then tomorrow we'll sit down and work out what's best to be done.'

'I'm not going to their house. They want me to sleep in the same room as Bro. He wakes up in the night and wants to play.'

Bea could feel Piers's amusement at this turn of events. She didn't feel amused, herself. She held back some sharp words. Bernice was clearly deeply upset. It was probably something as world-shattering as a tiff with her best friend. But, whatever it was, it must be treated with the seriousness Bea would afford to an adult's problem. She said, 'We can't talk now. We'll make some phone calls when we get back and find time to talk this evening.'

She made mental notes; she must ring the child's mother, and William Morton – who ought never to have let the child out of his sight – and perhaps Alicia, too? And the school. Would the house be clear of guests by now? What was really going on in the Rycroft family?

They got off the train. Bernice stalked ahead of them, back rigid.

Piers said, 'Do I come with you?'

'Do you want to?'

He nodded.

She said, 'Thanks. I could do with some moral support. Let's hope the house is empty of our tiresome guests by the time we get back.'

And in fact, it was. Bea hadn't set the alarm when she left, so that didn't sound off when she let them back into the house. That was to be expected. But there was no sound of voices to greet her return either.

Bernice stomped up the stairs without looking back. 'I'm going up to my room for some peace and quiet!'

Piers watched her, shaking his head. 'Twelve years old, going on twenty-five.'

'Mm.' Bea went into the living room, taking out her phone to start ringing people. First she must ring Bernice's mother, to reassure her . . . but what was this? There was an absence of guests, but a chair had been overturned and a cushion had been placed on the floor and left there.

Her call to Bernice's mother went to voicemail, so Bea quickly left a message to say that Bernice had returned and that Bea would ring again later. She noted that two chairs that normally stood around the dining table had also been pushed awry, and a mug of coffee had spilt its contents on the mahogany, which was going to cause a nasty stain. It had dripped onto the carpet, too. Bother! She'd have to clear that up in a minute. First she must ring William . . . she pressed buttons. Again his phone went to voicemail, so she left another message to say Bernice was safe.

And now what? She must ring the school to tell them that Bernice would not be back tonight. And then have a chat with that little . . . girl . . . about her conduct. But first she must deal with the immediate problem. What had been going on in her absence?

Piers stood in the doorway, hands on narrow hips. 'This scene is evidence of something, though I don't know what. An assault? No, I don't think so. Do we ring the police and report our visitors missing? Have they been hoicked up into outer space? Do we care?'

Bea shook her head. 'That cushion. It looks as if someone lying on the floor had the cushion put under their head. See the indentation?'

As one they turned to the kitchen. Nothing appeared to be out of place there, except that a cupboard door hung ajar. As did the back door. Bea knew she'd left it not only locked but bolted.

'Someone's in the garden?' The door let onto a cast-iron balcony from which a staircase descended to the garden below. There didn't appear to be anyone in the garden, and there was no sign of an intruder, except that a plant pot containing spring bulbs – which normally stood by the pool – had been knocked over and left on its side.

She pointed. 'Look!' The door of the shed at the bottom of the garden was shut and a wrought-iron bench placed against it.

'You stay here. Let me!' Piers brushed past her and bounded down the stairs to the garden.

Bea followed, more slowly. She was amused and annoyed that Piers should think a man should lead the way.

Winston the cat appeared from nowhere, stretched fore and aft, and followed Piers down to the shed. Piers tried to see through the window. Winston leaped up onto the sill, and peered in, too.

'Is anyone there?'

Something or someone thumped; once, twice.

Bea said, 'Someone's been locked in there? Watch it, Piers.'

He bent to drag the bench away from the door. She helped him. He pulled the door open and vanished inside.

Winston and Bea looked at one another and then peered in, too. It was dark inside.

Piers was struggling to do something . . .

Bea stepped inside. Someone had been tied to a garden chair with garden twine. He or she was making moaning noises. Piers wasn't getting anywhere, trying to undo knots. Bea looked for something to help him . . . ah, a pair of kitchen scissors had been demoted to garden use some time ago, and now resided in a nearby plant pot. She passed them to Piers.

The figure moaned. It had been gagged, too.

Bea ripped out the gag and the woman spat, or tried to. Tried to speak, and failed.

Piers got her upright but she couldn't stand by herself.

Again, she tried to speak. And failed. And winced. She was in pain from returning circulation.

'Come out into the sunlight.' Piers carried her out of the shed.

She made protesting noises. He let her stand on her own two feet but she would have fallen if he hadn't held her up.

She lifted a wavering hand, pointed her forefinger at Piers and mimed someone fainting.

'Someone came at you with a syringe?' said Piers.

Magda shook her head. And mimed the attack again.

Bea shivered. 'It's a gun? No, a taser? Someone used a taser on her?'

Magda nodded.

Piers put Magda's arm over his shoulder, and helped her up the garden path towards the house. The woman mewed with pain. Piers carried her up the stairs and into the kitchen where he put her on a stool, and began to rub her arms and legs to restore her circulation.

Bea got Magda a glass of water, which she gulped down. Tears leaked from her eyes. She mouthed the words, without sound. 'Taser! Take care!'

'Indeed we will,' said Bea. 'Piers, how about double-locking the front door? We don't want any unauthorized persons walking in on us, do we? Magda, do you think you can walk up and down for a bit to get your legs moving again?'

Piers nodded, and disappeared.

Magda clung on to the central unit and walked round and round it, groaning to herself. Her wrists and ankles had been rubbed raw, and there were red marks across her face where she'd been gagged. Apart from that, she seemed unharmed.

Piers returned. 'Do we yell for the cops?'

'First we find out who did this. Magda, what happened?'

Magda shook her head. Grabbed the water and drank again. 'Man! Laughed!'

'Lucas?'

A violent shake of the head. Magda rested against a stool. Drank some more. Worked her mouth. 'Never seen him before. Doorbell rang. Mrs Tarring let them in. Shirley came first. Cousin, right? And a strange man. Lucas said I was leaving.

Shirley said "no", that only I knew where the jewels were. Lucas said, "Not now, Shirley. That's for another day." He said the jewels were his responsibility and not hers. The man laughed. He's . . . weird. Is he Shirley's brother? But not quite right?'

'His name is Hilary,' said Bea, putting the kettle on and reaching for the aspirins. 'So Shirley and Hilary came here looking for the jewels?'

Magda wailed, 'Why did Mrs Tarring let them in?'

'Divided loyalties,' said Bea.

Magda mourned. 'She's worked for the Rycrofts for ever. She's their trusted right-hand woman. Why would she throw all that away?'

Bea shrugged. Why, indeed?

Magda stretched arms and legs. She twiddled her hands and her feet. 'Lucas tried to defuse the situation. He said they must all meet some time soon and have a good talk. But they, that man Hilary in particular, had something else in mind. He brought out this thing, it looked like a gun of some sort. I've never seen anything like it and I don't think Lucas had, either. But Mrs Tarring knew what it was because she said, "No, Hilary, you mustn't! This has gone far enough!" And do you know what he did? He turned on her, pressed it to her arm, her eyes rolled up and she fainted. Just like that!'

Piers nodded. 'A taser.'

Magda said, 'I thought she'd fainted. I got a cushion from the settee and put it under her head and straightened her skirt. All the while that man was laughing. Lucas stood still. I could tell he was thinking, hard. He almost closes his eyes when he does that. The girl, Shirley, she said to the man, her brother or whatever he is, "You shouldn't have done that!" But she didn't really mean it. She was smiling.'

Piers said, 'Then they turned it on you?'

'Lucas tried to stop them. He looked straight at me, and said, very quietly, "Miss Summerleys" – and he'd been calling me "Magda" earlier, so I knew he wanted me to pretend he hadn't been that friendly to me – "Miss Summerleys," he said, "this game is not worth the candle. I don't want anyone else hurt. I think it would be a good idea if you tell them where the jewels are."'

She moistened her lips again. 'So that's what I did. I told
them how I'd hidden them in the studio under Lucas's gown,
and then brought them here. I said I'd put them in the garden
shed behind some pots.'

'Ah,' said Piers. 'You didn't know—'

'That they'd been moved. No. I led the way down to the
garden and into the shed, but the pots were all over the place,
and the cases were there, but empty. I couldn't believe my eyes!
Lucas gave me one keen look, and I know he wondered, just
for a second, whether I'd double-crossed him, but then he realized I was as surprised as he was. And he nodded to me. He
knew I wouldn't. Mrs Abbot, do you know where they are?'

'Yes. Piers and I hid them in a safe place, thinking someone
might come after them. And they did, in the middle of the
night. But didn't find them.'

Magda said, 'Shirley screamed, "I told you they weren't
there!" She must have known someone had been here last
night and found the boxes empty. She was furious. She
demanded to know what I'd done with them. She turned to
the man, her brother, and he lifted that gun thing towards me
and I stood there with my mouth open, knowing he was going
to taser me and that I couldn't do a thing about it. That's when
Lucas said, "I know what she's done with them! She took the
jewels out of the cases and hid them at the studio. Right,
Miss Summerleys?"

'I could see he was trying to gain time, to protect me, so I
followed his lead. I said, "Yes, that's right. When the twins
came looking for them, I took them out of their boxes and
hid them under your robe, and the twins searched the studio
but they didn't find the jewels, and when I left I was so scared
that all I could think of doing was getting away before they
returned. Only after I was on my way here I still had the boxes
in your briefcase, but I'd left the jewels themselves on the
artist's stand."

'I was shaking. I didn't dare to hope they'd believe me, but
if Lucas thought it would buy us some time, I'd go along with
that. Then someone called out from the head of the stairs up
here and we all looked up. It was Mrs Tarring. She was very
wobbly but she called down to us, "Where are you all? What's

happening? I must have come over all faint!" I don't think she realized what had happened to her. She sounded so weak and unlike herself. Lucas called back, "We're all going to go back to the studio, Mrs Tarring. Miss Summerleys was very clever and hid the jewels there." Mrs Tarring nodded and went back inside.'

Magda took another drink, rolling the liquid round her mouth.

Bea said, 'Why didn't they take you with them when they went back to the studio?'

'Lucas arranged that I should be left behind. He asked if Shirley had her car with her, or if should they take a cab. He said there was no need for everyone to go, and they could leave Mrs Tarring here with me. I suppose he thought Mrs Tarring would see sense and call the police, tell them about the taser. But that didn't work. Shirley said she didn't trust me, and her brother . . .' Magda swallowed. 'He held the gun thing up and pointed it at me again.

'He said, "Bang!" Just like that. "Bang!" He put the gun to my neck. He was grinning. He likes hurting people, I think. I waited for him to fire it. I thought I'd faint. But Shirley said, "No, don't use it on her yet, my dear. You can be a little too enthusiastic with that thing, remember? Let's go and see if the gems are where she says they are, and if not . . . well, you can have a go at her later, right?"'

'Lucas said to let me go, that he guaranteed I wouldn't talk. But Shirley told her brother to tie me up and leave me in the shed so I couldn't raise the alarm. Lucas said to go easy because I was his housekeeper and he didn't want me damaged, but . . .' She rubbed her jaw and her wrists. 'You saw what the man did.'

Bea said, 'Back up a minute. You're a good witness, Magda. You have excellent recall. What exactly did Shirley say when she stopped her brother using the taser on you?'

'She said, "You can be a little too enthusiastic with that thing." Why? Is that important?'

'It may be,' said Bea. 'It sounds as if he's used the taser before on people. Can you kill with a taser?'

'Yes,' said Piers. 'There've been a couple of incidents when the police tasered someone with a heart condition and they died. And, I suppose that if you turned up the volume, it could lay you out good and proper.'

'So who was Shirley thinking about when she said that her brother had been too enthusiastic with the taser?' said Bea. 'Not Kent. He was hit with a blunt instrument. Not Lord Rycroft, who ran into a tree while driving. Not the twins, who drank something nasty. There's only one person whose death Shirley could be referring to,' said Bea. 'Does everyone agree?'

Piers said, 'Owen Rycroft? The cuckoo in the nest?'

Magda gaped. 'But, why?'

Bea said, 'Because he was pure poison. It was his arrival that started all the trouble. He used his position as favourite to try to push out all the other little birds in the nest with the object of leaving himself in control of the Rycroft money. He started with his father; he got people to think Lord Rycroft was developing Alzheimer's, ordering goods that he didn't need on the Internet. He wanted Lucas's flat. He tested both Kent and Lucas but found them too honest for his purposes, which was why he thought up that scheme to involve them in the supposed theft of the jewellery.

'There were easier targets; he agitated about the twins' business methods and debts. How much longer would they be able to get their debts cleared by the Rycroft Trust with him in charge? He considered Hilary and Shirley a waste of space, and said so. There was another man who worked in the office whom he didn't like, wasn't there? Ferdinand Redbreast. Owen threatened to cut them all off at the knees. He also threatened Mrs Tarring.

'But he did have some success and one piece of good luck. Young Ellis – who would in the ordinary course of events have inherited the title and stopped Owen in his quest for power – was killed in a traffic accident. If Lord Rycroft continued to show signs of incompetence, he might well have been sidelined into an old people's home. But there was a groundswell of opinion forming against Owen. The twins got together with the other members of the family who were under attack, because if Owen had managed to cut off their income, what would they have done? Are any of them employable?

Ferdinand and Shirley might be but, from what you say, Magda, Hilary is not entirely stable, and as for the twins . . .!'

'Yes, I suppose you're right.'

'We know that the younger members of the family were all talking to one another, exchanging news and views about Owen, creating alliances which in themselves were not strong enough to dispose of the man, but which fuelled their anger and their greed. Think of a network of people all hating Owen, and all phoning one another the whole time. Who was in that network?'

Piers counted them off on his fingers. 'The twins, Hilary and Shirley, and Ferdinand.'

'Who else?'

Magda wasn't sure. 'Mrs Abbot, you don't really think Mrs Tarring was involved?'

'She'd been threatened with losing her job, hadn't she? She knew what was going on, all right. How much she actually did to help the others, I don't know, but I think we can take it that she fed them information when she could, helped to pass around what information each of them gleaned, and was slow to assist any action which might have made it clear what they were up to. Now, these disaffected family members tried to get Lucas to join them, but he wouldn't. The network seethed but had no real idea how to deal with the situation. Then everything changed because Hilary acquired a taser. How do you think that happened?'

It was Piers who answered. 'They're illegal here, but if they're available in America I'm sure you can get hold of them somehow. We heard that the twins had blotted their copybooks with some strong-arm tactics. They beat someone up, didn't they? They had contacts through the clubs which could have helped them source a taser. Why did they give it to Hilary? Well, he's not too bright, but I can see they might think he'd be useful as an enforcer.'

'It seems to me,' said Bea, 'that giving someone like Hilary a lethal weapon was tantamount to encouraging him to kill, but it's possible the twins didn't intend him to go that far. Only, Hilary spun out of control. Owen had a subtle mind. It amused him to get his own way by drip-feeding falsehoods, not by the use of fisticuffs. I think Owen had some kind of confrontation with Hilary on the Friday, and he reacted by using his taser "too enthusiastically". And that's how and why Owen died.'

Magda said, 'But that doesn't explain who—'

Bea said, 'Let's take it step by step. There's a tangle of motives here, none of them pure. I think that when Owen was killed, certain members of the network decided to take up where he left off, partly to pay off debts because they were short of money – that's the twins – and partly to get rid of some of the other members of the family who stood in their way. They all knew, because of the phone bugging, that Owen had planned for Kent and Lucas to take the jewellery out of the bank, and they saw how this could be turned to their advantage. They saw, as Owen had done, that if they could only intercept the package, then Kent and Lucas could be blamed for its removal from the bank. What fun! They could get Kent and Lucas, those oh-so-pure Rycrofts, charged with theft. And out they'd go. So the twins descended on the studio in search of Lucas and the jewellery . . . and missed them.'

'That sounds about right,' said Piers. 'While Shirley and Hilary were putting Owen in Magda's bed, the twins were hot on the trail of the jewels.'

'Keep thinking "network". They were all on the phone to one another, listening to what was recorded on the bugs that Ferdinand had placed in different houses, exchanging information all the time, hearing about Owen's death, hearing about the jewels being taken out of the bank, and knowing that Lucas was going to be out that morning.'

'I still can't get my head around Hilary putting Owen in my bed,' said Magda, disbelieving. 'I'd never even met him then. Why should he want to embarrass me?'

Bea and Piers looked at her, and wondered how blind a nice woman could be.

Bea said gently, 'Look, Hilary killed Owen or tasered him, and then smothered him – possibly with Shirley's help. He wouldn't have done anything as subtle as putting him in someone else's bed himself. It was Shirley who had the brains and took control of the situation. She got Hilary to put Owen

in your bed because she thought His Lordship might be getting
too fond of you.'

Magda went fiery red. 'Oh, really. As if Lucas has ever . . .!
Honestly, it's never crossed his mind. Nor mine, either.'

Piers put her arm about her. 'You're a pretty woman. Why
wouldn't it?'

Magda blushed pink at being called a pretty woman. And
yes, she glowed at the compliment. But she still fought off
the suggestion that Lucas might become interested in her.

'You don't understand. Mrs Tarring told me all about Lucas
having a really bad experience with his sister-in-law many
years ago, and that he's not shown any interest in women
since. Poor man. No, you must be mistaken. He's never looked
at me that way. Really, he hasn't!'

Bea smoothed this over. 'I think Shirley misunderstood the
situation.'

'Yes, of course,' said Magda in a constricted tone.

Bea considered that now the thought had been placed in
Magda's mind, she would not be able to throw it off. The next
time she and Lucas met, perhaps she would be even more
aware of him.

'Wait a minute,' said Magda. 'How did they know the place
was going to be empty? Normally I'd have been there all
morning. Lucas only decided to take me with him at the last
minute.'

'I think that was fortunate for you,' said Bea. 'If you'd been
at home when Hilary toted Owen's body upstairs, you might
have met the same fate as him.'

*And been put in the same bed as Owen. And wouldn't that
have been a nice morsel for the gossips? That hasn't occurred
to Magda. Luckily.*

Bea continued, 'Let's follow Shirley and Hilary. They
have put the body in your bed and Shirley is on the phone to
the twins, who've gone to the studio to intercept the jewels.
She hears that the jewels are not at the studio, so she searches
Lucas's place on the off-chance that he'd taken the stuff back
home before going on to the studio. And that's when it occurs
to her to take the jade. Not only could she use the money their
sale would bring in, but also to give the police – when they

were eventually summoned – the impression that Owen's death had been due to a burglary that had gone wrong.'

Magda said, 'So the twins followed me here and tried to frighten you, Bea, into saying where the jewels are. They didn't know I was already here and that I'd hidden them in the garden shed.' She wailed, 'But where are the jewels now? Did the intruder who came in the night take them, and is now keeping quiet about it?'

Bea said, 'It's all right. Piers and I heard you tell Mrs Tarring where you'd put them, and thought they'd be safer in another place. Don't worry, we can get them back whenever we want. Meanwhile, back to the action. When the twins left here empty-handed, they heard that Shirley had searched Lucas's place and not found the jewels. The twin who was still conscious told me – and I believe he spoke the truth – that when they left me here, they decided to search Lucas's place for themselves. They went to the office to get some keys and found it locked up, so that didn't work. They tooled around a bit in the car, drinking from a bottle they found there. They ended up back here. One twin began to be really ill, and the other got him down to the agency and broke down the door. He set off the alarm, but at that point I was helping Piers move house and I wasn't around. The twin who was not so badly affected ought to have called for an ambulance, but he didn't. I did, when I got back, but feared the worst for both of them. It seems I was right, for one has already died and other is still in hospital. So who put the drugged drink in the twins' car?'

Bea went to the window and looked out onto the street. 'By the way, they said they left their car outside my house, so it should still be here, if it hasn't been towed away. Anyone know what their car looks like? It was an open sports car, I think.' She looked left and right and couldn't see one. Perhaps it had already been towed away?

Magda said, 'But who would have wanted the twins out of the way?'

Piers was frowning. 'The only people left who might have had reason to do it are Shirley and Hilary. I suppose that while the network had one aim in mind, they worked together, but when Owen died the jewels were up for grabs. Finders keepers.'

'Could be,' said Bea, favouring the idea. 'By the way, which hospital did they end up in? I think someone told me.'

Piers said, 'Charing Cross. But, hang about. Drugging the twins puts them out of the running for anything else that happens. If they didn't go back to the studio, and Shirley and Hilary are otherwise engaged at Lucas's place, then who killed Kent?'

'Indeed,' said Bea. 'Who else is hanging around?'

'No one,' said Magda, looking blank.

'Back to basics,' said Bea. 'There is someone. What about Ferdinand, to whom Mrs Tarring appears to be somewhat partial?'

'But why would he?'

'Look, he's involved in whatever anti-Owen plots have been going on, isn't he? We know that because he bugged Lucas's desk and he's the prime candidate for listening in to the phone conversations. Remember that although most of the family wanted Owen out, they all had different reasons for doing so. Ferdy had his reasons, too, didn't he? Didn't Mrs Tarring tell us how Owen used to make fun of him, call him "Robin Redbreast" and threaten him with the sack? Ferdy would be one of the founder members of the "Hate Owen" club.'

'But to kill Kent!'

'Consider the timing on Saturday morning. The twins, Shirley and Hilary are all rushing around disposing of Owen's body and trying to find the jewels. Ferdy doesn't seem to have been involved in that, but he's keeping himself up to date, as they are. He learns that the twins haven't found anything either at the studio or here at my house. He learns that Shirley hasn't found them at Lucas's place. He knows that Kent is planning to meet Lucas at the studio. Does he know that Hilary has killed Owen? If so, he must be in a terrible state of anxiety. No one was meant to get killed. All that the conspirators aimed for at first was to neutralize Owen, and look what happened! Hilary murdered him.

'Panic! The twins had gone off by themselves. Shirley and Hilary had put Owen in Magda's bed and fixed things up to look like a burglary. Ferdy knew that Lucas and Kent were to meet at the studio and he didn't know that the venue had been changed because the alteration to that meeting had been done

on people's mobiles, not on their landlines. So he went along
to the studio, perhaps to try to deflect suspicion, perhaps to
grab the jewellery, or perhaps he even meant to make a clean
breast of it . . . ?

'I don't think he meant to kill Kent. But when he got there,
he found the door open and Kent surveying the damage the
twins had done. Kent challenged Ferdy because there was
absolutely no reason for the man to have been there if he
hadn't been involved in the plan to get the jewellery out of
the bank. Kent threatened to call the police. He turned his
back on Ferdy, who panicked, picked up the iron cockerel
doorstop, and knocked Kent out. His instinct was to flee, to
remove any connection with the Rycrofts. So he took Kent's
identification papers and mobile phone and left him there for
Piers to find on his return. Muddled thinking. But none of
them could earn the title of Brain of Britain, could they?'

Magda whispered, 'Ferdy killed Kent? Oh, that will upset
poor Mrs Tarring.'

Bea huffed. 'The least of her problems. I have a feeling
she's known – or guessed – what happened all along. I don't
mean that she knew who killed whom, but she knew that there
was a network of Rycrofts who were working against Owen
and she has been trying to find reasons not to suspect them.
And so she helps us a bit. But not too much. Perhaps she just
does some listening in, and relays the odd message? Perhaps
she helps Shirley get keys to all the properties? She probably
rationalizes what she's doing as being careful, being loyal to
the Rycrofts, not knowing anything at all, really. Hilary knew
she was involved, and that's why he tasered her when she tried
to calm things down.'

Piers said, 'Who tried to break into the agency in the middle
of the night?'

Bea said, 'Ferdy, I think. If it had been Hilary, I think that
somehow or other, he'd have managed to get in.'

Magda sighed. 'I don't like thinking ill of Mrs Tarring.
She's been so good to me in the past.'

Bea said, 'I know. But she's . . . conflicted. Doesn't know
what to think.'

NINETEEN

Sunday afternoon

Bea had an idea. 'Magda, when we were all talking about who might have done what, it seemed to me that Mrs Tarring was being protective towards Ferdy. She's a widow, isn't she? Or divorced? Didn't she say that Ferdy was a widower, with no children? She's free to marry again now. Do you think she has her eye on Ferdy?'

Magda shrugged. 'I don't know. Maybe, it did sound as if . . . but I don't get to the office and I don't know the gossip.'

Bea looked at her watch. *Bernice! I must ring the school! William hasn't rung back. I'll kill him!*

And then . . . 'Piers, you did double-lock the front door, didn't you? I have a horrid feeling that when Lucas and Co. fail to find the jewels back at your studio, they'll be back here to have another go at Magda.'

Piers nodded. 'Double-locked. Shall I shoot the bolts on the front door as well?'

Someone twisted a key in the lock of the front door. And twisted it again.

Bea shot to her feet. 'The cupboard in the kitchen was hanging open. I told Mrs Tarring where I kept the spare keys! What an idiot I am! She's taken one so they can get back in whenever they wish!'

Bea, with Piers close behind her, ran for the hall to bolt the door, but was too late. The intruders were already in.

Lucas appeared first, with Hilary at his shoulder. Lucas was narrow-eyed, hands hanging loosely at his side. His hair was not as smooth as before and there was a yellowing bruise on his neck. He walked stiffly, under threat from the taser which a thickset youngish man was pushing into his neck. This was Hilary?

Hilary was enjoying himself. A man who'd found his true metier in life.

Behind him came Shirley . . .

. . . who was grasping Mrs Tarring by her upper arm. Mrs Tarring was uncertain on her feet. Her hair was all over the place, there was a bruise colouring up on one cheekbone, and her lip had been split. Her eyes were wild. Bea could hardly recognize the competent administrator in this broken creature.

'Back! Get back in there!' said Hilary, waving at Bea and Piers with his free hand.

They backed into the big room.

Magda rose to her feet with a cry of alarm when she saw Lucas.

His eyes flashed when he saw her. And then narrowed again. Had he sent some sort of message to Magda? Yes. She clapped both hands over her mouth, her eyes huge.

'Sit!' said Shirley, swinging Mrs Tarring round to sprawl onto the settee. 'The rest of you, too!'

A stir in the doorway.

An apologetic little man stood there. He looked totally inoffensive. Narrow-boned, wearing a shabby anorak over brown trousers. A dark red T-shirt showed at his neck. Ferdinand Rycroft. Ferdinand the Meek. Ferdinand, the arch-conspirator?

Bea stumbled back into the big chair by the fireplace.

Hilary gestured to Piers to take a seat. He obeyed, but he chose an upright chair over by the window instead of sitting on the settee beside Mrs Tarring.

Bea sent her mind searching for contact with Piers's mind . . . and found it. She understood that he'd chosen to sit at the opposite end of the room to her so that Hilary could not keep them both covered at the same time. If an opportunity arose, they could attack from two sides.

But not yet.

Not while Hilary had his taser so close to Lucas's neck.

Lucas stood. Mute. Eyes almost shut. Considering his options.

Magda bit her fingers in distress.

Shirley looked around. 'Everyone sitting comfortably? Then let us begin. The jewels were not in the studio. The police had taped the front door, but there was no one on duty, so we went round the back and broke in through the kitchen. The jewels were not on the dais. They were not anywhere in the house, full stop. So, Miss Summerleys, we have to assume that you have been wasting our time. And what happens to people who waste our time? Tell her, Mrs Tarring.'

Mrs Tarring gave a stifled sob. She tried to make herself small. She drew up her legs and put her arms over her head. A foetal position. Wishing herself a baby back in its mother's womb.

Shirley said, 'Lucas, tell her what happens to people who waste our time.'

'They get tasered,' said Lucas. 'Then they drink something to send them to sleep, and then they're smothered with a pillow. Which they say is what happened to Owen.'

Shirley said, 'That's exactly it!'

Mrs Tarring was so frightened that she began to sob. 'I didn't mean . . . I didn't think . . .! Please don't hurt me again!'

Hilary laughed. He took the gun away from Lucas and aimed it at Mrs Tarring. 'Shall I give her another couple of seconds?'

His sister shook her head. 'Don't waste time. Our priority is to find the jewels. After that you can play with them as you wish. But don't kill them. We want them to be alive but in a drugged sleep, when the end comes.'

Lucas said, 'There's too many of us for that to work. The police won't believe in accidental deaths for all of us.'

'Oh, I don't know. A little party, Mrs Abbot entertaining friends. Some stupid person laces the brandy and starts a fire.' She looked around with critical eyes. 'Yes, a fire will probably be the best way to finish them all off. Once they're asleep, we'll leave, but set a timer for about ten o'clock. They won't know anything about it. They'll all be dead asleep by that time.' She laughed. 'Dead asleep! That was clever of me, wasn't it? That suit you, Ferdy?'

A little jerk of the head. No words. Ferdy's eyes were everywhere, sweeping the room from left to right and back again to Hilary and the taser. And off again. Searching for . . . what?

'What she means,' said Lucas, speaking through stiff lips, 'is that once she has the jewels, she'll make us drink a sleeping draught and set a timer to start a fire in which we'll burn to death.'

'Correct,' said Shirley. 'But first we get the truth from little Miss Innocence here. She's not nearly as clever as she thinks, is she?'

'And then,' said Lucas, in the same dead tone, 'Ferdinand will betray his brother and sister to the police, which will get him off the hook and leave him as King of the Castle.'

'What?' said Hilary, waving his stun gun around. 'What did you say?'

Shirley laughed. 'Don't be absurd, cousin Lucas. Why would he do that?'

Ferdinand stifled a laugh with his hankie over his mouth.

Lucas said, 'Don't be fooled by Ferdy's meek and mild appearance, Shirley. He'll let you do your worst. You'll find the jewels and destroy anyone who can bear witness against you. And then you'll be of no more interest to him, so he'll turn you in. He's not particularly interested in the jewels, you understand. What he's after is—'

'Shut up!' said Ferdinand. He turned to Hilary. 'Give it to him! Longer, this time. I've never liked him. Do it! Now!'

Hilary wavered, looking from his brother to his sister and back again. 'Shirley . . .? What's Lucas on about?'

Lucas almost smiled. 'Have I got it right, Ferdinand? On Friday morning you were a long way from achieving your dream. You weren't the prime mover in the plot to grab the jewels. Owen was. But you'd danced around on the fringes, helping the conspirators by planting the bug under my desk, and maybe one at Kent's house and another in Owen's new flat, too?'

'No, no!' A stifled laugh from Ferdy. 'Not me.' Yet it was clear that he had done just that.

Lucas said, 'Tell me; were you responsible for the death of Kent's son Ellis? Way back last year? Perhaps you were.'

'No, not me.' Ferdinand produced a red hankie and mopped his brow. 'Believe me, I had nothing to do with that.'

'Or tampered with my brother George's car?'

Another snigger. 'No, no. Not I. That was Owen's little trick. He knew about cars, didn't he?'

'And you know that . . . how?'

'By listening in on his landline, of course. He told Kent that their father was going round the twist and that he, Owen, wouldn't be at all surprised if he had an accident in his car, the crazy way he drove.'

'That's not evidence.'

Another snigger. 'No, and you can't prove I've done anything wrong.'

'I believe you. On Saturday morning you had nothing on your conscience, except bugging various houses. At that point you learned that Owen had been killed, and that your brother and sister and the twins were all going to see if they could pick up where Owen had left off, and grab the jewels. You knew Kent and I were going to meet at the studio. And you went there . . . to do what? To tell Kent that you knew what had happened to Owen? To grab the jewels for yourself? What happened?'

'He wanted to know why I was there, and how I knew Owen was dead. He was going to call the police. It was an accident. I didn't mean to hit him, but he shouldn't have accused me of doing anything wrong. It wasn't my fault.'

'Oh yes, it was. And then, by great good fortune, that very morning my brother killed himself in a car crash. You say you weren't responsible. Well, the police will be looking into that, won't they?'

Ferdinand gave a hoarse cry. 'No, I never! What do I know about cars? Shut up, shut up! Hilary, give him a good one!'

His brow wrinkling with the effort to think, Hilary looked from Ferdy to Shirley and back. And hesitated.

'And suddenly,' said Lucas, 'you realized that you were a couple of lives nearer to the prize.'

Shirley's eyes sharpened. 'What! What prize?'

Bea tried to watch everyone at once.

Was that the front doorbell? Did no one else hear it?

Bea made as if to move from her seat, only to have the taser swing round and point at her.

'Back!' Hilary meant it.

Bea moved back into the depths of her chair but kept her hands on the arms so that she could shoot to her feet when the opportunity arose. *If* it arose.

Lucas said, 'Yesterday morning, Ferdy, there were three lives between you and what you dreamed of. You seized your chance to complete the good work, didn't you, when you met Kent at the studio? Next on your list were the twins. You were in touch with them by phone. They kept you updated. You knew they were still searching for the jewels and hadn't found them. You knew Shirley was busy that day, first disposing of Owen's body, and then searching my place and Kent's. You touched base with the twins at some point, and put a drugged drink in their car. As far as you were concerned, it didn't matter when they drank it, so long as they did so. You were only partially successful, however. One of them died, but the other survived, according to Mrs Abbot's information.'

Ferdinand shook his head, sniggering into his hankie. 'Wrong! Neither of them made it!'

Lucas blinked. 'Both died? Really? Then there's only one life between you and the prize. And I'm it.'

Shirley's mouth drooped open. She looked puzzled. 'Ferdy . . .? You didn't kill Kent, did you? And the twins?'

Ferdy tittered. 'Didn't you guess? Silly you. Yes, there's only one life to go now. Sorry, Lucas. Sorry. But you do see it's necessary, don't you?'

'What's he on about?' asked Hilary, genuinely bewildered.

'The title,' said Lucas. 'Ferdy didn't start off to kill everyone who stood in his way, but after Owen died he saw that he was one step closer to the title. When my brother George died, the title descended to his son Kent. When Kent died the title descended to me, as I was next in line. But if Ferdy could get rid of me and the twins, then he would inherit both the title and the Rycroft fortune.'

Ferdy giggled. 'I only wish that Owen were still alive to see it. That would teach him to make fun of me.'

'Your problem now,' said Lucas, 'is that you still haven't found the jewels.'

'That's true. Ferdy, we'll have this out later. In the

meantime,' Shirley turned on Magda, 'we're wasting time. Where did you put them?'

Magda looked up at Lucas. 'As God is my witness I put them, in their cases, in the garden shed. I did not betray you.'

Lucas opened his eyes wide. 'I believe you.' His voice was rich, and low. A declaration of trust. A commitment?

Magda continued to look at him, but spoke to Shirley. 'Taser me as much as you like. I do not know where the jewels are now.'

Lucas said, his eyes still on Magda, 'Taser me again, too, if you like. I don't know where they are, either.'

Bea shot her eyes round to Piers. He was smiling faintly, sitting forward in his chair, ready to spring . . . or to run for it? But where could he run?

The doorbell rang again.

Everyone jumped.

Who can that be?

'Nobody move,' said Shirley. 'They'll go away if we don't answer it.'

Lucas said, 'You've run out of time, Shirley. Tell your brother to put his toy away.'

'Not I!' Hilary flourished it, first at Lucas and then at Magda. 'Who gets it first, Shirl?'

The doorbell rang again. Longer. Louder.

Bea thought it was time for a distraction. 'Hilary, when did you last put the battery on charge?'

'What!' He swung round on her.

'The battery,' said Bea. 'I believe that a stun gun is powered by a battery. You've been using it a lot, haven't you? Have you bothered to recharge it between whiles? I doubt it. I think the battery on your taser must be pretty low by now. Can you work out how many times you've used it, and for how long?'

'Well, I . . .' He looked at it as if he'd never seen it before.

A childish voice spoke from the doorway. 'Isn't anybody going to answer the door?' Little Bernice, full of righteous indignation.

Everyone swung round to look at her.

And, the alarm went off. YOWL!

Piers charged at Hilary in a rugby tackle, sweeping him off balance and to the floor.

The taser shot from his hand and landed in the hearth.

Shirley lunged for it.

Bea went for Shirley, knocking her sideways . . .

But there was Ferdy, eeling his way past Bea to pick up the taser . . .

THE NOISE!

Lucas picked Ferdy up from behind and held him high with his feet dangling.

Ferdy's legs pumped the air.

And the alarm stopped as quickly as it had begun.

Everyone breathed heavily, recovering.

Lucas said, 'Magda, could you . . .?'

Magda made a little jump to seize Ferdy's wrist, the one that held the taser. She clung to it while Ferdy screamed thinly, trying to twist it round to press the trigger against her . . . And failed.

A new voice made itself heard. 'Mrs Abbot? Which is the householder? Police Constable Gordon, Constable Smart.'

Two large women, who looked as if they could each go ten rounds with a heavyweight boxer.

'We had a complaint about your alarm.' The women were holding up police badges. They had sharp eyes, and were heavily muscled.

Bea yelled, 'Look out! That's a taser in his hand!'

The constable had her mobile phone out. 'Back-up needed. Back-up needed.'

Hilary rose to his knees and collapsed. Deprived of his power, he looked as if he were going to cry. 'Shirlee . . .?'

Bea clambered to her feet, pulling herself up by the mantelpiece. She caught the foremost constable's eye. 'I'm Mrs Abbot, the householder. You are more than welcome. Yes, my alarm has been malfunctioning. I will personally apologize to the neighbours, but I can't get anyone to see to it till Monday morning. In the meantime, do you think you could remove that instrument of torture from Ferdy before he uses it again?'

Hilary knelt and reached out with both arms for Shirley,

like a toddler wanting reassurance from his mother. 'Shirlee
. . . tell them to go away!'

Shirley ignored him to make a break for it. She had almost
reached the door when Bea cried, 'Stop her!' and the second
constable stuck out her foot. Shirley tripped and fell heavily.

'What did you do that for, you nasty girl?' Hilary said, and
began to weep.

Bea shouted, 'You idiots! The taser! Someone, get it!'

The constable stepped over Shirley to yank the taser from
Ferdy's hand. With due care.

Shirley stirred. Slowly, she sat up, legs asprawl. She began
to weep, too.

Lucas said to Magda, 'Are you all right?'

Magda nodded. She passed a trembling hand over her
forehead.

Lucas held Ferdy out at arm's length, and let go. Ferdy
dropped to the floor, a limp bundle of bones held together by
his clothing.

Lucas brushed his hands off, one against the other. He looked
down at Magda. 'Well done.'

She nodded and smiled up at him. Tears stood out on her
cheeks. She'd been through a lot this last couple of days.

He patted her shoulder.

Ah!

Constable Gordon said, in the penetrating voice of one
accustomed to control unruly crowds, 'Would someone kindly
tell me what's been going on here?'

'With pleasure,' said Bea. 'Let me introduce you to some
people who are – or perhaps I should say – ought to be, on
your wanted list.'

The constable looked annoyed. 'And the taser? You do know
they're illegal – except for the police?'

Bea said, 'I'm delighted to hear it. Now, starting from the
bottom . . .' She pointed the miscreants out in turn. 'Yesterday
morning that man, Ferdinand Rycroft, murdered his cousin
Kent by hitting him with a blunt instrument. After that he was
responsible for killing his twin cousins by way of a drugged
drink. Don't be fooled by his meek demeanour; he's poison.
The man crawling over to his sister is Hilary Rycroft. Hilary

is Ferdy's younger brother. He's the one who's been laying about him with the taser. He's dangerous, too. He killed Owen Rycroft, who was found in Magda's bed yesterday. Hilary takes his orders from his sister Shirley, who's now sitting there, crying. She's probably not guilty of murder, but is guilty of assisting her brother in the disposal of a body. Although, come to think of it, you might also get her for smothering Owen after Hilary had knocked him out. But that's conjecture and I don't know which of them actually did the dirty deed. However, if you can't get her for murder, you can certainly get her for stealing Lucas's jade collection. Please take the stupid creatures away and do what you like with them. I have had it up to here and beyond! Oh, and do be careful with that taser; it's killed and tortured more than one person so far.'

'And I'm the Queen of Sheba,' said the constable, not taking in a word of this. 'And the rest of you are mere bystanders, are you?'

'No,' said Bea, exercising patience. 'The rest of us are heroes. That big man there is Lucas, Lord Rycroft. It was in his flat that a man was found dead yesterday morning, and he owns the jade which Shirley stole. No doubt you'll find it stashed away at her place. The man who looks as if he's been bashed about a bit is my ex-husband, Piers, and it was at his studio that another Rycroft was found, dying, yesterday morning. That pretty woman is Magda Summerleys who has been tortured twice by those minions from hell.'

The police constable said, 'It all sounds most intriguing. Now, you've introduced everyone except that woman over there on the settee. What has she been up to? Drug dealing and white slave trafficking, I suppose?'

Mrs Tarring was huddled in a corner of the settee, eyes peering out from under dishevelled hair. Half out of her mind.

Bea was merciful, and looked to Lucas for a lead.

He said, 'I'm Lord Rycroft. The woman on the settee is the administrator for my family trust. I believe she was the unwitting dupe in all this. She did suspect something, but I don't think she's actually broken the law. She's suffered enough, poor creature. Leave her be.'

The larger of the constables had her notebook out. She

gestured with her chin to Bea. 'Let's start at the beginning, shall we? You say you are the householder. Your name please?'

'Bea Abbot.' She spelled it. *Was that the doorbell again? Whatever is going on here?*

'Now, Mrs Abbot, you have identified yourself as the house-holder, right? We've received a report about an alarm sounding off at all hours.'

Bernice spoke up from the doorway, hands on hips. 'How many times have I got to answer the door? There's two police cars outside, full of big, sweaty men, who all want to know why they've been called out on a Sunday afternoon. Honestly, I turn my back for five minutes . . .! And, what are we going to have for supper, eh?'

TWENTY

Sunday evening

Later, much later, after statements had been taken and the police had removed Ferdy, Shirley and Hilary, and Mrs Tarring had been taken to hospital to be checked over . . .

Long after Bernice's family had been reassured that she was safe . . . and William had been informed that Bernice was back in the arms of her family . . .

After the family's solicitor had finally surfaced and been put in the picture . . .

And after Bea had taken notes of the personnel Lord Rycroft would like the agency to produce for interview; at least one more housekeeper, another administrator and more personnel for the office . . .

After all that, while Bea was thinking about what she could scratch together for supper, she and Piers stood at the window overlooking the garden and watched as Lucas, Lord Rycroft, jacket off and sleeves rolled to his elbows, fished in the pool for the hidden jewellery while Magda stood by with clean tea towels to dry the objects off as they were handed up to her.

Piers had dropped them into the water when they'd needed to find a good hiding place for the jewels. The sparkle of the fountain had multiplied the brilliance of the diamonds, but a casual eye wouldn't have seen anything unusual in the water. And nobody had. As Bea had said, only an artist would appreciate the cleverness of hiding diamonds in water.

Now and then Lucas looked up at Magda and said something which made her smile and shake her head.

Piers said, 'A shame we can't hear what they're saying.'

Bea smiled. 'Do we need to? Isn't it clear what's going on?'

Lucas and Magda counted out the spoils of their fishing expedition. They moved to sit on the bench nearby. Magda began replacing the jewels in their boxes, while Lucas put his arm along the top of the bench behind her. Magda's eyes were on her work.

Lucas said something to her and she lifted her face to his.

A sleek head inserted itself between Piers and Bea. The unmistakable aroma of cheese and tomato filled the air.

Bernice crunched on the large slice of pizza she was holding. 'You were so long, I got something out of the freezer for myself. Is he going to kiss her? Is he going to lay her down on the grass and have his wicked way with her?'

What on earth has she been reading?

Piers sighed. 'If he doesn't, he's a fool.'

Bernice said, 'I don't understand why kissing with tongues is supposed to be so good. It doesn't do anything for me.' She slurped from a tin of Coca-Cola.

Bea and Piers looked down at Bernice. Then they looked at one another. In shock.

Piers said, 'You're a bit young for it yet, brat.'

Bernice didn't take offence. She nudged Piers with her elbow. 'Tom cat!'

Piers laughed. He wasn't taking offence, either.

Down below in the garden, two people experimented with a kiss.

A long, long kiss. Then Magda was lifted onto Lucas's knee, and the jewellery was forgotten.

Bea stirred herself. 'Come along. That's private. Bernice, is that going to be enough for your supper? Piers, what about you? And oh, heavens! I forgot. Bernice, I have to ring the school and tell them you won't be back till tomorrow.'

'Not!' said Bernice.

'Quarrelled with your best friend, have you?' said Piers, with considerable affection in his voice. 'Want to stick pins into her? What's she done to upset you?'

Bernice avoided that. 'I want to learn Mandarin. The future lies in trade with the Far East. They don't do Mandarin at that school. I asked. So I need to change schools.'

Bea said, 'No, you don't need to change, Bernice. I'll organize you a tutor in Mandarin. The family fund will pay. And, unless I'm mistaken, your headmistress will be over the moon to be able to tell parents that she can now offer Mandarin, in addition to other languages.'

Bernice slurped Coca-Cola again, making rude sucking sounds. Hadn't she heard what Bea had said? Yes, of course she had. So there was something else bothering her?

'Puberty!' said Bea. 'Of course. Alicia's hit puberty and you haven't, yet. Don't worry. It will happen soon enough.'

'She's disgusting,' said Bernice. 'She's gone all pink. I hate pink.'

Piers fidgeted. 'I don't paint children. You're violet and gold. With a slash of silver.'

'What?' Bernice gave him an old-fashioned look. Then to Bea, 'What's he talking about?'

Bea said, 'He wants to paint you. It's going to drive him nuts till he does.'

'I don't paint children,' said Piers, striding about the room. 'I never have, and I never will!'

Bea said to Bernice, 'Take no notice. He gets like this when inspiration strikes.'

Bernice said, 'Will my picture be in the Summer Exhibition? I wouldn't mind that.'

Bea said, 'One in the eye for Alicia?'

Bernice smirked. 'I'm sorry I caused so much trouble this weekend. Only, it was upsetting. I thought you and William were going to get married and live in his country house, and I liked that idea. But now he's all over this fat, greasy woman who took us sailing. She's got an awfully bad complexion but he seems to like her and Alicia is pleased about it. How could she!'

Bea rubbed out a smile. Even if she didn't want William any more, it was pleasant to know that her replacement in his life had bad skin.

Piers said, 'I do *not* paint children! Ever. This is ridiculous!'

Bernice set down her empty Coke tin. 'Why did you and Piers break up, anyway?'

'What?' Piers stopped pacing. He looked from Bernice to Bea, and slowly crimsoned . . . and as the colour had faded, he looked tired. 'Yes, I suppose this is as good a time as any to confess.'

Bea flushed. 'No, don't. It's all right. Bernice, this is no business of yours.'

'Yes, it is,' said Piers. 'At least, it might be if . . .' He swallowed. 'All right, this is the truth. Bea and I got married far too young. I was fresh out of art college and hadn't yet earned a penny, while Bea took on any old jobs to keep us fed and watered in that horrible little flat. My ego couldn't stand Bea being the provider in the marriage. My stupid pride! It ate away at me. I offered to go and get a job in a supermarket, but she wouldn't have it. She said I would make good one day, but then we had a child and she had to work harder than ever. I just couldn't take it.

'When women smiled at me it made me feel better, so I rationalized my bad behaviour. I pretended that I responded to women in order to get a fee for painting them, but that wasn't it, really. I didn't give a toss about them. I could see I was hurting Bea but I went on and on . . . and yes, I felt guilty, but I couldn't seem to stop. And then she threw me out. I saw it coming, but . . . I always thought that I'd get her back some day. Only she met Hamilton just as I was beginning to earn a decent living and that was that. And I've been hanging around wanting to say I was sorry ever since.'

Bea told herself that she wasn't going to pass out. She wasn't the fainting sort.

She wondered if she could get away with killing him with her bare hands. Perhaps she could bury his body in the garden.

All those years!

She'd had a wonderful, loving relationship with Hamilton, of course. She didn't regret marrying him, not for a minute.

She'd been luckier in love than Piers, if it came to it. He'd had nothing but a string of short-term relationships which hadn't lasted.

She supposed she'd always known Piers would want to come back at some point.

She didn't have to take him back.

No way!

On the other hand . . .

He was part of her. Always had been. She missed him.

He was looking at her with a mixture of defiance and guilt.

He was trying to pretend that he didn't care what she said. But he did, didn't he?

He was expecting her to throw him out.

And she could. Of course she could. Her life was just perfect as it was. She didn't need him, or anyone.

Bernice said, 'Well, say something! Kiss her, why don't you?'

Bea didn't know how she felt. She said, 'I don't know. I really don't know . . .'

Piers said, 'We could, perhaps, talk about it?'